Praise for the Liz Talbot

W9-BZD-091

"The authentically Southern Boyer writes with heart, insight, and a deep understanding of human nature."

– Hank Phillippi Ryan,
Agatha Award-Winning Author of *What You See*

"Boyer delivers a beach read filled with quirky, endearing characters and a masterfully layered mystery, all set in the lush lowcountry. Don't miss this one!"

– Mary Alice Monroe,
New York Times Bestselling Author of *A Lowcountry Wedding*

"A complicated story that's rich and juicy with plenty of twists and turns. It has lots of peril and romance—something for every cozy mystery fan."

– *New York Journal of Books*

"Has everything you could want in a traditional mystery...I enjoyed every minute of it."

– Charlaine Harris,
New York Times Bestselling Author of *Day Shift*

"Like the other Lowcountry mysteries, there's tons of humor here, but in *Lowcountry Boneyard* there's a dash of darkness, too. A fun and surprisingly thought-provoking read."

– *Mystery Scene Magazine*

"The local foods sound scrumptious and the locale descriptions entice us to be tourists...the PI detail is as convincing as Grafton."

– *Fresh Fiction*

"Boyer delivers big time with a witty mystery that is fun, radiant, and impossible to put down. I love this book!"

– Darynda Jones,
New York Times Bestselling Author

"Southern family eccentricities and manners, a very strongly plotted mystery, and a heroine who must balance her nuptials with a murder investigation ensure that readers will be vastly entertained by this funny and compelling mystery."

– Kings River Life Magazine

"*Lowcountry Bombshell* is that rare combination of suspense, humor, seduction, and mayhem, an absolute must-read not only for mystery enthusiasts but for anyone who loves a fast-paced, well-written story."

– Cassandra King,
Author of *The Same Sweet Girls* and *Moonrise*

"Imaginative, empathetic, genuine, and fun, *Lowcountry Boil* is a lowcountry delight."

– Carolyn Hart,
Author of *What the Cat Saw*

"*Lowcountry Boil* pulls the reader in like the draw of a riptide with a keeps-you-guessing mystery full of romance, family intrigue, and the smell of salt marsh on the Charleston coast."

– Cathy Pickens,
Author of the Southern Fried Mystery Series

"Plenty of secrets, long-simmering feuds, and greedy ventures make for a captivating read...Boyer's chick lit PI debut charmingly showcases South Carolina island culture."

— Library Journal

"This brilliantly executed and well-defined mystery left me mesmerized by all things Southern in one fell swoop... this is the best book yet in this wonderfully charming series."

– Dru's Book Musings

Lowcountry
BONFIRE

**The Liz Talbot Mystery Series
by Susan M. Boyer**

LOWCOUNTRY BOIL (#1)

LOWCOUNTRY BOMBSHELL (#2)

LOWCOUNTRY BONEYARD (#3)

LOWCOUNTRY BORDELLO (#4)

LOWCOUNTRY BOOK CLUB (#5)

LOWCOUNTRY BONFIRE (#6)

Lowcountry
BONFIRE

A Liz Talbot Mystery

Susan M. Boyer

HENERY PRESS

LOWCOUNTRY BONFIRE
A Liz Talbot Mystery
Part of the Henery Press Mystery Collection

First Edition | June 2017

Henery Press
www.henerypress.com

Trade Paperback ISBN-13: 978-1-63511-227-6
Digital epub ISBN-13: 978-1-63511-228-3
Kindle ISBN-13: 978-1-63511-229-0
Hardcover ISBN-13: 978-1-63511-230-6

Printed in the United States of America

For my daughter,
Melanie Marie Boyer Shilling,
with much love

ACKNOWLEDGMENTS

Heartfelt thanks to...

...each and every reader. Because of you, I can live my dream.

...booksellers. You are rock stars. To those of you who stock the Liz Talbot Mysteries and recommend them to your customers, I am forever in your debt.

...Jim Boyer, my wonderful husband, best friend, and fiercest advocate. Thank you could never cover it, nevertheless, thank you for everything you do to help me live my dream.

...everyone at Henery Press—Kendel Lynn, Art Molinares, Erin George, Rachel Jackson, Amber Parker, and Stephanie Savage. This book is better because of all of you. Thank you for all you do. I count myself as very fortunate to be a Henery Press author.

...the world's best sister, Sabrina Niggle, who finds my mistakes when I can no longer see them.

...the world's best mom, and very likely the world's most voracious reader, Claudette Jones.

...Gretchen Smith, my dear friend and partner in a great many shenanigans—you know what you did.

...my dear friends John & Marcia Migacz. John knows about things I don't, like gunshot wounds and helicopters. Marcia has eagle eyes.

...my dear friends Martha and Mary Rudisill, eleventh and twelfth-generation Charlestonians, respectively, thank you for your continued enthusiastic assistance.

...Claire McKinney and Larissa Ackerman at ClaireMcKinneyPR.

...Jill Hendrix, owner of Fiction Addiction book store, for your ongoing support.

As always, I'm terrified I've forgotten someone. If I have, please know it was unintentional and in part due to sleep deprivation. I am truly grateful to everyone who has helped me along this journey.

ONE

The dead are not much given to hysteria. The morning Tammy Sue Lyerly piled her husband's clothes into his Raven Black 1969 Mustang convertible and lit a match, my friend Colleen stayed oddly nonchalant. She'd been dead eighteen years and had seen a thing or two.

For her part, Tammy Sue was pitching an F5 hissy fit. She dug all ten fingers into her 1980s pile of long red hair, clutched her head, and bellowed, "*Let it burn.*"

Four Stella Maris volunteer firemen cast her worried looks but went about the business of hooking up the hose to the fire hydrant. We stood in a loose huddle a safe distance from the burning car in the Lyerly driveway.

"I asked you what you were doing here," said Blake.

My brother, Blake, was the Stella Maris Police Chief. My husband, Nate, and I were private investigators, and Blake purely hated it when we meddled in his business.

"I called her," said Daddy. "I overheard at the flea market that your sister'd done some work for Tammy Sue recently. Thought maybe she'd want to know." Daddy shrugged, looked innocent. Mamma and Daddy lived across the street from the Lyerlys, so naturally Daddy was first on the scene. Mamma had come with him. She raised an eyebrow to let him know she had his number. It wasn't yet eight o'clock. Daddy sipped coffee from a large insulated stainless steel travel mug, all nonchalant like.

"For cryin' out loud, Dad. We don't need the whole town out here this morning." Blake gave his head a shake. He scanned the neighborhood we'd grown up in. Folks gathered in clumps under the shade of massive live oaks in bordering yards. They'd all come out to see the show. The audience was growing fast. It was early on a Tuesday in the middle of June. Some of those folks were missing work. Blake lifted his Red Sox cap, ran a hand through his hair, and resettled the cap.

Tammy Sue grabbed my arm with one hand and clutched her chest dramatically with the other. "Well, I want her here, and you don't have a single thing to say about it. This is my property."

"Yours and Zeke's." Blake kept his tone easy, casual. "Where did you say Zeke was again?"

"He's with that cheap hussy, Crystal Chapman." Tammy's eyes glowed with crazy. She leaned forward and hurled the words at Blake. "And he'd better by God not come home unless he wants me to light his ass on fire too."

A particularly flammable piece of clothing caught fire in a *whoosh*. The flames climbed, crackled, and popped.

Blake closed his eyes.

"I just don't see Zeke Lyerly being worth all this fuss, do you?" Colleen's expression telegraphed her boredom. It was a slow morning otherwise on the island. Colleen was our guardian spirit. If she'd had anything better to do, she would've been elsewhere—she wanted that on the record.

I raised my brows and blew out a breath. Nate and I had worked a great many domestic cases. One thing I knew for sure: when love soured, it could turn sane people into raving lunatics.

Colleen said, "Everyone thinks he's so good looking. I don't see it."

"Seriously?" I squinched my face. Zeke was a fine example of the Southern male. I'd give him that much, and I was happily married and didn't generally notice such things. Tall and lanky, with sun-kissed brown hair cut close to keep it from curling, mischievous blue eyes, an easy, movie-star smile, and a down-home drawl, Zeke was prone to flirt. He was a charmer.

Nate quirked an eyebrow. A grin teased the corners of his mouth.

Damnation. I'd responded to Colleen out loud. No one but Nate and me could see or hear Colleen. I used to be her only human point of contact. But as soon as Nate and I were married in December, he was added to the family plan.

A wayward lock of dark blond hair brushed his forehead. His eyes were shockingly blue against his tanned, sculpted face. He kept his honeyed drawl low, where only I could hear. "We should never've given Tammy Sue those pictures."

I cast him a look that said, *Give me a break*. We'd had no choice in the matter. Tammy Sue hired us to find out if Zeke was cheating. In my heart I just knew we'd find some crazy Zeke thing—he was a certifiable character, no doubt. But I would've bet he was true to Tammy Sue and our investigation would prove that, just like the last time she'd hired us. Unfortunately, I would've lost that bet.

Pete Carter, one of the volunteer firemen, trained the hose on the car and doused the flames.

Daddy's face was grim. "Shame to destroy such a pretty car like that." He gave Tammy Sue a reproachful look. "That's a collectible."

Tammy's crazy eyes widened.

"Now Tammy Sue." I smoothed words on her like balm. "I

understand you're upset—anyone would be under the circumstances. But really, all you've accomplished here is destroying a marital asset—a valuable one at that."

"I couldn't care less about the money." Tammy Sue's voice was harsh. Then she softened it to a stage whisper. "My whole world has just fallen to pieces." Tears pooled in her eyes.

"But you will care about the money," said Nate. "When you've had time to process everything, trust me, the money is going to matter. It always does."

"Boy howdy," said Colleen. "You mortals are all about the money."

Clay Cooper, Blake's second in command, crossed the wide Lyerly front lawn. "Blake, I taped off the area. You want me to take statements?"

"Nah, I think it's pretty clear what happened here," Blake said.

"What happened here is that cheap tramp seduced my husband and destroyed our lives. Can't you arrest her for something? Alienation of affection?"

"That might be a cause for civil action, but it's not against the law," said Blake. "On the other hand, if Zeke wants to press charges for destruction of property—"

"He wouldn't dare." Something flickered behind Tammy Sue's eyes. She wasn't completely sure of that, was my guess. She clutched her heaving chest and looked at me, a question in her eyes.

"I seriously doubt he'd do that." I gave Blake a withering look.

Nate rubbed a spot on his neck above the white collar of his Columbia shirt. "I guess it depends on how attached he is to that car."

"Sure is a pretty car," said Daddy. "It's one of only three like it in the world, Zeke told me. Sixty-nine was when they came out with the Mach 1. That car—with the GT Equipment Group and 428ci Cobra Jet—it's rare."

Mamma piped up. "Frank, your automotive trivia is not helpful in the slightest. Tammy Sue doesn't need to be burdened with your appraisal of the car this morning. Why don't you find something helpful to do?"

"Well, Red Bird, the fire department has things under control, it looks like to me." Daddy gestured with his mug towards the soaked, smoldering car. Red Bird was one of his pet names for Mamma, an homage to her auburn hair. "What did you have in mind?"

"Perhaps you could go and find Zeke." Mamma raised her chin, extended beyond her five feet two inches. "Maybe he stayed at the shop last night."

Zeke owned and operated Lyerly's Automotive, a repair shop, over on Palmetto Boulevard.

"Why would he do that?" asked Daddy.

"*Frank.*" Mamma gave him The Look—the one she usually reserved for Blake, me, and our sister, Merry. All three of us had her cobalt blue eyes. None of us communicated as effectively with them.

"Carolyn, Zeke has never spent the night in that shop. Not one time," Daddy said.

"I didn't know you kept such close tabs on Zeke's sleeping arrangements. Do you do that for all your poker buddies, or just the ones more than ten years younger than you whose gun collections you admire?"

Mamma turned up the volume on The Look. I could read her mind clear as day. Surely Daddy could too. She was thinking as to how she didn't care *where* Daddy found Zeke—just that he found him lickety-split.

"Well, I'll go check then," said Daddy. He didn't move.

Pete Carter stepped forward, but kept his distance. "Tammy Sue? Could we get the keys to the car? We cut the battery cables. The flames are out, but just to be on the safe side, we need to fill the trunk with water to keep any sparks away from the gas tank."

Tammy Sue took a step towards him, yelled, "I hope the gas tank catches and the whole thing burns 'til it's nothing but a chunk of melted metal. You hear me? When it cools off, I'm going to move it into the grass and plant flowers around it."

Pete blinked.

Blake said, "Tammy Sue, I think it's safe to say you've made your point with Zeke. Enough's enough."

Nate said, "Here now, why don't you let me have the keys?"

She crossed her arms, gave her head a stubborn shake. "I want him to see it burning."

"Have you called him?" I asked Blake.

"Tried. He's not answering his cell," said Blake.

I said, "Tammy, if the gas tank catches fire, there could be an explosion." I knew this wasn't true, that cars rarely exploded when the gas tank caught fire. But I was betting Tammy didn't know that.

Defiance settled into carved stone on her face. "I hope it bursts into a sky-high, brilliant blaze of red and orange spangled glory with shooting stars and blows that car straight to kingdom come on a moonbeam."

Blake looked at the ground, inhaled slowly. "Of course you do."

"I'll get the crowbar." Pete backed away a few steps, then dashed off.

"We need some fireworks." Tammy raised her voice and hollered, "Anyone got fireworks?"

"Oh, dear," said Mamma. "I'm afraid you're overwrought."

"And a twenty-one-gun salute." Tammy spun towards Daddy, her expression fevered. "Frank, get your guns. We'll have a tribute for the car."

Daddy tilted his head towards his shoulder, made a face like maybe he was considering her request.

"Frank." Mamma's tone held a warning.

I said, "Tammy Sue, why don't we get you inside?" I nodded towards her and Zeke's creamy painted brick ranch.

"No." She shook her head, then nodded. She trembled, seemed to buzz with manic energy. "I need to watch."

Mamma clucked. "My gracious. The humidity's gotten to you, is what it is." She put an arm around Tammy. "How about a glass of iced tea? Maybe with some soothing mint? Do you want me to call someone for you?"

A look of consternation washed over Mamma's face. I wondered who she might call and reflected how she was wondering the same thing. Tammy Sue wasn't originally from Stella Maris. Her family was elsewhere. Who were her close friends? She and Mamma were neighbors and friendly, yes. But Tammy was in her early forties, more than ten years younger than Mamma. They ran in different circles for the most part.

For a split second, Tammy held her ground. Then she crumbled, put her head on Mamma's shoulder, tucking in to her embrace. "Thank you so much, Carolyn."

Mamma patted Tammy's head, then gentled her towards the house. "There, there now."

"I'm going to go inside with them," I said to Nate.

"All right. I'll just—"

"Ah, hell—" Blake stared towards the car.

Pete backed away from the open trunk, dropped his crowbar. "Dear Lord, no."

Tammy raised her head, turned, and let loose a primal scream. "*Zeke.*"

Nate lunged and grabbed her just before she hit the ground, nearly taking Mamma with her.

I stepped towards the car.

There Zeke Lyerly was in the trunk, clearly quite dead, his body frozen in a strange position with his back and neck stiffly arched and his limbs tucked behind him. Mercifully, at least for the rest of us, the fire hadn't reached the trunk. He wore his work clothes, jeans and a shirt with his name on the pocket. His face was frozen in a ghastly grin, his eyes wide open.

I fought the urge to look away and studied him closely. A clamor of shock erupted behind me.

"How did I not see that coming?" Colleen sounded confused, indignant.

"Father in Heaven, help us," said Mamma.

"Zeke..." Daddy's voice was thick with grief.

Next to me, Blake muttered a few curse words. "All right. Everyone step back, but no one leave the area. Coop?"

"Yeah, Blake," Clay Cooper called from beside the fire truck.

"Looks like we need those statements after all." Blake pulled out his cell phone.

I backed away from the car. Poor Zeke. Could this be real? Maybe a horrible prank?

"I've got to check in." Colleen faded out.

Nate met my gaze. "Probably for the best she's out from under foot."

"Come again?" Blake looked at Nate sideways.

I fought my way out of a stunned stupor. "You'll want our help on this."

Murders were rare in our small island town off the coast of Charleston, South Carolina. My brother was not an experienced homicide investigator. Nate and I had worked many murder cases, most of them as a part of the defense team, granted. But this was the kind of situation Blake and the town council had anticipated when they retained us as outside investigators.

Blake pursed his lips, sighed, and nodded. "I'll call the county and get a forensics team out here right after I get ahold of Doc Harper." He tapped his phone and raised it to his ear. "Hey, Doc. I need you right away at Zeke Lyerly's house."

Nate and Mamma murmured back and forth and ministered to Tammy Sue.

"I'm taking Tammy across the street to your parents' house," Nate said. "We need an EMT." He scooped her up and carried her, still unconscious, across the yard.

"Roger that," Blake said. "Nah, Doc. It can't wait. We've got a death here, and it doesn't get much more suspicious than this. Right. Thanks."

Mamma trailed behind Nate. "Frank, help Nate. As soon as we get Tammy settled, I need to set out some drinks and get lunch together."

That's my Mamma. She knew her role, and by golly no one would go hungry on her watch. I turned back to Blake, kept my voice low. "I think Zeke's been poisoned."

"Poisoned?" Blake screwed up his face in a look that called my common sense into question.

"Strychnine, unless I miss my guess. There are no obvious wounds, but his body looks like it's in mid-spasm. Strychnine causes violent convulsions. Victims' bodies are often contorted like Zeke's. His face...They call that a death mask. If it was strychnine, it was a horrible way to die. And almost certainly not an accident."

"No, that damn sure doesn't look like an accident to me." Blake wore a sick expression, like he'd eaten bad food himself.

"Technically," I said, "he could've died accidentally, then someone hid his body in the trunk. I'm not saying that's what I think happened. But it's possible. We need Doc Harper to tell us for sure. Be right back."

I circled the Mustang, leaving a wide swath, snapping pictures at every angle. I stopped in the driveway, faked a FaceTime call by holding the phone a foot from my face and chatting to thin air while I tapped "video," and got a panorama of the throng of neighbors pressing as close as they dared to the crime scene tape. Was Zeke's killer among them?

I walked back to where Blake waited in the grass.

"Are you going to have a conflict here?" he asked.

"What do you mean?"

"Your client has a damn fine motive. Former client. The town of Stella Maris is your client now. If Tammy Sue—"

"Tammy Sue did not do this," I said. "She's positively stricken—didn't you notice how she fainted dead away?"

"What I noticed is that she has a flair for drama."

"You think that was an act? Her passing out and almost pulling Mamma to the ground?"

"Simplest solution. You're the one always trottin' out Occam's razor."

"That's not the simplest solution. That's simpleminded, is what it is," I said.

"Well, until you bring me a better suspect, she's the only one I have. You'd better get to work."

I pulled out my iPhone, unlocked it with my fingerprint, tapped "Phone," then Nate's name at the top of my favorites list. It took him five rings to pick up.

"I know you've got your hands full," I said, "but Blake has it in his head that Tammy is guilty until we prove her innocent. I'm thinking one of us needs to talk to Crystal before word spreads. But one of us needs to be here."

"Agreed," he said. "You go. Your mamma is taking over things here. I'll head back across the street and wait with Blake for Doc Harper and the forensics team."

"It'll take hours for them to process everything."

"No doubt it will. Go on now, find Crystal. See what you can learn. For all we know she's already left town."

I glanced at poor Zeke, at the soaked, burnt-out, remnants of his Mustang. "Whoever did this is a stone-cold killer. I hope they make our job easy by leaving town in a hurry."

TWO

Crystal Chapman worked as a masseuse over at Phoebe's Day Spa. We'd exchanged pleasantries on occasion while Phoebe foiled my hair, adding several shades of blonde to the sandy color I'd inherited from Daddy. I called Phoebe on the way to make sure Crystal was there, but I didn't tell her what I wanted with her. Aside from the fact that I knew from my recent case Crystal had been having an affair with a married man, I didn't know much about her. I hadn't done an in-depth profile. All Tammy asked for was proof of Zeke's infidelity.

Zeke. I mulled him as I zipped over to the business district.

Zeke's exploits were legendary, although the more colorful accounts were the ones he told himself—the ones no one could actually confirm. These were the tales that did not have the resounding ring of truth to them—such as his vivid reports of his days as an Army Ranger, his adventures as a prize-winning bull rider in the rodeo, and his heyday as an almost famous NASCAR driver.

By far the most outrageous story he'd ever told purportedly occurred during his years with the DEA, fighting the drug war in the South American jungles. It involved an anaconda, a nuclear missile, a sexy French missionary, and the crazed drug lord who had been holding her hostage. According to Blake's calculations, if everything Zeke Lyerly said were true, he'd have to be 235 years old.

Much of the fodder, however, that Zeke generated for the local gossip circuit was a matter of public record, having resulted in complaints being sworn out, both civil and criminal. A recurring theme in Zeke's local escapades was the creative use of his shotgun. In that respect, he sometimes seemed to be in an undeclared contest of one-upmanship with Daddy.

Zeke used his shotgun to expedite things. When his next-door neighbor installed an outdoor light that shined in Zeke's bedroom window and disturbed his sleep, rather than wake his neighbor to complain, Zeke simply opened his window and shot out the offending light. When the drink machine at Carter's Exxon declined to produce the bottle of Coke he'd paid for and Pete Carter was busy on the phone with a vendor, Zeke simply retrieved his shotgun from his truck, shot the lock off the machine, and collected his drink. When he found a nest of yellow jackets in his front yard, rather than bother with the usual chemical methods of extermination, he and Daddy shot a few rounds each into the rotted tree stump where the yellow jackets had made their home. This proved much more harmful to Zeke and Daddy, who each suffered a couple dozen stings, than to the yellow jackets.

To the best of my knowledge, Zeke had never shot a person—although at least twice he'd come close enough that charges of assault with a deadly weapon had been brought. Both times the charges were dismissed: the first time because Zeke somehow convinced Hank Johnson, the presiding judge, that there was no way Zeke could've missed Jackson Beauthorpe, his ex-wife's boyfriend, from his lawn chair if he'd really been *trying* to shoot him—the sonavabitch was barely twenty yards away, sneaking in Zeke's backdoor; and the second time, in a related matter, because Zeke's ex-wife had left town for an undisclosed location and could not be produced to testify against him.

Zeke was a colorful, but generally affable, guy, who told unbelievable but entertaining stories. The last time Tammy hired us to follow him, I had cause to reassess whether his tales might not have more truth in them than most people thought. But that was a whole nother story, and at the end of the day, all I had to show for it was a suspicion I could neither prove nor disprove. Zeke was an enigma wrapped inside a Southern cliché.

It was nine o'clock when I parked on Palmetto Boulevard in front of the spa. Lyerly's Automotive sat almost directly across the street. I took a few deep breaths to steady my nerves. Many of our cases involved dead bodies. It was rare for me to be on hand when they were discovered—rarer still for them to turn up in a neighbor's yard so early on a Tuesday. I climbed out of the Escape and went inside.

"Do you need a massage, or what?" Phoebe asked as I walked through the door. She was about the same age as me— mid-thirties. With her signature three-inch platform shoes, she was eye-level with me. That morning, the wide stripe in her black hair was magenta. Living in Stella Maris for thirteen years had done nothing to dilute her Brooklyn accent. "Crystal's booked this morning, but she could take you at two o'clock."

"Not today, thanks. Where is Crystal?"

"She's back with Winter Simmons. Ain't she your cousin or somethin'?"

"Something." Winter was married to my first cousin once removed, Spencer.

"I'm confused," said Phoebe. "Massage is the only service Crystal offers."

"You might be surprised," I said. "Does Zeke Lyerly come in for massages?"

Phoebe raised an eyebrow. "Come on now. You know Zeke. He doesn't like people knowing I cut his hair. If he did come in for massages, he wouldn't want me blabbin' about it."

"Yeah, well...Phoebe, Zeke is dead." It was a wonder I'd beaten the news to the day spa.

"*What?*" Phoebe drew back and her eyes popped open wide. "What happened?"

I thought about Zeke in the trunk of his Mustang. "Honestly, I don't have the first clue. But I came here to find one. Was Zeke a massage client?"

"Here? Why in the world would you look for clues here?"

"Phoebe. Please. Was Zeke a massage client?"

"Well, yeah." She spread her arms wide, palms raised, and gave me a look that asked *so what?* "He started comin' in a couple-three months ago. Said he had a pinched nerve, okay? Crystal saw him three times a week at first. Now it's once a week, if that."

"Did he come in asking for Crystal or for a massage?"

Phoebe seemed to ponder that. "I can't remember. Both, I think."

"Are you aware of any other relationship Zeke had with Crystal?" I asked.

Phoebe cut her eyes toward the ceiling. "What do you mean? They were friends, I guess."

I gave her my best *Oh puh-leeze* look. "Maybe you should go get Crystal. I'm sure Winter will understand, under the circumstances."

"All right, fine." Phoebe walked towards the hall where the treatment rooms were situated.

"Don't tell her about Zeke." I pulled my iPhone from my

purse, opened a voice memo to record, and slipped the phone, microphone up, into the outer pocket.

"I won't, already."

"After you get Crystal, send Winter on to work."

Phoebe muttered something under her breath. She knocked on the door. A few minutes later she returned, trailed by Crystal, a miniature but well-rounded blonde I pegged at early thirties. She wore a garnet Phoebe's Day Spa logoed smock, jeans, and tennis shoes.

"Hey, Crystal." I offered her my brightest smile. "I'm so sorry to bother you, but I need to talk to you for a few minutes if that's okay. Phoebe, can we use your office?"

"Yeah, sure." Phoebe waved towards the back.

Crystal cut me a look that asked, *what the hell?* Nevertheless, she followed me down the hall to Phoebe's office at the very end. We settled into opposite ends of a blue leather sofa.

"My goodness, you've lived here a while now, haven't you?" I asked in my chatty voice.

"Right at eleven years." Her patience expired. "What's this about?"

I smiled again. "Where are you from originally?"

"Charlotte."

"That's a pretty city," I said. "How'd you end up here?"

"I came down to Isle of Palms with friends after high school graduation. We took the ferry over one afternoon. I fell in love with this place. Now are you going to tell me what this is about? I know you're a private investigator, but why are you asking *me* questions?" Her tone was sharp. Her hazel eyes telegraphed that she was fully pissed off.

"Of course," I said. "I'm so sorry—I didn't mean to upset you. I need to ask you about one of your clients."

"Ah, I'm sorry, but that's a big 'hell no.' And speaking of my clients, I have one waiting right now." She started to rise.

"Phoebe asked her to reschedule," I said. "This is about Zeke Lyerly."

She prickled, lowered herself back into the sofa. "What about him?"

"Were y'all seeing each other before he became a client here, or did the affair start sometime after that?"

She flushed bright red. "I never said we were seeing each other at all. I—"

"I'm going to save us some time, Crystal. See, Zeke's wife hired my firm a while back to find out if he was having an affair. I know, in vivid detail, all about your relationship with Zeke. I have pictures."

Truthfully, we'd stopped snapping pictures after we got several closeups of the two of them glommed onto each other in what looked like an octopus mating ritual as Zeke came through the front door of Crystal's apartment. He'd slunk out two hours later with wet hair and a torn t-shirt. I had no need to know the sordid details of what had transpired in the interim.

"What?" She raised a hand to her face.

"But I don't know how long all that's been going on. So why don't you tell me?"

"Why would I tell you anything? You've ruined everything." She stood up, took a step towards the door.

"Crystal, please sit down."

"I have nothing more to say to you. Stay out of my business."

"Crystal—"

Her hand was on the door knob.

"Crystal," I said gently, "Zeke is dead."

She froze, then turned towards me. "*What*? No...no, you're

just saying that so I'll...I'll...I don't believe you."

"I'm terribly sorry, but it's true. Please sit down."

Her face went white. She moved back to the sofa in slow motion and eased herself back down. "What happened?" She bit back a sob. Her shock and grief seemed genuine.

"I'm trying to find that out. How long had you been seeing Zeke?"

"Why do you want to know?" Her voice rose. "What happened to him?"

"Please answer the question. How long?"

"Couple months," she said. "He started coming here about that time."

"And when was the last time you saw him?"

"Sunday night. He came over after dinner. I can't believe this."

I nodded. He'd been there Sunday night—that much was true. We'd followed Zeke to Crystal's apartment in an older Victorian over on Jasmine Drive.

"What time did he leave?"

"A little after ten." She fixed her gaze on a spot on the floor.

That was also true. "And you haven't seen him since then?"

"No."

"Have you spoken with him?"

"No."

"Do you know of anyone he had trouble with?"

She lifted her eyes, met my gaze. "Just Tammy Sue." It came out hard, mean.

"What kind of trouble did he have with Tammy Sue?" I asked.

"He wanted a divorce. She wouldn't give him one." Her words were defiant, as if she thought I judged her harshly. But at the same time she sounded detached, undone.

"He told you that?" Tammy hadn't mentioned Zeke asking for a divorce, and if he had, I wondered if she wouldn't've just hired an attorney instead of investigators.

"Yes."

"When?"

"The first time I talked to him."

I scrunched up my face. "The first time he had a massage appointment?"

"No." Her head moved slowly from side to side. "We talked before that, at a party back in March—at the Robinsons."

Margie and Skip Robinson owned the marina and lived beside it on the north side of the island. They'd both grown up here.

"You're friends with the Robinsons?" I asked.

Crystal shrugged. "I know them. Margie gets her hair done here like every other woman in town. But Coy Watson invited me. Skip invited him."

Coy Watson was a bartender at The Pirates' Den. "So you talked to Zeke at this party. Was Tammy Sue with him?"

"Yes. But he went for a walk on the beach with me. We hit it off."

"I see. Were you and Coy Watson dating before that?" I asked.

"Sometimes. It wasn't serious."

"And while you were walking on the beach, Zeke told you—right after you met—that he wanted to divorce his wife, who was back at the house you'd just left?" I knew Zeke Lyerly. Casually volunteering personal information was not his style. If she'd said he'd told her about parachuting into Chechnya on a top secret mission to rescue visitors from Krypton, that I would've believed—that he said it anyway.

"We'd met before that. I mean, I knew him. He knew who I

was. He worked on my car a couple times."

I nodded. "Why do you think he confided in you that he wanted to divorce his wife?"

She cut her eyes away. "So maybe it wasn't then that he told me. It might've been later. But I know what I know. "

Was she rattled by the news of Zeke's death or being deliberately contradictory? "You went for a walk on the beach, you talked, and then...what? He came for a massage?"

"That's right. I told him he should. He said he had a pinched nerve. I told him a massage would help."

"At what point did your relationship become...social?"

"A few days later. I took him some homemade cookies. Tammy couldn't be bothered to bake for him."

This was inconsistent with what I knew of Tammy, who shared recipes with Mamma. "Did Zeke tell you that?"

"Not in so many words. But I can tell when a man hasn't had cookies in a while. If she baked for him, he wouldn't've been hungry."

Was she still talking about cookies? "When was the first time you saw him privately?"

She looked at the ceiling. "I guess you could say it was then."

"I'm sorry?"

"When I took him the cookies. We saw each other *privately* then."

"That same day? You mean at the garage?" Surely she meant something else.

"In his office. Cookies weren't the only thing Tammy didn't have time for."

I coughed, took a deep breath. Was she trying to shock me? "And after that, you saw him regularly?"

"Couple times a week."

"Where? At your place?"

"Usually. Sometimes I stopped by the garage to take him treats."

"More cookies?"

"Sometimes a pie. Whatever he wanted. Are you going to tell me what happened to Zeke? Did she hurt him?"

"Who?"

"Tammy Sue. He said she was crazy."

"He was afraid of Tammy?"

"I wouldn't say afraid. Zeke could take care of himself. He was an Army Ranger."

I moistened my lips, nodded. "That's what he said. What exactly did he say about Tammy?"

"It's not so much what he said."

"I'm not following. Did he tell you he was afraid of what Tammy might do?"

"Not in so many words."

"What exactly did he say, and in exactly which words?"

"I don't remember." She leaned in close to me and her voice rose with each word. "What. Happened. To. Zeke?"

"I told you, I don't know. I only know he's dead. Did you work yesterday?"

"Yes."

"What time did you leave?"

"Six fifteen."

"After that? Where were you last night?"

"Good grief, you don't think I killed him?"

"Did you?" I gave her a level look.

"Of course not." Her voice softened. "I loved him."

"Where were you last night?"

"I was at home, all right?"

"Alone?"

"Yes, alone. What of it?"

"Did anyone call or stop by?"

"You mean do I have an alibi?"

I shrugged. "Do you?"

"No. Do I need one?"

"It would be helpful," I said.

"Well I'm sorry I can't be more helpful, but even though I don't have an alibi, I did not kill Zeke."

I sighed. "Do you have any idea who might've—aside from Tammy Sue? What about Coy Watson? Was he upset when you started seeing Zeke?"

Crystal gave a dismissive wave. "He had no way of knowing. I certainly didn't tell him. I told you. It wasn't serious between me and Coy."

"And Zeke never mentioned anyone he had a disagreement with?"

"No." She raised her brow in an innocent expression, shook her head. "Well. Like I said. Just Tammy Sue."

THREE

Colleen met me on the sidewalk in front of Phoebe's. "I would've thought they'd've given me a heads up or something if someone on the island was in mortal danger." Her voice was pensive, her green eyes troubled. Since she died, Colleen favored sundresses. That morning she wore a gingham number that matched her eyes and set off her ginger-red hair.

Before I spoke, I pulled out my iPhone and ended the voice memo. "If you're telling me there's a glitch in the system at work, that's disturbing on a great many levels." As a guardian spirit, Colleen's afterlife mission was sponsored by The Almighty.

"Of course not." She gave me an exasperated look. "It's just...I guess I'm still learning the ropes."

I mulled that. "You really were surprised this morning?"

"You could've knocked me over with a feather. I went to check in—see if I'd missed something. Nope. I was told this isn't my concern. I kinda think they're making a point."

"What do you mean?"

"Well, I have been pushing the boundaries of my position a bit. My mission is to protect the island. Keep the population at current levels or lower."

I made a rolling motion with my hand, nodded. I was well acquainted with Colleen's mission, though I thought it was more the people who lived here she was protecting than the island itself.

"I'm not supposed to be helping you with your cases," she said. "I have to be more careful. I could get reassigned."

"But you haven't been helping me with my cases—just occasionally watching my back. And *I'm* certainly grateful."

"Well, someone must think I've crossed the line."

"They've clipped your wings, have they?"

"I told you, I'm no angel. But, yeah, I guess."

I shrugged. "We'll manage. Nate and I are good at our jobs, you know."

"I never said you weren't. Where are you going now?"

I nodded towards Lyerly's Automotive. "Across the street."

"Oooh. I'm coming too."

"That 'more careful' thing didn't last long." I looked both ways and stepped into Palmetto Boulevard.

"I'm fine on the island. Anything going on here could relate to my mission. I think maybe I've been spending too much time in Charleston."

"Your call. I just don't want you to get into trouble." I crossed the sidewalk into the parking lot of Lyerly's Automotive. The original building was a brick rectangle, circa the early 1900s. Zeke added on three service bays with oversized garage doors when he bought the building after he came home from his stint in the Army, or whatever he was doing. An older burgundy Subaru was parked in front of the service bay on the far right.

"I can handle my business," said Colleen.

"You sound like Blake." My brother took every opportunity to share that sentiment with me. I retrieved my phone, started a new voice memo, and slid the phone back into the outer pocket of my crossbody bag. I'd had to pare down what I carried with me, but I'd come to rely on the hands-free style of purse as an investigative tool.

A doorbell chimed as I opened the door and stepped inside. The reception area held a metal-legged desk and the kind of sofa and chairs they must sell only to car dealerships and repair places. The air smelled vaguely of grease. No one was around. "Hello?"

"Someone's here," said Colleen.

"Someone had to open the place," I said. "Unless it was never locked up last night." Had Zeke been killed here?

"No, I mean, I can sense it. Someone's here," said Colleen.

"Hello?" I stepped towards the door against the back wall. Somewhere beyond, a toilet flushed. A door opened and closed. Footsteps. "Hello?"

A young man sporting James Dean hair and the matching sneer stepped into the room. "Sorry, I was in the back. What can I do for you?"

The name on his shirt was Price. That rang a bell. "Are you Price Elliott?"

"I sure am. And you're Liz Talbot." He looked me up and down, grinned.

"Seriously? Is he even of drinking age?" Colleen levitated. She raised her arms slowly. A breeze blew through the room, riffling a stack of work orders on the desk.

Price's grin flickered. He glanced around the room.

"That's right." I smiled real friendly. "How're your mom and dad?" Grant and Glenda Elliott had both lived in Stella Maris all their lives. They went to St. Francis Episcopal, the church I'd grown up in.

He shrugged. "Fine, I guess."

"Did you open up this morning?" I asked.

"Yeah. Zeke should be here soon. Normally he's here before me. But I have a key just in case." He crossed to a bookshelf that housed a stack of magazines and picked up a coffee mug and a cell phone from the top.

"Was the building locked when you got here?"

He took a long sip of coffee. "Why wouldn't it be?"

Was everyone I talked to today going to have an attitude? "Just curious. That your Subaru out front?"

"Yeah."

"So, you're a mechanic?"

"Dad thinks so, I reckon. This was his idea, not mine."

College must not've worked out for Price. Vaguely, I remembered hearing he'd gone to University of South Carolina for a while. "When's the last time you saw Zeke?"

"I left at five yesterday. He was still here. Why?"

"How long have you worked for him?"

He sighed heavily. "A year or so. Do you need your car looked at?"

"No, thanks. Anyone else work here besides you and Zeke?"

"Tammy Sue does the books. But she does that mostly from home. Why do you ask?"

"Do you mind if I take a look around?"

He made a face that could've meant any one of several unpleasant things. "Zeke wouldn't like that." He sat on the edge of the desk, glanced at the screen of his cell phone.

I stepped to the door to my right, which led to the first bay. The top half of the door had a window. "Who does the Accord belong to?"

"Connie Hicks. Works at the bank. Car was leaking transmission fluid."

I knew Connie. "When did she bring it in?"

"Yesterday about noon."

"Was anyone supposed to come by to pick up a car last night after five?"

"Yeah. Connie was supposed to come by after work—around six, she said. Car's ready. Zeke filled out the service ticket." He nodded towards the desk.

"Anyone else?" I asked.

Colleen passed through the door we'd come in. Where was she off to?

"Nah. Most of yesterday's work was oil changes. All of those were picked up before I left. Any particular reason you're asking all these questions?"

"Let's just say—"

The door opened and in walked Colleen—solidified. Price could see her. And he seemed to appreciate what he saw. He stared slack-jawed at her.

Forever seventeen, Colleen had changed into jeans, a blue and pink patchwork shirt, and converse tennis shoes. Her hair fell in molten curls around her shoulders to halfway down her back. She looked like she'd stepped out of an Urban Outfitters catalogue.

What on earth was she up to? Price was too young to remember Colleen, but if someone older walked in...Would they recognize her? Her afterlife body was a perfect version of the one she'd occupied when we were in high school, her skin clear and luminous, her figure slim. Still, I had recognized her right off when she first appeared to me a few years back. Materializing in public was risky.

"Do y'all have rental cars?" Colleen's voice was all sultry, theatrical.

"Ah...well, let's see..." Price licked his lips.

Go. Colleen threw the thought at me. "My car broke down over at the ferry dock? I'm going to need to see about getting it fixed. But I need a rental car in the meantime."

"I'm going to take that look around while you help this

customer," I said.

"Yeah, sure. Go ahead," said Price.

I opened the door and stepped into the service bay. Connie's silver Accord sat above the hydraulic lift. Oversized garage doors on the front and back could be opened to allow cars to pull in one side and out the other.

The area was neat. Zeke appeared nearly as fond of organization as I was. The tools were put away. Rolling tool carts were closed and pushed to the walls. The floor was even clean. Aside from that, it looked like every repair shop I'd ever visited. Nothing testified to foul play.

A walk-through door near the back led to the next bay. I continued my tour. The second garage was empty and just as neat as the first. Another door identical to the one leading from the first to the second work bay led to the last. It was vacant and clean as well.

I headed back towards the office. As I approached the door leading to the reception area, I crouched, slipped over, flattened myself against the wall, and peered through the window in the door. *Get him outside.* I threw the thought to Colleen.

"I need some fresh air," she said, perhaps a little too loud.

"Hey, we have that. Right out here. You want a Coke?" Price opened the door for her.

Colleen was doing exactly what she just got through telling me she wasn't supposed to be doing. And it wasn't like I couldn't have talked Price into letting me look around the shop without her help. She and I needed to have a talk. There were times I really needed her. She didn't need to be getting into trouble doing things I could easily do for myself. She was having fun, is what it was.

I shook my head and walked through the pass-through door into the reception area. Quickly I stepped through the door in the back. I was in an office with a large double pedestal desk—looked like oak to me. The kind of desk school teachers had when I was in school. Zeke's desk.

I reached into my purse, pulled out a pair of latex gloves, and slipped them on. Then I stepped around the desk and slid into the chair. A large blotter-style calendar took up most of the surface. May was still on top. I studied the last month of Zeke's life.

Each day had eight lines. Customers' last names were written in a neat block print. It looked as if business had been good. Nothing stood out, but I snapped pictures of May and June in sections for my records. If nothing else popped, I could work my way through his last few weeks of business. Perhaps there'd been a dispute. But poison...If I was right about the poison, that required planning, which meant it wasn't a spur-of-the-moment crime of passion.

I slid open the top drawer. Its contents—the usual paper clips, note pads, and whatnot—were neatly organized. Nothing interesting. I felt underneath. Nothing taped there. Systematically, I worked my way through the desk. The most interesting thing was a bottle of Makers Mark in the bottom right-hand drawer.

I sat back in the chair, scanned the room slowly. In front of the desk were two leather sling chairs with exposed metal frames. The wall behind them held a calendar sold by the Little League and two framed photos of a beach that brought the Caribbean to mind. On the wall to my right was a short section of cabinets with a coffee maker on a black laminate counter. The wall to my left held file cabinets. I'd likely be back to go through those. No time for that now.

My eyes slid back to the counter. Had Zeke been poisoned here? I swiveled around, stood, and took a closer look at the coffee supplies. Beside the Cuisinart, upside down, in a black silicone case that had been camouflaged by the countertop, was a cell phone. Zeke's? Price had his phone. Personal electronics were often treasure troves of information. I took a picture of it, showing where it had been found, then picked it up. It was an iPhone.

I pressed the "Home" button. The wallpaper was a photo of Zeke and Tammy Sue on the beach at Devlin's Point. I pressed "Home" again. The passcode screen displayed. Shit fire. I pulled an evidence bag from my purse, labeled it, dropped the phone inside, and slid the bag back into my purse.

The coffeepot was on, with three-quarters of a pot in the carafe. I opened the two wall cabinets wide, drew back, maybe jumped a little.

Right there on the shelf, front and center, was a bag with a skull and crossbones.

I snapped a picture.

Death Wish Coffee Company. I examined the bag, which proclaimed it to be the world's strongest coffee, fair trade and USDA organic certified. I opened the bag. It looked like regular coffee to me, and the bag was more than half used. If it turned out Zeke had been poisoned, this would be a sad piece of irony. I returned it to the shelf.

The coffee cabinet also contained Jamaican Blue Mountain, Molokai Hawaiian Midnight Roast, and certified Kopi Luwak coffee, "wild and cage free." Hell's bells. Was that what I thought it was? I picked up the bag, read the back label. Yep. Zeke had a bag of that coffee that was eaten and digested by civets before it was roasted. I opened the bag. It did not look like regular coffee one bit.

I prowled through the rest of the cabinet and the drawers, finding nothing more interesting than colorful pottery coffee mugs. I scanned the room again.

There were two doors in the back wall. The one on the left stood slightly ajar. I walked over and pushed the door open. A bathroom. The door on the right appeared to be an exterior door. I opened it slowly and stepped outside. To my left was a small parking area. To my right was the driveway cars exiting the service bays used.

Zeke's white Ford F-350 pickup was parked in the first spot. He'd typically driven the truck to work. This was common knowledge. Something—someone—had prevented him from leaving as usual last night.

There were three more parking spaces behind the building. A tow truck occupied the last spot. Two spaces sat empty between Zeke's truck and the tow truck. A pair of mature magnolias screened the small parking area from the parking lot of the Baptist Church. Access to the back of the building was from Anchor Way on my right. To the left, the back of the bakery walled off the area. I walked to the edge of the lot. Someone could've accessed this area from behind the bakery, but they'd have gotten scratched up. A thick stand of bamboo grew close to the back of the building. If someone parked back here and loaded Zeke into a car or truck to move him, they would've had to've driven in from Anchor Way.

Had someone driven the Mustang over here? Or had Zeke been moved to the Lyerly home in another vehicle and then moved to the back of the Mustang? Why would anyone do that?

I needed to talk to Tammy Sue.

I looked into the window of Zeke's truck. The glass was tinted, but I could see inside. It could've been sitting in a showroom—it looked that clean. A garage door opener was clipped to the sun visor. I tried the door, but it was locked.

I studied the asphalt.

Two faint scratches, maybe eighteen inches apart caught my eye. They trailed from near the door to the end of the second parking space.

I pulled out my phone and tapped Blake's name in my favorites list.

He answered on the third ring. "Yeah, Sis."

"I think Zeke's shop was the crime scene. Looks like drag marks on the asphalt out back. Have forensics check the heels of Zeke's boots."

"Anyone there today?"

"Price Elliott." I gave Blake the highlights of what Price had told me. "What did Doc Harper say?"

"He can't tell anything yet, blah blah, but it could've been strychnine. He's not going to say much until he's done an autopsy, got his test results."

"I'm heading back over there in a few minutes. Soon as I lock this place up, send Price home. We need to get forensics in here."

"Sounds good. I'll tack that way, bring the team from the Sheriff's office when they finish here."

"Any news?"

"Tammy came to, but then they had to sedate her. She's still at Mom and Dad's. I haven't talked to her yet. Nate seemed to think you'd handle her better regardless. Mom's got lunch ready, got trays of sandwiches, fruit, hell, I don't know what all. I haven't had time to eat myself."

"Has Doc Harper taken custody of Zeke?"

"Yeah, they're just leaving."

"You going to have the car towed back to the station?"

"Thought I would, after the forensic team finishes up."

"Should I see if Price can drive Zeke's tow truck, or do you want to have Pete tow it?" Pete Carter ran the only other tow service in town.

"I'll get Pete to do it. What's your take on Price?"

"If he didn't kill Zeke—and I don't have any reason to think he did, yet—he was probably the last person to see him alive aside from the perpetrator."

"Tell him not to leave town."

"Roger that. See you soon." I ended the call with Blake and walked around the building to avoid traipsing back through Zeke's office.

As I rounded the corner, Colleen and Price came into view. *Time to go.* I threw the thought in her direction.

She said something I couldn't hear, then started down the street. Price darted after her.

"Price?" I called out.

He ignored me, jogged a few steps to catch up with Colleen.

"Price, we need to talk," I called.

He turned back to me with pure rage. "I don't know what in the hell you want, but I'm done talking to you."

And less than an hour ago, he'd gazed upon me with unambiguous lascivious notions. Another girl might be hurt at how fast he'd lost interest in her. "I'm afraid not."

Colleen disappeared into thin air while his back was turned.

He snarled at me, then pivoted. "What the hell? Where'd she go?"

"You've got way bigger problems than that," I said.

FOUR

I had to park two blocks away from Mamma and Daddy's house on Sweetgrass Lane. Both sides of the street were lined with every emergency vehicle the town of Stella Maris owned, plus a white Tahoe with the Charleston County Sheriff's Office emblem—the Crime Scene Forensics unit. Behind the official vehicles were those of curious island residents who didn't live in the immediate area. I wended my way past huddled groups of somber-voiced friends and neighbors.

Nate's Explorer was still in the driveway. My Godmother's, Grace Sullivan's, Cadillac was parked behind Blake's dark green Tahoe. I didn't recognize the other cars crowded in behind them. I climbed the steps and crossed the deep front porch of Mamma and Daddy's rambling Lowcountry cottage.

"Mamma," I called out as I opened the door.

"I'm in the kitchen," she said.

I headed down the hall towards the back of the house. As I stepped into the kitchen, Grace lowered a platter of sandwiches onto the island. She wore her signature St. John pantsuit. Not a single hair in her platinum bob was out of place, and her understated makeup looked freshly applied. She looked awfully spiffy for someone who'd been working in the kitchen, is what I'm saying. Her and Mamma both.

"I'm starved." I moved towards the sink to wash up.

"Hey, Sugar," said Grace. "These are chicken salad. I just finished pulling things out."

"There's tomato sandwiches, pimento cheese, deviled eggs, potato salad, shrimp salad, and fruit salad," said Mamma. "Watch that water now. You're going to scald yourself. My gracious. What do you want to drink?"

"I'll get some tea." I dried my hands and slathered on some Purell. Then I picked up a blue stoneware plate and commenced piling it high. "Only you could pull together this kind of spread spur of the moment."

"I couldn't've done it without Grace," Mamma said.

"That's nonsense," said Grace. "All I've done is get in the way."

They argued the point while I settled onto a counter-height stool and tucked into lunch. I savored my first bite of home grown tomatoes, thinly sliced sweet onion, and Duke's mayonnaise on soft white bread. "Mamma, are these your June Pinks?" June Pinks are my favorite heirloom tomato.

"Yes. I only had a few. It's early yet." She set a glass of iced tea by my plate.

"Thanks, Mamma," I said. "Let's hide those tomato sandwiches, why don't we? How's Tammy Sue?"

Mamma and Grace shook their heads in unison.

"That poor thing," said Mamma. "She's in a bad way, bless her heart."

"Where is she?" I asked.

"On the sofa in the den," said Mamma. "I wanted her close by where I could hear if she called."

"Did she say anything more about what happened?" I asked. "Anything I need to know?"

"No." Mamma shook her head. "She's beside herself, quite

naturally."

I took a bite of chicken salad sandwich.

"You're not going to try and ask her questions now are you?" asked Mamma.

"I have to," I said. "There's not going to be a good time, and I want to keep her from having to endure legal problems on top of losing Zeke."

Grace said, "Really, Sugar, can't that wait a day or two?"

"Unfortunately not," I said.

They both frowned at me.

"Grace, are you getting any kind of a read on this?" I asked. Grace was our island psychic—not the kind with a sign out front. Grace ran the bed and breakfast. But after a near-drowning in her teens, she had the gift.

"Well, I can tell you that poor child didn't kill anyone, if that's what you mean," said Grace.

I nodded. That "poor child" was somewhere north of forty. "I figured. Has Nate had lunch?"

"Why yes, of course," said Mamma. "I insisted. I took him and Blake both plates out. Your brother hadn't touched his last I looked. Surely you can't talk to Tammy after she's been sedated."

I wanted to linger over lunch, but made short work of it while Mamma and Grace continued to make their case for me letting Tammy sleep. It wasn't that I disagreed with them. In the best of all perfect worlds, Tammy should have time to grieve before we started asking her questions. But she couldn't grieve properly from jail, and I needed to keep her from being further traumatized.

I set up the voice memo app, then took my tea and a glass for Tammy into the adjoining den. She was stretched out under a quilt on Mamma's buttery yellow leather sofa. Chumley,

Daddy's Bassett Hound, slept on the floor beside her.

"Tammy?" I set the tea down on the coffee table and placed a hand on her shoulder. "Tammy Sue?"

She blinked, stirred.

I took the wing back closest to her.

Tammy gasped, as if remembering her loss. Her lips trembled.

Chumley woofed a soft bark.

I patted him on the head, then spoke softly. "Tammy, honey, I need to talk to you."

She squeezed her eyes closed. "I can't."

"It's important. You want to help me find out what happened, don't you?"

"I just can't." Her voice was a shaky whisper.

"You've got to be strong, now. I can't even imagine what you're going through. But I need your help to get justice for Zeke."

"What am I going to do?" She pulled the quilt closer, up around her ears.

"You're going to take this one day at a time. Right now, we need to figure out who might have meant Zeke harm. Do you have any ideas at all?"

"All I can think of is maybe Crystal, you know, if she was pressuring Zeke to divorce me, but he wouldn't. Maybe she got angry."

"Did you and Zeke ever talk about divorce?" I asked.

"Never. Zeke loved me. I know he did. This was...I don't know what this was. But he did love me."

"Of course he did." I pulled the clear plastic bag with the iPhone I'd found out of my purse. "Do you recognize this phone?"

She nodded. "It looks like Zeke's case. I mean, I guess there are a lot of iPhones with black cases. Where did you find it?"

"On the counter in his office. Do you know the passcode?"

"Yes. It's 8764. It stands for 'Tammy Sue is My Girl.'" Her voice trailed off into a keen.

"Stay strong, now," I said. "When was the last time you saw Zeke?"

She took a deep breath, gathered herself. "Yesterday at lunch time."

"Did you speak with him after that?"

Tears spilled down her cheeks. She shook her head. "Normally we talked several times during the day. But things have been tense these last few weeks."

"Walk me through this. We gave you the pictures yesterday morning at ten. Did you confront Zeke at lunch?"

"That's right. I was very upset, naturally."

"Naturally. What did he have to say for himself?"

Tammy negotiated herself into an upright position. "The usual things men say. It didn't mean anything. He loved me. He was sorry. He promised not to see her anymore."

"Did you believe him?"

"That he loved me, yes. And I believed he was sorry. He seemed very...subdued. Which was unusual for Zeke, as you know. I'm not sure I believed it didn't mean anything. It meant a lot to me. If you love someone, really love someone, you're not drawn to other people in that way. You know what I mean?"

"I do," I said. "But these things are complicated. The important thing to remember now is that he loved you. Tammy, did the two of you have an argument at lunch?"

"Boy, did we ever. You know we're both—we were both—passionate people." She dissolved into noisy tears.

"I know, Tammy. Now, focus for me. What time did Zeke come home, and what time did he leave?"

"I called him right after you and Nate left. I told him I needed him to come straight home. He did. He arrived about eleven fifteen. I confronted him. He admitted he and Crystal had been having an affair for the last couple of months. He begged me to forgive him. I...I needed to work out my anger."

"How did you go about that?"

"I hit him a couple of times. He let me at first. Then he grabbed my wrists. We struggled. I scratched his cheek. It wasn't my finest moment."

Fresh scratches on the victim's face. Not good. "How long did this argument last?"

"He left to go back to the shop a little after one."

"And you didn't speak to him after that?"

She sobbed, shook her head.

I patted her arm. "What time does he normally come home?"

"About six thirty."

"Did you try to call him when he didn't come home?"

"No. I thought he'd picked her. Gone to her house. I never thought—" She dissolved into sobs and heaves.

I gave her a minute. "I bet you were up all night."

"I was. How could I sleep? I thought he loved her more than me. But the whole time, he was already *gone*." The sobs got louder.

Mamma and Grace peeked in from the kitchen. Their expressions announced their grave disappointment in me. Mamma crossed her arms. I stroked Tammy Sue's hair.

"When did it come to you to light a fire in the car?" I asked.

"When it started getting daylight, I suppose. He loved that car so much. It was his very first car. He hardly ever drove it, kept it in the garage all the time. I wanted to hurt him."

"It was in the garage last night?"

"Yes."

"How many sets of keys to the Mustang are there?" I asked.

"Two. We each had a set on our keychains."

"You were up all night? You didn't doze off at all?"

"I didn't close my eyes, not once."

"Did you hear anything in the garage at all?"

She was quiet for a moment, thinking. "No. Nothing. But I did have the music on pretty loud. I was hurting. I was listening to Johnny Cash."

"Were you maybe sipping a little something for the pain?" I asked.

"Well, yes. Who wouldn't?"

"You make an excellent point. Is there any way someone could've taken the Mustang from the garage without you knowing?"

She shook her head. "I would've heard something or seen something if anyone took it out of the garage. That car is loud."

"But you had the music up and you'd had a drink or two..."

"I'm telling you, that car is loud. The whole house shakes when Zeke starts the engine."

"Okay. About what time did you pull the Mustang out into the driveway this morning?"

"I guess it was a little after six."

"Did you notice anything amiss in the garage?"

"No, but I was too distracted to care about anything like that."

"Was the top already down?"

"No, I put the top down after I moved it outside."

"And then what did you do?" I asked.

"Well, I put a pile of his clothes in the backseat and lit a match. Then I went inside and got more clothes. I made several trips. I filled up the back and started on the front seats. I had to relight the fire several times. It didn't catch right off. We didn't have lighter fluid, anything like that. It had just started burning good when your daddy showed up. Not long after that, here came your mamma, then Blake. I guess you know the rest of the story."

"Tammy, can you think of anyone who Zeke had bad blood with? Anyone who had a reason to hurt him?"

"No one who would have done *this*."

"But he did have a falling out with someone?"

"Well, he nearly fired Price Elliott."

"When?"

"Maybe a week ago. Price was always late. And he was always wanting to leave early, had some excuse. His work ethic isn't what it should be. Zeke took him on as a favor to Grant and Glenda when Price failed out of college. Zeke's been very frustrated with him. Finally Zeke told him if he wanted to keep his job he'd have to show up on time and act like he wanted a job there. Price was angry. They argued. But I can't see him doing this thing."

"Is there anyone you could see doing it?"

"Well, no, of course not."

"Nevertheless, someone did. Was there anyone else Zeke had trouble with?"

Her face lit with recollection. "Coy."

"Coy Watson? What was that all about?" Did Coy find out about Zeke's relationship with Crystal after all?

"It was stupid. I'm not saying Coy would've hurt Zeke. But if you ask me who he had trouble with…that was Coy."

"Okay. What was the problem?"

"Coy had one of those stupid drones. It looked like a little spaceship. He flew that thing all over the island. You must have seen it…"

"I can't say I have."

"Well, he seemed to like to torment Zeke best. He'd fly that infernal thing into the backyard in the evenings while we were outside having a drink, enjoying the breeze. It made Zeke so mad. He tried talking to Coy about it. Coy told him it was a free country."

"You said Coy *had* a drone? Did something happen to it?"

"Well, yes, actually. Zeke took his shotgun and blew it out of the sky Thursday night. Coy came running over here. He was livid. He said that drone cost thousands of dollars."

"What did Zeke do?"

"He told him to get out of our yard before he blew him to kingdom come just like his toy. He said that's what Coy got for spying on people."

"The drone had a camera? Did Coy tell you that?"

"Zeke said it had to have one. That's the only way Coy could know for sure who he was aggravating the fool out of."

"Did Coy show either of y'all any pictures he'd taken with it?"

"No. Well, he didn't show them to *me*. Zeke never mentioned it."

"Did Coy leave then? When Zeke told him to get out of your yard?"

"He did. But on his way, he told Zeke he was going to kill him. It was just loose talk, is all. At least, that's what I thought at the time."

"Can you think of anyone else Zeke had trouble with?" I asked.

"Not a soul. He was a good man."

"I know," I said. "What about his friends? Who was he closest with?"

"Well, he was friendly with everyone. He played poker with

your Daddy and that bunch. He and Pete Carter were good friends. Spencer Simmons. Skip Robinson. Humphrey. I think he was closest to Humphrey Pearson."

"Really?" I scrunched up my face.

"Elizabeth." Mamma flashed me The Look.

I smoothed my face. Mamma worried a good bit over me getting wrinkles. She was forever telling me not to crumple up my face like that.

I said, "I wouldn't have thought he and Humphrey would have much in common." Robert Pearson's older brother Humphrey was a poet. He'd arrived too late for the sixties, but most folks thought of him as a flower child. He played guitar, sang in a few local bars, and was an activist for environmental causes and drug legalization. Occasionally he did carpentry work to pay the bills. He was also an avowed nudist, though typically not in public.

"It does seem strange, doesn't it?" said Tammy. "But they had lunch a couple times a week. Zeke asked me every so often if I had a friend we could introduce Humphrey to."

I mulled that. "Can you think of anyone else?"

"No, but I'm not functioning well right now. I'll think about it. Right now I can't get it out of my head that when I drove that car into the driveway and lit that fire, poor Zeke was in the trunk the whole time. What if I killed him? What if he was alive until he breathed in all that smoke?" The wailing began in earnest.

Mamma and Grace came and took up positions on either side of Tammy Sue and shooed me away. But I had enough to get me started.

FIVE

Back in the car, I grabbed my iPhone and cued up a playlist I'd named "Thinking Music." The opening beats of "Be as You Are" by Kenny Chesney wafted through the car's speakers via the Sync system. Breathe in. Breathe out.

The Sheriff's Office's forensics unit was still on site.

I simply had no choice. I called Blake.

"Before you send the forensics team over to Zeke's shop, have them process Tammy's hands and nails. My guess is they'll find Zeke's skin cells. They had a hell of a fight yesterday."

"I'm going to have to arrest her. You know that, right?" he said.

"She's not a flight risk." I prayed I was right about that. "Give me a little more time. I'm relatively certain she didn't kill Zeke. And I have a few other suspects."

"Who might that be?"

"I need more time. Hey, listen. I've got Price's set of keys to Zeke's shop and Zeke's iPhone. Both are evidence. I've bagged and labeled them. I'll drop them off at the station and log them in as soon as I've had a chance to dig through the phone."

"Fine, but—"

"I've got to run. Talk soon." I ended the call before he could press me for details on my other suspects. The investigation was only hours old. Casting suspicion on anyone was premature.

Breathe in. Breathe out. Keep moving.

It was nearly one thirty. I headed to the island's information hub.

The doorbells pealed a cheery welcome as I stepped inside The Cracked Pot, Colleen in tow. She was in transparent mode that afternoon—her default setting. But since she'd learned to solidify, an advanced skill, and could eat while in that form, she never missed a chance to score ham biscuits.

"I wondered why you didn't show up at Mamma's house," I said. "She and Grace had a massive spread going on."

"I had business to take care of," she said. "Order me two ham biscuits to go?"

I gave her the side eye. "Okay, but you'll owe me."

She rolled her eyes with drama only teenagers could muster.

"Hey there, Liz." Moon Unit Glendawn was in the weeds. She and two waitresses in starched pink dresses hustled between the counter, a row of booths by the window, and a section of brightly painted, mismatched tables and chairs in the middle. "Sit wherever you can find a spot. I'll be right with you."

I spotted Connie Hicks by herself at the end of the counter. She was roughly my age, with smooth, medium brown shoulder-length hair. Her crisp navy skirt suit was likely a size sixteen.

"Hey, Connie," I said. "Have you already ordered?"

"Hey. How are you? Yes. I'm just waiting on my cheeseburger."

"Would you mind joining me in a booth?"

Connie and I weren't close enough to be lunch buddies, but she didn't seem surprised by my suggestion, which meant word about Zeke had spread. "Sure, if one's empty. This place is even more packed than usual today."

I scanned the room. Everyone in town knew this was where

you came to get the scoop. Humphrey and Robert Pearson looked like they were finishing up, but they were at a table in the middle of the room. Brenda Carter and Margie Robinson stood at the third booth. Brenda was what Mamma would call willowy. She had a graceful way about her. Her ash blonde hair was cropped short and chic. Brenda said something I couldn't hear. Margie looked at me, then quickly away.

"Gossipers," said Colleen. "Like everyone else in here."

To Connie I said, "I see a booth. I'm going to grab it."

"I'll just ask them to send my food over," she said.

I started towards Margie and Brenda. They had their heads together in conversation. Before I reached the booth, they had wended through the crowded room towards the door.

Within moments, the table had been cleared and my tea was on the way. Colleen situated herself beside me, next to the window. I'd placed an order for her ham biscuits. Satisfied, she studied something on the other side of the glass.

"I don't understand what you're doing." I followed her gaze, spoke under my breath.

"I'm looking out the window," she said. "It's a beautiful day."

You know what I mean. This time I threw the thought. *You just got through telling me you'd gotten in trouble for meddling in my cases. And you turn right around and pull that stunt with Price Elliott. You're gonna end up reassigned if you're not careful.*

She was quiet for a moment. "I'm not gonna let that happen."

I know you won't mean to. But what if you cross the line one too many times? That stunt this morning was completely unnecessary. Colleen...I'd miss you something awful. Please be careful.

She turned a mulish look on me. "Here comes Connie."

Connie settled in across the table from me. With violet eyes, delicate features, and creamy porcelain skin, Connie was a classic beauty.

"Did you hear about Zeke?" I asked.

"I did. It's just awful. I saw him only yesterday. It gives me cold chills. Poor Tammy Sue." Connie shook her head. "Bless her heart."

"I wanted to ask you about yesterday," I said.

"What about it?"

"What time did you drop your car off?"

"On my lunch break. I went early. Around eleven."

"And you were supposed to pick it up yesterday at six?"

"That's right. I was late. My drawer didn't balance. I got there about twenty minutes past six. Zeke said he'd wait 'til I got there. But the door was locked and no one answered when I knocked."

"Did you see anyone else?"

She shook her head. "Not a soul."

"Was there a Subaru out front?"

"Price Elliott's car? No, I gathered he'd gone for the day."

"Did you look in any of the windows?" I asked.

"I tried. I was thinking maybe Zeke couldn't hear me, but since he knew I was coming, he must still be there. I was going to try to get his attention. But I never saw him."

"Did you walk around back?" I asked.

"No. I had on heels. I called a friend to come get me. Figured I'd missed Zeke and I'd get my car today."

"Did you see anything that struck you as out of the ordinary?"

"No. I wish I could help."

"That's the gospel truth." Colleen startled me.

Reflexively, I looked at her.

Moon Unit set my tea and Connie's cheeseburger on the table. "Ham biscuits will be up in a minute." She whirled away.

"You know this place is busy when Moon Unit doesn't have time to gossip on a big news day," said Colleen.

What's the gospel truth? I threw the thought at Colleen.

"Connie here wishes she could help. She'd love to know something—anything—she could tell you to be a part of things. I feel bad for her. I know how that feels."

Guilt washed over me. As a teenager, I hadn't been a model friend to Colleen.

"Is it true what they're saying?" asked Connie.

"What are they saying?"

"That Zeke was murdered?"

"It's early yet. Doc Harper will tell us the cause of death."

"Come on, Liz. You surely must know if he was murdered."

"Well, he was in the trunk of his car," I said.

"That's what I heard. It's a safe bet he didn't crawl in there and shut the trunk himself."

"Stranger things have happened." I didn't believe he'd done any such thing. But I was on a fool's errand to stem the tidal surge of gossip.

"You know," said Connie, "I might know something that could help after all." She took a bite of her cheeseburger.

"Really? What's that?"

She raised a finger, finished chewing, and took a sip of her Coke. "You should talk to Spencer Simmons. Wait...isn't he your cousin?"

"Once removed. His father is my Gram's brother. Spencer and Zeke are—were—friends, I think."

"That's right. They were friends. I was at this party back in late March over at Margie and Skip's?"

"Okay?"

"Oh boy," said Colleen.

Hush up. I gritted my teeth. *I'm trying to hear what she's got to say.*

"Spencer and Winter were there. Winter was flirting with Zeke, making a real show of it. Spencer was livid. He got all up in Zeke's face."

"Wait. Winter was doing the flirting you said. But Spencer was mad at Zeke?"

"I didn't say Zeke didn't like it. He ate it up with a spoon. He flirted back. Ask Tammy Sue. She wasn't one bit happy about it."

"I'll ask her. Was there a fight or anything?"

"No, but you could tell tempers were flaring. Zeke went for a walk on the beach to give Spencer a chance to cool down, I guess. Things blew over after that. But there might be something there. With Zeke being murdered and all, you might want to look into it." She picked up her cheeseburger.

Colleen looked down her nose at me, all superior like. "She's resorted to mudslinging. That's always a mistake. When you start slinging mud, there's no way to predict who it's going to stick to. More often than not, it's all the wrong people."

I kept my eyes on Connie. "I'll check it out. Thanks. You'd better make arrangements for someone to take you home this afternoon. I don't think they'll let you take your car until they finish processing the shop."

"Processing?"

"Looking for evidence. The forensics team will be there soon. Nothing can be disturbed until they're finished."

"You don't think Zeke was murdered *there*?"

"I didn't say he was murdered at all."

"But if they're looking for clues, they must think something happened there. I could've been there when it happened." Connie set her burger down and grabbed her Coke glass with both hands. She took a long gulp.

I didn't think she missed it by much.

SIX

After I left the Cracked Pot, I checked in with Nate. He was still with Blake and the forensics team from Charleston County. I headed home to organize what we knew thus far—and to spend quality time with Zeke's phone. Rhett, my golden retriever, greeted me out front with a frisbee.

"Hey, Buddy." I petted him thoroughly.

He jerked his head, waved the frisbee at me.

"I wish I had more time to play." I tossed the toy a half dozen times, promised Rhett a walk later, then climbed the steps to our front porch. Several of the potted gardens and hanging baskets drooped in the heat. I stopped long enough to water them, but ignored the call of the waves crashing on the beach out back and the lure of the hammock in a shady corner of the porch. I headed inside.

I poured myself a Cheerwine—regular, I'd given up artificial sweeteners of any kind—and took it to my office. Nate and I had considered renting office space in the business district, or even in Charleston, where most of our cases came from. But we struggled to pay taxes, insurance, and upkeep on the fifty-plus-year-old beach house Gram had left me as it was. We didn't need the extra expense of an office.

The dry erase boards we used for complex cases were still in place in what used to be Gram's living room, but now served as my office and the place where Nate and I worked together. His office was on the second floor in a former guest room, but he rarely worked there. I settled at the desk, turned on my laptop, and created an electronic case file.

Since we had an ongoing agreement with the Town of Stella Maris, we didn't need a new contract. I typed up my account of what had happened that morning—I'd been there when Zeke's body was discovered, so I was technically a witness. Then I transcribed my interviews with Crystal Chapman, Price Elliott, Tammy Sue Lyerly, and Connie Hicks.

Next I set to creating profiles of everyone involved in the case, starting with Zeke. Here's what I knew about Zeke Lyerly to begin with: he'd lived across the street from Mamma and Daddy for the last nine plus years; he was well-liked; he was a decent and honest mechanic; most folks in Stella Maris considered him to be a loose cannon, but I wasn't so sure.

From public records and subscription databases, I pulled the parameters of Zeke's life. He was born on Stella Maris, April 14, 1969, and graduated from Stella Maris High School. He enlisted in the Army straight away. That much was in the local newspaper archives.

His parents, Zane and Emily Lyerly, were both deceased. He had no siblings. He married his first wife, April Lynne Fox, in Arlington, VA, in June 1997. They divorced in 2007, not long after they returned to Stella Maris and Zeke opened the auto repair shop. He married Tammy Sue the next year.

There was not one word, aside from his marriage to April, about the years between him joining the Army in 1987 and him opening Lyerly Automotive in March of 2007. What had he been doing for twenty years?

He and Tammy Sue jointly owned their house and the shop. There were no mortgages on either and no claims for collection.

The Lyerlys seemed financially solid. Zeke had no children with either of his wives.

I pulled up Tammy Sue's Facebook page. She and I were "friends." I was Facebook friends with a few dozen people from Stella Maris who I knew but didn't spend much time with. As far as I could tell, Zeke didn't have his own Facebook profile. I would've been surprised if he had. I scrolled through Tammy Sue's photos—she'd posted hundreds. Zeke wasn't in a single one of them.

I went to the website for Lyerly's Automotive. It was bare bones—just a home page with an address and phone number, and no smiling photo of the owner. I went on a mission to find a picture of Zeke online and couldn't. Lots of folks were shy about the internet. My sister, Merry, had a fit when I posted a picture of us together at Christmas. Still.

We'd taken dozens of recent photos of Zeke for Tammy Sue, but most had Crystal in them as well. Finally I found a headshot of just him, one I'd snapped Sunday evening as he climbed out of his truck at Crystal's apartment. Now his expression struck me as thoughtful, even conflicted. I printed the picture and attached it to the center of the dry erase board.

The holes in Zeke's background were telling. Most people left a trail of property transfers, inquiries to rental agencies, utility bills, and all manner of other electronic footprints in their wake. The fact that Zeke's history had so much blank space pointed to either scrubbing or extended periods of time spent out of the country. And while there was no reason to think his death was related to anything that had happened in the twenty years he'd been gone—after all, he'd been back for nearly a decade—there was no reason to discount it entirely either.

What might I learn from his first wife's profile? He'd been married to her for the last ten years he spent away. I returned to my desk and went to work on April Lynne Fox Lyerly. An hour later, all I knew about April was that she was born in Goose Creek, had married and divorced Zeke, and her last known address was at 3 Queen Street in Charleston—a condo in the French Quarter. The holes in her background matched his perfectly. What exactly had the two of them been up to, and where had they been?

April was a part of Zeke's local history only for a brief time. Had she not liked life on Stella Maris? How had Tammy Sue felt moving into a house another woman had picked out? How had Zeke met Tammy to begin with? She wasn't from here, but he'd married her after he returned.

I reached for Zeke's iPhone, slipped it out of the bag, and typed in 8764.

Bingo.

Who had he spoken with in the last few days? I pulled up his recent calls. The last person he'd spoken to on his cell was Tammy Sue, at 11:13 a.m. the day before. Before that, there was a call from Carter's Exxon at 10:57 a.m. There were several calls from Tammy Sue over the last few days, and double that from Crystal. Zeke had called Humphrey Pearson Sunday afternoon. And he'd called a number from our local area code without a saved contact identifying the number Friday morning. I scrolled through the older calls. The same names repeated, with occasional calls to and from Price Elliott, the mayor's office, Coy Watson, Pete Carter, Skip Robinson, Spencer Simmons, and to other local businesses.

Whose was the number that didn't belong to a saved contact?

I dialed the number. After five rings, a pre-recorded message announced that the number I'd dialed had not set up their voicemail box.

Zeke's contacts held no surprises. I moved on to his email. His inbox was empty. That in itself was suspicious. Who on earth had an empty inbox? Zeke must not've given out his email address to everyone who asked like I did.

I opened the drafts folder. There was one email to mr.Smith@gmail.com from mr.Jones@gmail.com, dated two weeks ago.

Dear Mr. Smith,

It has been a long time. I am currently relocating to a nearby city. I tell you this to avoid misunderstandings should we run into one another on the street. I wish you well, and harbor no hard feelings toward you or yours.

Sincerely,
Mr. Jones

Hell's bells. What was that all about? The email was in Zeke's drafts and it was signed "Mr. Jones." Who the hell were Mr. Smith and Mr. Jones?

This was beyond strange—almost like a joke, but who would the joke be on? It's not like Zeke anticipated someone would be snooping in his cell phone.

I massaged my temples. I had no idea what to make of Zeke's email account. For the moment, I set it aside. Unlike me, Zeke had very few apps on his phone. In addition to the standard Apple apps, he had a couple weather apps, one for local news, and Fly Delta. I prowled through the phone with wild abandon, but was disappointed. Why did he even have a smart phone? He used very little of its capabilities from what I could tell.

I opened the Safari browser. Zeke had no favorites, no

bookmarks, and no browsing history that I could see. Did he always use private browsing, or did he not use the internet with his phone at all?

Rhett padded in to check on me. It was nearly five o'clock. I stretched, decided I needed to clear my head. Rhett and I went for a romp on the beach.

An hour later, as I crossed the boardwalk over the dunes, Nate came out the back door onto the deck. The sleeves of his white button-down collared shirt were rolled up showing off tanned, muscled forearms. Late afternoon sunlight glinted in his dark blond hair. I was a lucky woman. Rhett raced ahead to greet him. I smiled and quickened my pace.

"Hey, Slugger," he said. "Did you have a nice walk?" His blue eyes, warm and happy, caught mine.

"We should've waited," I said.

He pulled me close to him, kissed me hello. Behind me, the ocean rolled and sluiced. I soaked in the moment, relishing the quiet, solid joy of this man, my husband, coming home to me at the end of the day.

"You are quite the distraction," he said.

"I was thinking the same thing about you." I nuzzled his neck.

Rhett ran in a circle around us.

Zeke, in the trunk of the car, flashed before my eyes. I heaved a sigh. "I'm not nearly through with profiles."

"What do you want for dinner?"

"Something quick."

"How about I grill us some salmon?"

"Sounds good. I'll throw together a salad."

"Teamwork." Nate brushed my face, slipped a lock of hair behind my ear. "Perhaps if I help you finish those profiles you'll allow me to distract you from work for a while, Mrs. Andrews."

As always, his husky drawl sent shivers dancing up my spine. My husband could seduce me with his voice alone. "As if I could stop you from it."

We set the case aside long enough to make and eat dinner. The breeze off the water died down, and the citronella candles weren't doing enough to discourage the mosquitoes. We ate at the kitchen table, but opened the window to listen to the surf.

After dinner, we took the rest of the bottle of Cloud Break pinot noir to the office. I settled into the sofa with my laptop, Nate on the other end with his.

Nate stared at the case board. "That picture from Sunday evening?"

"Yeah."

"For a man on the way to visit his much-younger mistress, does he appear to you to have a lack of enthusiasm?"

"I thought the same thing. But he sure was happy to see her when she opened the door, remember?"

"There is that. As displays of affection go, that was downright voracious," he said. "Why don't we start with forensics?"

"Sounds good. What did they find?"

"At the house, not much. The only fingerprints were Zeke's and Tammy Sue's. No sign of forced entry into the house or garage. They looked around for anything with strychnine in it. Nothing there. They took both computers—"

"Damnation. I figured they would."

"They found the pictures we took of Zeke and Crystal. They've been logged into evidence. And guns—three shotguns and ten handguns. Zeke apparently had a fondness for Glocks."

"I would've been shocked if they hadn't found shotguns. I would've expected rifles as well. But that many handguns? That's crazy."

"What was more interesting was the way they were hidden."

"What do you mean?"

"The handguns were all attached underneath furniture, well hidden but within reach, by magnets in the drawer bottoms and shelves. They were scattered throughout the house, as if Zeke always wanted to have a gun within reach."

"He was afraid of something—someone. That's interesting."

"This looked more like full-blown paranoia to me. One of the shotguns was strapped underneath the bed. We knew Zeke liked guns—like your daddy. But your daddy has his gun collection on display. Zeke had his hidden but handy. At any rate, the guns were the headline at the house. At the shop, they found a chip off a coffee mug on the floor. Brown ceramic. No sign of the mug. Took all the coffee in for testing."

"Did you get a look at the coffee?" I asked.

Nate rolled his lips in, nodded. "I did. He had exotic tastes, to be sure."

I shuddered. Who wanted to drink coffee ground from beans an animal had eaten and digested? Who even thought that up?

Nate said, "Looks like someone cleaned up a recent spill pretty aggressively in Zeke's office. We need to ask Price if he knows anything about that, if any mugs are missing. Tammy too. Fingerprints, out front there're too many to count, most unusable. Zeke's office was wiped clean."

"A broken mug and a spill," I said. "Assuming for a moment that there is no other, more innocent explanation for that, our working theory of the crime is that the killer likely poisoned Zeke in his office. Zeke dropped the mug and broke it, spilling poison on the floor. The killer then cleaned that up."

"As interesting as Zeke's coffee supply is, it's unlikely the killer poisoned a bag of it, or delivered a bag laced with strychnine. There would be no way to be sure of who you were killing, or when. Someone was there, watched Zeke die, cleaned up the mess, and moved his body."

"Strychnine is extremely bitter," I said. "The killer likely put it in coffee already brewed. That might've disguised the taste long enough for Zeke to consume a lethal dose."

"Workday was over. Zeke was in his office doing paperwork or what have you. Someone comes in with, what, a thermos of coffee? Offers Zeke some. Pours some into Zeke's mug. He drinks it, and either notices it tastes wrong right off and drops the mug, or a few minutes later when the poison starts to take effect he drops the mug then."

"He'd have started twitching, then had spasms that got progressively worse until he asphyxiated. It's odd he didn't call for help. He must've known he'd been poisoned. And here's something else. I didn't find a single gun at the shop. Did the sheriff's office?"

"No, now that you mention it."

"The way he stashed guns all over the house, it doesn't seem like he would've not had one within reach at work."

"Indeed, it does not. Someone who knew the gun or guns were there must have removed them earlier. When Zeke realized he'd been poisoned, he may have tried to call 911, but maybe the killer had a gun for backup. Zeke went to get his, but it wasn't there. Time ran out."

We both mulled that for a few minutes.

"What did they say about the scrapes on the asphalt?" I asked.

"The back of Zeke's boots were scuffed up. They have to run some tests, but it looks like he was dragged from the backdoor to a vehicle parked behind the building like you thought. What's your take on Crystal?"

I filled him in on my interviews with Crystal, Price, Tammy, and Connie. "I'm afraid I haven't gotten very far with profiles. I spent hours looking into Zeke and his first wife, April. I found what I could, but there isn't much there. And his phone was nothing but a frustration." I told him about the odd draft email.

Nate's forehead creased. "That is peculiar. Who do you want me to start with?"

"Why don't you take Tammy Sue? I'll start with Crystal. Then I'll take Price if you'll take Coy."

"What about your cousin, Spencer?"

I wrinkled my nose. "I'm not sure Connie's gossip rises to the level of something that would put him on a suspect list. I need to follow up on that before we go there."

"As you wish."

We worked in silence for about an hour. Then I grabbed the photos we'd printed and took them to the case board. In a line under Zeke's stand-in, I put headshots I'd found online of Tammy Sue, Crystal, Coy, and Price.

"Tammy Sue had motive, sure." I wrote "jealousy" under her name. "But means and opportunity...I'm reasonably sure we're dealing with strychnine. Did you see the way Zeke's back was arched?"

"I don't know about that, Slugger. He has long limbs, and he was folded up in the trunk of a '69 Mustang."

I shook my head. "It was more than that. Strychnine has a tell. And I'm not sure Tammy could've gotten Zeke into the trunk by herself."

"I bet she could've. She looks strong. Doesn't she work out with your Mamma?"

"Yeah, she's in her Jazzercise class. They do use weights."

"I'm not saying Tammy did lift him into that trunk, mind you. Only that she's capable. What about opportunity? Tammy

Sue was home alone. Can anyone confirm that?"

"Shoot. I forgot to ask her that. She was so upset. I'll talk to her again tomorrow. Crystal doesn't have an alibi."

I wrote "Jealousy" under Crystal's name and stepped back.

"Anything in her background that jumps out at you?" Nate asked.

"Not really. My opinion is that she's a little volatile. But that's all it is—my opinion."

"Your instincts are good. We certainly can't rule her out. But for my money, Coy Watson looks good right now. He has two motives, if he knew about Crystal and Zeke. And since he was spying on Zeke with his drone, he could've found that out without Crystal knowing."

"Agreed." I wrote "Jealousy" and "Revenge/Anger" under Coy's name. "He lives in an apartment over Skip and Margie's garage. Maybe we should see if Skip has any rat poison around."

"About that," said Nate. "I did some checking. Island Hardware doesn't have inventory online. We'll need to check with them in the morning to see what they carry. But if you go over to Lowes in Mount Pleasant and look for rat poison, your only choice is a refillable trap with bromethalin pellets. A few others I've found online have diphacinone, bromadiolone, or warfarin. Any of that will kill people if you give them enough of it. But you won't have the violent convulsions you get with strychnine. And I couldn't find anything with strychnine in it that you can ship to South Carolina. I suspect, but haven't been able to confirm, that it's illegal, or at least against DHEC regulations, to use it here. I don't know how your average person with homicidal intent would get their hands on strychnine these days."

"Where can you ship it to?"

"Mostly states west of the Mississippi," he said. "But also

Florida, Alabama, and Maryland. They'd be the closest places."

"So someone knows folks that live in one of the states you can ship it to."

"Could be, I guess. But it sure seems like there'd be an easier way to kill someone if you felt like it had come to that."

"Maybe. But poison tells you something about the killer. He or she didn't want to come at Zeke directly. Poison is a stealthy weapon."

"Less chance of Zeke turning the tables on an assailant that way. Could point to a woman."

"Not necessarily. With Zeke's history, no one with sense would pull a gun or a knife on him."

"Fair point. Anything intriguing in young Price's profile?"

I listed "Revenge/Anger" as a motive under Price's picture. Zeke had come close to firing him and they'd argued a week before Zeke's death.

"Not really—nothing related. He had a DUI a couple years ago. I'm not sure I think he's enterprising enough to acquire strychnine. But we can't rule him out just yet either."

I drew a box the size of a four by six photo in line with the other persons of interest and labeled it "Someone from Zeke's Past," and listed "Revenge" as a motive. "This is a long shot," I said. "But I think we have to consider it given the holes in Zeke's background. The fact that he and April were both off the grid for twenty years—that's huge."

"Agreed," said Nate. "It's significant. Anyone else we should look at?"

I drew in a deep breath, let it out slowly. "This party at Skip and Margie Robinson's house keeps coming up. It might not mean anything, but it bugs me. What did you find out about Tammy Sue? It's possible someone wanted Zeke out of the way so he could pursue her."

"Hmm...well, she's originally from Roswell, Georgia—it's a suburb of Atlanta. She owned a hair salon there until she married Zeke and moved here. He was her first husband. No restraining orders against ex-boyfriends, nothing like that. Her parents still live in Roswell. And she has two brothers that live there with their wives. Two nieces, three nephews."

"That's interesting. I don't recall ever hearing about them visiting. I wasn't sure she had family. But as far as someone who might be smitten enough with her to do away with Zeke...she'd likely know about that. Someone like that would at least be paying her attention, surely. I'll ask her about it." I drew another box and labeled it "Someone Smitten with Tammy Sue."

I sensed Nate behind me. He wrapped strong arms around my waist and kissed the back of my neck. My skin tingled, and love, solid and warm filled my chest.

"I think we're finished for the evening," he said. "And I am smitten with you, Mrs. Andrews."

SEVEN

The next morning, Nate, Rhett and I ran our customary five miles on the beach. At five a.m., the air was balmy. By the time we made it back to the house, the heat and humidity bore down on the morning. I dressed in a sleeveless blue blouse, capris, and comfortable sandals.

We took coffee with us and headed to Mamma and Daddy's house. There was no sense in fixing breakfast at home when that would just upset Mamma. I smelled the country ham when we walked in the front door.

"We should've run ten miles," Nate said.

"I'm not sure we can outrun Mamma's cooking."

"We may have to hide her cast iron."

"Sugar, your cheese eggs are on the stove," Mamma said as we entered the kitchen. "Nate, you want yours over medium?"

"You shouldn't have gone to all this trouble," said Nate.

"You act like you're new here." Blake sat at the kitchen table, a platter of breakfast in front of him.

"Mornin', Tutie," Daddy called from behind the newspaper. "Nate." For whatever reason, Nate was one of the few people Daddy didn't have a nickname for. Tutie was short for Fruity Tutie, a jab at my aversion to germs.

Mamma said, "It's no trouble at all." She cracked two eggs into the sizzling cast iron skillet.

Nate cut me a look.

"How's Tammy this morning?" I moved to the sink and lathered my hands.

"About as well as you could expect," said Daddy.

"We got another dose of Valium in her," Mamma said. "But it must've worn off. She woke up about three and didn't want to take anything else."

"Has she eaten?" I asked.

"Not a bite," said Mamma. "It's all I can do to keep her hydrated."

"I'll go look in on her." I dried my hands and slathered on a thick layer of hand sanitizer.

"Here." Mamma handed me a plate piled with cheese eggs, country ham, grits with gravy, and a biscuit with butter and strawberry jam. "Eat your breakfast first. You need your strength."

"I would've gotten that, Mamma," I said. Either I hadn't moved fast enough to suit her, or she'd decided I was unqualified to fix my own plate. "I'm not cutting timber." I took the plate and slid into my chair at the breakfast table.

In self-defense, Nate fixed his plate and waited by the stove for his eggs.

"Looks like you may be right," said Blake. "Doc Harper tested Zeke for strychnine. Results aren't back yet, but preliminarily—he stressed that preliminary part—he seems to think it's a safe bet that's what killed him. Initial window is between four and eight p.m. yesterday."

"Price says he left at five and Zeke was there and alive," I said. "Connie Hicks came by the shop at 6:20 to pick up her car. She didn't see anyone. The shop was locked and Zeke didn't answer her knock."

Nate joined us at the table. "Anything more from

forensics?"

"Not yet." Blake forked a bite of grits and gravy, looked at me. "Tell me about these other suspects of yours."

I constructed the perfect bite of eggs, grits, gravy, and ham. The problem with investigating crime in a small town is that the suspect pool was often made up of friends and family. I didn't want to discuss this in front of Mamma and Daddy just yet. I caught Blake's gaze, gave my head a small shake.

"Let her eat her breakfast, son." Mamma settled into her chair. Her plate had one egg and one spoonful of grits with no gravy.

"Have you talked to your sister?" Daddy asked.

"Not in the last few days," I said. Merry had taken a leave of absence from work to teach a workshop at UNC-Charlotte. She was also spending time with her fiancé who lived nearby. "Have you?"

"Your mamma talked to her. I guess she's all right up there." He sounded skeptical. Daddy regarded anyplace else one of his children lived as a dangerous place.

"Daddy," I said, "you and Zeke were friends. Can you think of anyone who might've done this?"

He dropped the corner of the newspaper. "I can't imagine who could've gotten the drop on Zeke. Nor who would've wanted to neither. You know, I saw him come home yesterday. Twice."

"What time?" I asked.

"Once before lunch. A little after eleven. Then he left again after lunch and came home at six thirty."

"Wait. What?" I said.

"He came home early for lunch," said Daddy. "Then again at his usual time, six thirty."

"You saw Zeke come home at six thirty?" Blake asked.

"Didn't I just say that?" said Daddy.

"Daddy," I said. "Tell me exactly what you saw at six thirty."

"What do you mean? I just told you three times. I saw Zeke come home at six thirty."

"Dad," said Blake. "Did you just hear me say that Doc Harper said Zeke was killed between four and eight?"

"Did you say that? I was reading the paper."

"Did you talk to him?" I asked.

"Nah. I was sitting on the front porch, me and Chumley."

"Okay then, you saw *someone* drive Zeke's truck into the driveway," I said.

He shrugged. "Someone drove Zeke's truck into Zeke's driveway at the same time Zeke does that every day. Had Zeke's cap on. Waved when he pulled in, like Zeke always does."

"Did he pull into the garage?" I asked.

"Well, he drove around back. I can't say whether he pulled into the garage or not."

I pondered that. The Lyerly's garage was on the back side of the house with a rear-loading door. You had to drive down the driveway and make a long U-turn into the garage. "His truck is still at the shop."

"I guess he went back," said Daddy.

"How long were you outside?" I asked.

"I came inside not long after he came home," he said.

"Did you go back out?" I asked.

"Nah. It was almost supper time," he said. "Time for my Jack and Coke."

"You didn't see the truck leave again?" I asked.

"No," he said.

I made eye contact with Nate, then Blake. This was significant. Given that the evidence so far pointed to Zeke being killed at the shop, Daddy had very likely seen the killer driving Zeke's truck. And Zeke had almost certainly been in the back.

"Is Tammy going to stay with y'all for a while?" I asked.

"As long as she needs to," said Mamma.

"Did she call her family?" I asked.

"She did," said Mamma. "I was surprised they didn't come yesterday. But Tammy said maybe they'd be here for the funeral."

"Poor Tammy. Now she's got a funeral to plan," I said. "Has anyone called to see about her?"

"Margie Robinson," said Mamma. "She's coming by later this morning."

"Are they close?" Nate asked.

"I had that impression," said Mamma.

"Anyone else call or come by?" Nate asked.

"No," said Mamma. "Just Margie. She heard from someone at The Cracked Pot that Tammy was here."

I cleared my place. "I'll take her some tea."

"She'll want it iced, with Splenda and some lemon," said Mamma. "And don't be burdening her with your theories about artificial sweeteners. She has enough to worry about right now."

Daddy kept the newspaper at full mast, hiding behind it. "Red Bird, did you fix Kinky a plate? Poor little pig has to eat too."

Kinky LeCoeur was the Vietnamese potbellied pig Zeke had helped Daddy adopt in a poker game-related transaction a couple months back. Mamma looked at me. Her gaze held me accountable for Daddy's fascination with potbellied pigs. I'd made the mistake of telling him about one that belonged to a client.

Mamma pointedly ignored Daddy. "Make sure Tammy Sue drinks that tea now. She needs the fluids."

Blake said, "Dad, I think you're going to have to take care of Miss Kinky."

I took a glass of iced tea up to the guest room and knocked gently. "Tammy Sue? It's me, Liz."

"Come in," she called.

I opened the door, walked in, and set the tea on the glass-topped wicker nightstand. The room seemed dark and stuffy. "Why don't I open these windows?"

She rolled over and pulled a pillow over her head, burrowing beneath a pile of quilts.

I raised the roman shade on the left-hand side of the bed and opened the window, then walked around the bed and repeated the process on the other side. Light spilled into the room. The air was fresh, but hot. I turned on the ceiling fan, then fluffed the pillows Tammy wasn't holding fast to. "Here now, Tammy. Why don't you sit up and have some tea?"

No response.

"I know you want to help me find out who took Zeke away from you." I moved the cushioned wicker chair closer to the bed.

She climbed out from under the pillow and quilts, wiggled into a sitting position. Her eyes were swollen, her mass of hair knotted and matted.

"Please drink some tea. Mamma's worried about you being dehydrated," I said.

"I don't want to worry her." Tammy reached for the glass.

I waited until she'd drunk a few sips. "We're all working real hard on finding out who did this. I need to ask you a few more questions. I'm really sorry."

"It's all right," Tammy said. "What do you need?"

"Walk me through what you were doing between five o'clock and six thirty on Monday." How had she missed Zeke's truck pulling in at the usual time?

"Well, after Zeke went back to work, at first I was just so mad at him. I stewed a bit. I was cleaning house like a crazy person. Nervous energy, I guess. Then I started thinking how he'd been so sorry...so...devastated that I'd found out about Crystal. I decided to fight for my marriage. I put myself together a home-spa afternoon. I did my nails, soaked in the tub, did a facial...I wanted to be really pretty when Zeke got home." She cried softy. "I put on his favorite lingerie and waited with a bottle of Champagne. I wanted to show him I forgave him and was recommitting to our marriage."

The light dawned. "And when he didn't show up..."

"I felt rejected all over again. I felt like a fool."

"And that's when you lost your temper," I said.

"That's right."

"Where in the house is your bedroom in relationship to the garage, the driveway?"

"It's on the other end."

"Can you see the garage from your bedroom window?"

"No. There's a window on the back of the house, but there's a big magnolia tree right outside. The window on the other wall looks out the end of the house."

"You can't see the driveway at all?"

"No, not from our bedroom."

"Did anyone call or come by to see you between five and eight?"

"Unfortunately not."

"That's okay," I said. "I'm just checking off my list. Are you close friends with Margie Robinson?"

"I'd say so. I'm as close to her as anyone here. Closer than most. To be honest, my life revolved around Zeke. I didn't spend a lot of time with anyone else. I kept the books for the shop, kept the house nice, sold crafts at the flea market three or four days a week." She shook her head. "I don't know what to do without Zeke."

"It's going to take time," I said. "Do you recall going to a party at Margie and Skip's a while back?"

She flinched. "That's when he started seeing her."

"Crystal?"

"Of course Crystal."

"Was there anyone else Zeke talked to at that party?"

"What do you mean? He talked to everyone there. Oh, wait...you mean Winter?" She rolled her eyes. "Winter was trying to get Spencer's attention. She flirted with Zeke a little, but it was harmless. Who told you about that?"

"Connie Hicks."

"Well, Connie's flirted with Zeke herself."

"Did it work? Did Winter get Spencer's attention?"

"Boy, did she. Spencer was livid."

"With Winter, or with Zeke?"

"Both of them, now that you mention it."

"Okay. You said you do the books for Zeke."

"That's right."

"Do you do that mostly from home, or do you go into the shop?"

"Mostly from home. But I go in Friday afternoons for a couple hours. Well, I used to. Recently I haven't as much." Her eyes welled up.

"Does Zeke have a special coffee mug? One he uses more often than not?"

"Yes, actually. He loves this pottery mug I got for him at the flea market. It's brown, and it has a funny face on the front. He used it every day."

"When's the last time you saw it?"

"The last time I was at the shop...maybe Friday before last?"

"Was Zeke particularly fond of coffee?"

"Was he ever." She shook her head. "The darker and

stronger, the better."

"He had some unusual brands in the cabinet," I said.

"Most days he kept a pot of Jamaican Blue Mountain brewed. That was his go-to. He had a few other, more expensive brands. Some Hawaiian Kona. That civet mess..." She closed her eyes, smiled. Then she covered her mouth. "That bag of Death Wish. I bought that on Amazon for him as a joke. He loved it. Oh my goodness. That looks bad, doesn't it?" Her eyes filled with tears.

"Not necessarily," I said. "You would hardly have bought it if you were contemplating poisoning him."

"I guess that's right."

"When did you buy it?"

"Back in April, I think it was. I could look it up on Amazon."

"Don't worry about it for now. Tammy, was Zeke camera shy?"

"He hated to have his picture taken. Occasionally, he'd let me take a picture for a frame or whatever. But I had to promise never to post anything online—Facebook, like that. He was very serious about it."

"Why do you suppose that was?"

"He always said the internet was an invasion of privacy. He hated the very idea of social media."

"Do you think that's all it was?"

"I wondered, you know, if he was afraid of someone he used to work with coming after him."

"Where did he tell you he worked before he met you?"

Her eyes were clear, guileless. "He was in the Army. I think some of that NASCAR stuff, all like that, that might have been a little embellished. But in the Army, he was overseas, and I think he was on some dangerous missions. I didn't ask too many questions."

"Do you know if Zeke used email?"

"Never. If places asked him for an email address, he told them the truth: He didn't believe in email. If they had mail for him, he told them to send it via Uncle Sam."

"This might seem like a strange question, but has anyone flirted with you? Paid you special attention?"

She raised her chin, squinted at me. "Not that I can think of."

"How about someone who just seems especially attentive or solicitous?"

She was quiet for a moment. "Humphrey has always seemed that way. I mean, more solicitous than Zeke's other friends. He helps with the dishes when he comes over for dinner. Compliments me outrageously. He jokes with me a lot, says if Zeke doesn't treat me right I should let him know, all like that. But he doesn't mean anything by it, I'm sure."

"Probably not." Tammy had told me the day before that Zeke and Humphrey were close friends. Was Zeke keeping Humphrey close to keep an eye on him? "But we have to run down every possibility. Have you ever met April, Zeke's ex-wife?"

"No, I haven't. And Zeke didn't talk about her at all."

"He must have told you something about her when you were dating."

She nodded. "He said they were too much alike to be married to each other."

A feminine version of Zeke? I tried to wrap my brain around that.

"How did you meet Zeke?"

"I went to the Dominican Republic with three of my girlfriends from back home in Georgia. The Iberostar Grand Bavaro in Punta Cana. We saved up our money. It was an all-inclusive resort. Very posh. Anyway, we were having drinks in the lobby bar right after we arrived, and Zeke came up to me and said, 'I can wait a little while if you really want a big wedding, but if it's all the same to you we could find someone to tie the knot right now.'"

"And that was the first time you'd ever seen him?"

"Yes." She smiled at the memory. "We just clicked. We spent the evening together, had dinner, walked on the beach. Then the next day we went sailing. It was love at first sight, for both of us. We spent most of that week together. I wanted to go back to Punta Cana—the two of us. We were going to. Maybe next year." She sniffled, wiped her eyes.

"When was that trip?"

"Spring of 2008. We got married in early September. We just couldn't stand to be apart."

I rubbed her arm. "Listen, I'm going to need to look around over at your house, is that okay?"

"Sure. My keys are in my purse." She nodded towards the dresser. A large leather purse sat in front of the mirror. "It's probably a mess. The people from Charleston County were over there all day yesterday. I told them it was fine—do whatever they needed to do. They would have anyway, I guess."

"Do you know of any secret places Zeke had where he kept things?"

"Just his top desk drawer. Maybe he had a hidey hole. It would be like him. But if he did, he never told me about it."

"How about a safety deposit box?"

She shook her head. "I don't know of one. He told me once that we needed to talk about things...just in case. But we thought we had plenty of time. We put it off."

"You don't know what things he meant?"

"I assumed the usual things. Insurance, maybe. I never

wanted to talk about life insurance. I always told him there wasn't enough money in the world to fix it if anything happened to him." She dissolved into sobs.

I slid onto the bed beside her, hugged her close, and let her cry.

EIGHT

Nate and I left Tammy in Mamma's capable hands and set to exploring the Lyerly home. It was a comfortable-sized ranch—roughly twenty-four hundred square feet was my guess—with a three-car garage, and a screened porch, patio, pool, and fire pit out back.

I unlocked the front door and we stepped inside the foyer. The floor plan was open, with the entry separated from the family room ahead and a dining room to the right by only a column and a change in ceiling height. In the vaulted family room, french doors on either side of the fireplace led to the screened porch. Light-colored bamboo flooring with a darker tiger stripe ran as far as I could see. The walls were painted a creamy ivory, the decor uncluttered, almost minimalist.

"This feels un-Zeke to me," I said.

"Were you expecting taxidermied wildlife?"

"Maybe."

"I'll go right if you want to go left," said Nate.

"Sounds good." I headed down the hall to the master bedroom at the end, then beyond that to the master bath. The forensics team hadn't left too much of a mess. Fingerprint dust on surfaces was the worst of it. The medicine cabinet held nothing more interesting than cold medicine.

The tiled shower, jetted tub for two, dual vanities, and

water closet were clean enough for a real estate showing. I ran my hands over the door and window trim. No keys stashed there.

I spent an hour in the master closet and had nothing to show for it except a hankering for a shoe rack like Tammy Sue's floor-to-ceiling shelf unit that held an impressive sixty pairs of heels, boots, sandals, et cetera. I moved to the bedroom.

The window on the back of the house was actually a large bay window in the sitting area. Right off I could see that the magnolia tree completely blocked the view of the garage and the part of the driveway that accessed it. Tammy Sue couldn't possibly have seen Zeke's truck pulling in Monday evening from the master suite. But whoever had been driving it had no way of knowing she was back here primping. What would he or she have done if Tammy had caught them in the act of transferring Zeke's body to the car? It was a reckless move.

I felt vaguely disappointed that none of the drawers in the dresser, chest, or nightstands had false bottoms. Nothing was taped underneath any of the drawers. The forensics team had taken the most interesting things—the guns. Zeke took prepared to a whole new level. But what on earth had he been prepared for? I scanned the master bedroom again, convinced it was holding out on me. Then I moved down the hall.

Zeke had made an office out of the smallest bedroom in the house. A wall of bookcases housed a built-in desk. I sat in his desk chair and tried mightily to get inside his head. Who were you really, Zeke Lyerly? I slid open the desk drawer—there was only one, just below the work surface. Paperclips, staples, a note pad, a flashlight, et cetera. It was so generic, it could've been anyone's desk drawer. If Zeke had secrets—and he must have—his desk would not confess them.

Of course Charleston County Sheriff's Office had taken the

computer. I did manage to find a gun they missed—a Glock hidden in a hollow shelf in the bookcase. Aside from that, the room was shockingly normal.

I was surprised at the amount of memorabilia Zeke had—the bookcase held everything from high school yearbooks to baseball trophies and a wicker basket full of baseballs with dates written on them in ink. In the file cabinet, along with the usual files of receipts, insurance policies, and the like, I found a folder of newspaper clippings. I flipped through them. Zeke had been a high school baseball standout.

None of the mementoes seemed related to anything that happened after high school except a set of decorative glasses—the kind resorts put fruity liquor drinks in—from Iberostar Grand Bavaro in Punta Cana. I knew the story behind those.

I went back to the newspaper articles. Most were about baseball victories. But *The Citizen*, the Stella Maris local paper, was a small-town paper. They still printed the honor rolls from the local schools. And Zeke had made straight A's all through school. He'd been his class valedictorian. That was unexpected.

The three most recent clippings in the folder were obituaries. Zeke's father had passed away in 2004, and his mother in 2005. The final obituary, from 2014, was less yellowed with age than the others. I felt my face scrunching. Harold Yates died October 23, 2014. He'd been seventy-four years old. No survivors were listed. He'd lived in Stella Maris his whole life, a plumber by trade. What had been his connection to Zeke?

I returned the file to the cabinet and picked up the high school yearbook from 1987, Zeke's senior year. I flipped through, stopping at photos of Zeke—his class picture, with the baseball team, the National Honor Society, student council. Then I scanned what people had written when they signed his yearbook.

The longest entry was signed with hearts, "Love always, your TB." Zeke's high school girlfriend had clearly expected to be Mrs. Lyerly. But everyone thought high school love was forever in the moment. There was a time when I was sure I'd one day be Mrs. Jackson Beauthorpe. Who was TB? I scanned the senior girls, then the juniors, sophomores, and freshmen. No one's initials fit.

I skimmed a few more entries. Half a dozen other girls wanted Zeke to "come see me this summer before you leave." The guys congratulated him on a great baseball season, mentioned specific games and home runs. Stella Maris High was a small school. Virtually everyone had signed Zeke's yearbook. He'd been popular.

"Run across any guns the forensic team missed?"

I looked up. Nate leaned against the doorframe.

"Just one. You?" I closed the yearbook and returned it to the bookshelf.

"One inside a fake box of cereal. He was definitely afraid of someone. It's not like we live in a high-crime town by any stretch. His fear feels specific."

"Agreed. Have you gone through the guest room?" I asked.

"Yeah. Tammy has a small desk in there, some needlework. The household bill files are there. Nothing of note really."

"Did you check out the garage?"

"Yes, I basically retraced the steps the Sheriffs' Office took yesterday. I specifically looked in the garage for anything that had strychnine in it. I also looked again in the pantry, laundry room, and under the kitchen sink. There's nothing."

"I feel like we're missing something. On the surface, this house doesn't seem to have as much potential for hiding places as some of the places we've searched. But since Zeke had it custom built when he moved back here in 2007, anything's possible. He could've had the contractor build in a secret compartment."

Nate thought for a moment. "He probably used a local contractor."

I winced. "He did. I know because Mamma and Daddy—"

Nate nodded. "Live right across the street and this is a small town. Of course. I guess you'd better call him."

"Him" was Michael Devlin. The local contractor. My former boyfriend. We had a complicated history, one that involved him being tricked into marrying my scheming cousin when we were all but engaged. And I might have pined for him a few years, but that was pre-Nate, and a whole nother story.

I would rather have had a root canal than call Michael. Nevertheless, I pulled out my phone, opened contacts, and tapped the "D."

"He's still in your contacts?" asked Nate.

I shrugged. "I've known him my whole life. I haven't called him in years. Do you want to call him?"

"Probably not productive. I doubt he'd come if I asked."

"There's that."

Michael answered on the second ring. "Liz?"

"Hey, Michael. How are you?" My voice sounded fake-nice to my own ears.

"I'm good. How are you?" His tone was overly casual, like we talked all the time.

Could this possibly be more awkward? "Fine, fine. Hey, listen. You built Zeke Lyerly's house, right?"

"Ah, yeah. I heard about Zeke. Damn shame."

"I'm helping Blake investigate. I'm going through Zeke's house right now."

"Oh. *Oh*. Right."

"Did he have you build in hidden storage?" I asked.

"He did. I'll have to show you. You going to be there a while?"

"Yeah. I'll wait here for you. Thanks for coming. This could be important." I ended the call.

Nate said, "I noticed how you didn't mention I was here."

"It seemed counterproductive."

Nate shook his head, studied the ceiling.

Fifteen minutes later, Michael pulled into the driveway.

"He came quick." Nate looked out the window of Zeke's office.

"Well I told him it was important." I rose from the leather office chair. Nate knew I loved him and only him. I was sure of that. But how could he ever forget the sight of Michael in our living room on one knee with a diamond? I could not have dreaded seeing Michael more. But we needed his help.

The doorbell rang.

"You want me to get that?" Nate asked.

"Let's both go." I kissed him on the cheek.

We walked together to the door and Nate opened it.

Michael pulled back like maybe he'd been punched.

"Buon giorno!" Colleen picked that moment to pop in. "He's still pining for you. He needs to find a wife. And he needs to be building houses somewhere else. We're full up here."

He'll likely leave town soon enough since you're putting him out of business. I threw the thought at Colleen. Michael had been unable to sell his most recent spec house due to Colleen's poltergeist antics.

Nate and I both smiled. It flashed across my mind to wonder if Nate was smiling at the idea of Michael leaving town.

"Thanks for coming so soon," Nate said.

Michael seemed to try to parse Nate's expression, but

looked confused. "Liz said it was important. But she didn't mention you were here."

"Is that a problem for you? Me being here with my wife?" Nate asked.

Michael looked away, took a step back.

"It is important." I stepped back, allowed him room. "Please come in."

Michael hesitated, then ambled through the doorway. "Shame about Zeke."

"Yes, a real shame," I said.

"A shame," said Nate at the same time.

Colleen blew the door closed just for fun.

Nate closed his eyes.

Michael looked at the door. "The wind pick up?"

"Must have," I said.

Colleen held out her hands, palms up. Silvery clouds formed in her hands and grew. They were kinetic—lit from within, with sparkling flecks of light.

Nate stared. He wasn't as familiar with Colleen's theatrics.

She flew up above Michael's head and poured the clouds out over him like a bucket of soap suds.

Michael shuddered, then looked over his shoulder and squinted. "There's something odd about this house." He swallowed hard, looked at me like maybe I was to blame.

I offered Michael my sunniest smile. "Right? Like I said. We need to know if Zeke had you build in any secret storage compartments."

"That's not what I—" Michael rubbed the side of his neck, seemed to shake off his misgivings. "Yeah, he did. Three. I'll show you. First one's in here." He moved quickly into the kitchen and opened the broom closet. "This has a false back." He moved several brooms and mops and a vacuum into the kitchen floor. "You just press on the top right hand corner of the sheetrock and it will release." He stepped out of the closet so we could see.

Well hell fire. The sheetrock in the back of the closet had swung open, revealing a closet behind the closet. A built-in, fully stocked gun rack filled the space. I counted a dozen guns, including six automatic rifles and two big-ass handguns. Sound suppressors in varying sizes along with night vision scopes and goggles laid on a shelf to the left. Ammunition lined another on the right. "Sweet reason."

Nate examined the opening. "That's well done. It recess into the garage?"

I raised an eyebrow at him. Now he was complimenting Michael's craftsmanship?

"Yeah," said Michael. "But you'd never know it. I'll show you."

"He was prepared," said Nate.

"For what?" I asked.

Michael shrugged. "Whatever, I guess."

"I'll let Blake know these are here. I don't have any reason to think they're illegal. But still." I was accustomed to guns. Daddy had a cabinet full in the den. The fact that Zeke had these hidden was what put me off. That and he'd already had an arsenal under the furniture.

In rapid succession, three kitchen cabinets banged shut.

"What was that?" asked Michael.

"What?" asked Nate.

Colleen burst out laughing—her signature bray-snort peals. I declare it sounded like a donkey cross-bred with a pig.

I shook my head at Colleen, but the look on Michael's face told me he'd interpreted it that I hadn't heard the cabinet doors slamming.

"You said there were three hidden compartments?" said Nate.

Michael nodded. "Next one's in the master bedroom." He moved in long strides through the family room and down the hall.

Nate and I followed. Colleen hovered above Michael's head.

Michael looked up, seemed to cower a bit.

What are you doing? I threw the thought at Colleen.

Helping him make a decision.

"This is actually a hidden access to the attic." Michael opened the walk-in closet and turned on the light. "This shoe rack swings out." He demonstrated, pulling on the shelf of shoes I'd admired. Then he pressed on the sheetrock. The panel swung in revealing steps that led up. "The roof is really high. Zeke coulda had a whole nother floor of house up here. Said he didn't need it."

Michael led us up the steps. At the top he flipped a switch and light flooded the attic. Plywood flooring ran the entire length of the house, but the area was mostly empty. There was a stack of half a dozen boxes to our left.

"I wonder what's in here," I said.

Nate pulled the top box off, opened a pocket knife on his keychain and cut the second box open for me. Then he cut open the box he'd removed from the stack.

I pulled up the flaps on the box in front of me. "This is kitchen stuff."

"Same here," said Nate.

Colleen flipped the light switch off and on.

Cut it out.

"Y'all need help?" Michael moved back towards the steps, clearly eager to leave.

"No, thanks," I said. "We can come back up here later.

Where's the third hiding place?"

"In the garage." Relief flooded his face. He practically ran down the steps.

We followed him to the garage, where only Tammy Sue's cream-colored Buick Enclave was in its spot. Nate admired the way Michael had recessed the hidden closet in the kitchen between two built-in storage units in the garage, but Michael wasn't interested. He was clearly eager to tell us what we needed to know and get out of there.

The third hiding place was a fake air return in the garage. "This was easy," said Michael. "Anyone can recess one of these between a couple studs. Piece of cake." He pressed the top of the metal grill and it popped out. He stepped back so Nate and I could see what was inside.

Yet another Glock and a bundle of hundred dollar bills. I fanned through them. "It's a full strap. There's ten thousand dollars here."

Michael whistled low.

I looked at Nate. Normally we don't like other folks witnessing a search, but we likely wouldn't've found this stash without Michael.

"Doesn't seem very secure," said Nate.

I was thinking how maybe this was Zeke's get-out-of-town-quick stash and he needed it handy. But why?

"Michael, thanks for coming out." Nate offered him a handshake.

Michael waited a beat, realized he was being dismissed, and seemed grateful. He shook Nate's hand. "Not a problem. Let me know if you need anything else."

He pressed the garage door opener, waited for the door to raise enough for him to duck under, and lit out of there like something was after him.

"What was all that about?" I asked Colleen.

"I told you. Michael builds houses. We don't need more of those here. I'm helping him make a difficult decision—to move. Besides, there's too much history here for him, some of it painful. He'll be much happier starting over somewhere else."

I studied her for a moment.

"You're not sorry to see him go, are you?" asked Nate.

"Of course not," I said. "It's just, I hate to see anyone run off from their home."

"This isn't his home," said Colleen. "It's his history. He needs to find his home."

"Arrivederci!" She faded out in a pouf of sparklers.

Nate and I looked at each other for a long moment. We'd gone a round or two over where exactly home was for us. In my heart, I knew Stella Maris was both my history and my home. Nate didn't have the roots here that I did.

"Why is she speaking Italian all of a sudden?" asked Nate.

"Your guess is as good as mine."

He lowered the garage door. "You want to finish going through those boxes?"

"Sure."

We made our way back to the attic. But there was nothing but ordinary household stuff in the boxes upstairs—a complete, almost new set of Lenox Stoneware, flatware, kitchen linens, et cetera. "It's like this stuff is a spare set of everything," said Nate.

"When Zeke moved in here, he was married to April. Not much more than a year later, he married Tammy Sue. She would've picked out her own things."

"And April didn't want this stuff? It all looks new."

"Well, I heard she left in a hurry. There was drama."

"Marital drama?"

"I'm afraid so. Zeke took a few shots at the other party

involved sneaking out of this very house."

"Is the other party involved still in town?" Nate asked.

"Well, yes." I sighed. "But that all happened nearly ten years ago. Surely it can't have anything to do with Zeke's death."

"Who is it?"

"Jackson Beauthorpe."

"Jackson...wait. Isn't that another one of your old boyfriends?"

"Well, it was high school, Nate." I loved living in a small town, truly. But some days it complicated things.

"Is April younger than Zeke?"

"No. They're the same age."

"And Jackson?"

"He's my age."

"April had a fling with a guy a decade younger?"

"Something like that," I said.

Nate headed down the steps and I followed. "Well, it probably wasn't serious. If something else doesn't pan out we can look into it."

"I figured we'd talk to April. She lives in Charleston now."

"She didn't go far when she left in a hurry."

"She did at first. They tried to find her to testify against Zeke. Looks like she came back to Charleston after the dust settled."

"And you'd rather interview her than your boyfriend?" Nate's tone was teasing.

"If we need to talk to Jackson we can. I don't have a problem with it."

"Maybe I should interview him." His eyes sparkled.

"Be my guest. It's a waste of time."

He stopped by the front door and pulled me close. "I don't see finding out everything there is to know about any man who's ever kissed you as a waste of my time."

"Who says I let him kiss me?"

"He's a fool if he didn't try." His mouth claimed mine, warm and possessive. He pulled back, caressed my face. "As long as he never tries it again."

NINE

We stopped back in at Mamma and Daddy's for lunch. Mamma was back in the kitchen, arranging platters and serving bowls filled with everything she'd served the day before plus a vegetable platter, pasta salad, and roasted corn salad. There was enough food for a family reunion.

I went to the sink to wash my hands. "Where's Daddy?"

"In the backyard," said Mamma. "He's clearing some brush along the tree line. I declare it's gotten so grown up back there. It's a snake nest."

A chill shuddered up my spine. I purely hated snakes. "Can't he hire professionals to do that? Folks with protective clothing and all like that?"

"He said he could handle it himself," said Mamma. "Call him in for lunch, would you, sugar? Nate, would you bring me the tea urn from the pantry?""

"Sure." Nate and I spoke at the same time.

I crossed the kitchen, went out the backdoor, and scanned the yard for Daddy as I moved through the screened porch and stepped outside. Old-fashioned grass—the kind you mowed but didn't fuss with too much—stretched from the porch across roughly two acres. Live oaks, magnolias, and pine trees dotted the landscape, with bunches of azaleas underneath the shady overhangs.

Chumley's outdoor retreat, comprised of an oversized dog house with a front porch inside a fenced area that we never referred to as a pen, was situated in the back left corner. A line of crepe myrtles that would bloom red soon bordered the right side of the yard.

The tailgate of Daddy's white Chevy pickup truck stuck out from the woods that ran along the back yard. It really was overgrown. It looked like an impenetrable tangle of vines, brush, and small trees had nearly swallowed the truck whole. Mamma was right. It was snaky. Chumley's bark was muffled. Was he inside the truck?

"Daddy?" I called. "Lunch is ready."

No answer.

I strolled across the yard. What was he doing?

As I got closer, I could see Daddy standing in the back of the truck, sawing on a limb over his head with a pruning saw. Chumley was in the cab, looking out the back window, barking up a storm. I stopped twenty feet away, leaving plenty of room between me and any snakes. "Whatcha doing?"

Daddy didn't immediately answer. When the limb came loose, he tossed it over the side. "There. That's almost got it."

"You stuck in there?"

"Nah. I could drive out, but I don't want to scratch my truck."

I pondered that. "How'd you get the truck in there?"

"I drove in."

"May I ask *why* you drove the truck into the thicket?"

"No, you may not." He delivered the line like I'd breached etiquette, asked him something deeply personal.

I nodded. No doubt it had seemed like a good idea at the

time. "Daddy, why don't you hire somebody to clean up back here?"

"Hire somebody? Why would I do that?"

"Because you're a retired salesman, not a landscaper?"

"Landscaper. Huh. Those people charge sky high prices, and they wouldn't do it to suit me. I can take care of my own yard."

I studied him, standing there in the truck, sawing on some kind of thick vine, thinking how there was surely a more efficient way. "It's probably full of poison ivy in there."

"Poison ivy? Nah."

"Frank, you need a hand?" Nate walked up behind me.

"Nate. Yeah. Tell you what. How about climbing in the truck. Back out real slow. Stop if I holler at you."

Nate analyzed the situation. "Sure thing."

"Don't go crawling in there," I said. "It's snaky. How in the world did you even get out of the truck, Daddy? Will the door open?"

"Enough to slide in, it will. Be careful, don't let Chumley or Kinky out. They've got no business in this jungle."

"*They've* got no business in it, but it's safe for Nate? And you?" I said. "Why are they in the truck to begin with?"

"They like to ride in the truck," said Daddy.

"Slugger, it's fine," said Nate.

"Mamma wants us inside," I said. "Lunch is ready."

"Go on," said Daddy. "We'll be in directly. We can't leave the hound dog and the poor little pig in the truck. It's too hot."

I sighed. "I'm not leaving the two of you out here like this. Someone needs to be here to call 911."

"That won't be necessary." Nate picked his way through the brush. "This won't take but a minute."

"Careful of the paint," said Daddy.

"Hand me your saw," said Nate, "and I'll cut a few of these branches away from the front door."

Daddy passed him the saw.

Chumley barked louder.

Heaven only knew what the pig was doing.

Poor Nate. I could scarcely think which idea I hated more: walking into that snaky mess of a brush tangle, or getting into the cab of a truck with a Bassett Hound and a pig that had been cooped up for who knew how long. It had to smell to high Heaven in there.

Fifteen minutes later, Nate had cleared the branches and vines away from both doors. I cringed as he climbed inside the truck. He started the engine and eased the Chevy back while Daddy hollered instructions at him. As soon as the truck was completely clear, Nate pulled to a stop and eased out the door.

"All set," he said.

Daddy climbed out of the back of the truck. "Well thank you there. 'Preciate it."

"Happy to help," said Nate.

I pulled him towards the house. "Come inside, now, Daddy."

"I'll be right there, soon as I get Chumley and Kinky settled."

Nate and I hustled across the yard.

"I am so sorry," I said. "And I'm afraid of the precedent this might set."

"I'd say it wasn't anything, but I think it'll work out better for me if I encourage you to figure out a way to make it up to me." He grinned, looking happy with the way things had worked out.

After another round of hand washing and a thick layer of Purell, I put Nate and me each a plate together with a chicken salad sandwich, pasta salad, and cream cheese and olive deviled eggs. Mamma fixed plates for her and Daddy, and we all settled back into our places at the kitchen table while she fussed at him about getting his truck stuck in the woods.

"What we need are a few goats, maybe a llama," said Daddy. "Keep all that mess eaten down."

Mamma stared at him, a chicken salad sandwich halfway to her mouth. This was about to escalate. In the wake of the incident where Daddy acquired Kinky—which was a whole nother story—Mamma had a well-publicized, hardline position about no more animals.

"Did y'all know Harold Yates?" I asked.

"Harold Yates?" Daddy made a face. Is that where I got it? "Why are you asking about him?"

"Did he know Zeke?" I asked.

Daddy shrugged. "He was a plumber. He knew everybody in town, I guess. He was the only plumber on the island for a long time. But he died several years ago. What does he have to do with anything?"

"Maybe nothing." I took a bite of my sandwich.

"He was crazy if you ask me," said Daddy.

"Frank." Mamma flashed him a quelling look as she took her seat. "Be nice. That poor old soul never hurt anyone." Her small plate held a scoop of chicken salad, a small scoop of potato salad, and several thick slices of tomato

I was going to have to pattern her habits better. But not today. I needed thinking food. I delivered a bite of potato salad to my mouth.

"What kind of crazy?" asked Nate. "Was he a character? Or was he ill?"

"He was always going on about flying saucers, aliens, all such as that," said Daddy. "Probably had him a tinfoil hat."

"*Frank.*" Mamma laid down her fork.

"Carolyn, I'm just telling them the facts," said Daddy. "They asked."

Mamma smoothed the napkin on her lap. "He never had anybody. It was sad. He never married or had children. He was an only child, and his parents died young. He was a lonely person. Imagine what any of us would turn into without each other. Have some Christian charity."

"How would you put it?" Daddy asked. "Why don't you answer the children's questions then."

Mamma used her fork to cut a bite of tomato. "He was a lonely soul. He passed away from a heart attack a few years ago. And he was a plumber. He's been to this house a number times. You've seen him, Liz. It's been a long time."

I squinted, tried to recall.

"Stop that," Mamma said.

I smoothed my brow. "I don't remember."

"You were a child," said Mamma. "He's been here more recently, but you were living in Greenville. I don't think he ever retired."

"Did he believe in UFOs?" I asked.

Mamma sighed. "Yes. I suppose he did. He didn't try to keep that quiet. He passed a lot of time watching the sky."

"Daddy," I said, "how familiar are you with Zeke's gun collection?" Daddy and Zeke had bonded over two things: poker and guns.

"He has a few nice shotguns. Why do you ask?" said Daddy.

"I'm just curious," I said. "Running down a few things. Do you know why he'd have silencers and sound suppressors?"

Daddy cut a glance at Mamma. "No, I don't know anything about that," he said, in the same tone he used when someone had left a godawful mess in Mamma's kitchen and everyone knew it was him.

I gave him a long look. I'd seen Zeke use a gun with a silencer once, the first time Tammy hired us. I caught him surreptitiously dispatching members of our wild hog population to the hereafter. He'd told me at the time that he'd been hired by "concerned citizens," one of them being my daddy. The porcine problem was highly controversial. Island matrons—my mamma was exhibit A—were fed up with the pigs rooting in their flower beds. On the other hand, they were far too tender-hearted to hear tell of the swine being harmed. If I wanted the straight scoop, I'd have to get it when Mamma was elsewhere.

The front doorbell rang. From the family room, Chumley went to woofing.

"Who in the world?" Daddy stood and went to find out. We heard him talking to someone.

A male voice.

"Sure, come on in," Daddy said.

Nate, Mamma, and I stood and stepped into the hall.

Robert Pearson, a family friend who also happened to be our family attorney, stood just inside the door. "Hey, Carolyn. Liz. Nate. I've got a package for Tammy Sue. I understand she's here."

"A package?" I said.

"Yes," said Robert. "It's confidential, I'm afraid."

He must've been Zeke's attorney too. Of course.

"She's upstairs in the guest room," said Mamma. "I don't think she's up to coming down."

"Do you mind if I go up?" said Robert.

"Nah, go on ahead," said Daddy.

"Can I get you anything?" asked Mamma.

"Thank you, Carolyn. But no, I'm fine. I won't be long." He started up the stairs.

"Maybe I should let her know you're here?" I scrambled up after him.

"That's not a bad idea. Thanks," he said.

I slid past him and knocked on the door to the first bedroom on the right. "Tammy Sue, are you awake?"

She didn't respond.

I knocked again, then opened the door and slipped in, smiling as I closed it behind me with Robert still in the hall. The shades had been lowered again, dimming the room. "Tammy?"

She stirred.

I walked over to the bed, placed a hand on her shoulder, and jostled her gently. "Tammy, Robert Pearson's here to see you."

"What does he want?" Her voice was thick with sleep.

"He has a confidential package for you."

She sat up. "What is it?"

"I don't know. He's right outside. Is it okay to let him in?"

"I guess."

I opened the door and admitted Robert, then waited a beat before taking a step towards the hall.

"Where are you going?" asked Tammy.

"The matter I have to discuss with you is confidential," said Robert. "My condolences on your loss."

"Thank you," said Tammy. "I need Liz to stay with me."

I paused.

"I have a package for you and an envelope from Zeke," said Robert. "Have you retained Liz to work for you?"

"I did, yes."

Robert nodded at me. I closed the door.

Robert approached the bed. I pulled the wicker chair over for him, then perched on the edge of the bed.

Robert said, "I'm Zeke's attorney. He asked that in the

event something happened to him, I get this to you within twenty-four hours." He handed her a sealed envelope.

"Do you know what's in here?" she asked.

"No," said Robert. "He prepared that envelope himself. I drew up his will. I have that of course. Zeke made you the executor and his sole beneficiary. He's already made his final arrangements. He didn't want you to have to worry about anything."

Tammy clutched the envelope to her chest. Tears rolled down her face.

I patted her leg.

After a minute, she turned the envelope over, worked the seal open, and slid out a single sheet of paper and a small key. She read quietly, sniffling occasionally.

"Is there anything more I can do for you?" Robert asked.

"No," she whispered. "Thank you so much for coming."

"My pleasure to be of service." He laid a larger manila envelope on the bed. "Copies of everything you'll need are in here. Judge Johnson signed the order appointing you executor this morning. The, ah, memorial will be Friday night at seven. If you need anything else, call me anytime." He stood. "I'll show myself out." He closed the door behind him.

Tammy read the page again, then handed it to me.

It was a letter.

January 14, 2010

My Darling Tammy,

If you're reading this, I've gone on ahead of you. Know that I'll be waiting to see you again someday. But in the meantime, I want you to enjoy every minute of this life. I hope in time you'll find someone to share it with. Someone who can be there for you and take care of you when I can't. The last thing I would ever want is for you to be alone.

Sweetheart, you know how I like to tell tales. But what I'm going to tell you now is the God's honest truth. I was in the Army for a short time, but they decided to send me to college. I graduated top of my class from West Point, but then the CIA wanted me, and the Army agreed to it. I spent twenty years as an operations officer, most of it out of the country. April was my partner, and my marriage to her was more of a business deal. You are the only woman I've ever loved. You can trust April. If you ever need anything, if you are ever afraid, go to April.

I think we covered our tracks pretty good when we got out, but you never know. We live in the age of WikiLeaks. Whatever happened to me, it probably doesn't have anything to do with my job at the CIA. If it does, best to just let it go. I don't want you to get hurt. With me gone, no one would have any reason to come after you.

I don't have secret files on anyone, nothing like that.

Talk to Michael Devlin, who built our house. There's some built-in storage you should know is there. You can have someone sell the guns. You won't need them. The people I was prepared for, well, they either got me (but I doubt that) or they're too late now. They won't bother you.

The key is to a safe deposit box at the bank in town. Open it for me just as soon as you can. You can toss most of what's in there. I won't need it now. Take the cash and go on a nice vacation or something. You'll find more cash at the house.

You said you didn't want to talk about life insurance, so I just bought some. You should be set. Also, I made arrangements for a big party at The Pirates' Den. Don't even think about carrying me in there in a casket. I have to be clear about this now: I don't want a damn funeral. I've taken care of everything, and this is how I want it. Robert will make the necessary phone calls.

I love you, sweetheart. Please be happy. Think of me every once in a while. I'll be keeping an eye on you.

Always,
Zeke

"He loved you so much, Tammy." That was quite clear to me. I tried to fit that knowledge with the other thing I knew for a stone-cold fact: Zeke had cheated on Tammy. Was it as simple as a mid-life crisis?

"He did, didn't he? When he wrote that letter, he really did love me. I just hope he still did."

"Of course he did."

"Do you think some spy came here and killed him?"

I pondered that for a moment. "I don't. Someone must've used Zeke's key fob or the garage door opener in his truck to open the garage door and put him in the trunk of the Mustang. This is not how spies do things. They would've been in and out, quick and clean."

"Should I call April?"

"Are you scared?"

"No. I mean to let her know. She and Zeke were married, after all. She was his partner. It probably won't be in the Charleston paper."

"Robert probably had an envelope for her too," I said. "Do you want me to make sure of that?"

"Yes, please. Thank you, Liz. I don't know what I'd do without you and your Mamma and Daddy." She sat quietly for a moment. "What do I do now?"

"Get a shower and get dressed."

"What for?"

"Because that will be quicker than getting a power of attorney so I can open the safe deposit box."

TEN

Nate headed over to the hardware store to get the skinny on locally available rat and gopher poisons. I figured it was going to take Tammy the better part of two hours to shower, wash all that hair, and get dressed. I used the time to zip over to The Pirates' Den to have a chat with Coy Watson, who typically worked the day shift on Wednesdays. On the way, I spoke with Robert Pearson again.

"Tammy and I were thinking how it's likely you have another envelope for April Fox, Zeke's first wife?"

"Now, Liz. You know if I did that would be a confidential matter," said Robert.

"But Zeke is dead, and Tammy is your client now, right?"

"Well, yes. But I have to follow Zeke's wishes."

"And based on the contents of the letter he left her, Zeke was most concerned with Tammy's comfort and welfare," I said. "He wanted Tammy to rely on April if she needed her. Tammy wants me to make sure April is notified of Zeke's death, and to make that introduction—you know, smooth things over between the two wives. Really, Robert, do you want to be in the middle of two of Zeke Lyerly's wives?"

He was quiet for a moment, seemed to ponder all that might entail. He sighed. "As much as I might rather delegate this, I feel like I have to handle it."

"Why on earth? The important thing here is what Tammy wants. What Tammy is comfortable with. Isn't that what Zeke would want you to do?"

"Zeke gave me explicit instructions. I don't have to wonder what he wanted me to do," he said.

I changed tactics. "Look, Robert. You know Nate and I are helping investigate Zeke's death, right?"

"I recall the contract the town entered into with your agency. I didn't know Blake had retained you on this specific case."

"Well," I said, "he did. And I need to speak with April. This gives me an entree with her. I could use your help here."

"I suppose if you are operating as an arm of local law enforcement, I would need to cooperate with you," he said.

"Exactly. And I truly do appreciate your cooperation."

"I'll leave the letter with my receptionist." He sounded worn down, but relieved.

I ended the call just as I pulled into a parking place at The Pirates' Den.

Coy Watson grew up in West Virginia. Like Crystal, he'd come down with friends and fell in love with the area. He'd been in Stella Maris since the summer he turned eighteen. He'd started out as a line cook, but was now a bartender for John and Alma Glendawn who owned The Pirates' Den. I'd known him for years.

The air conditioning was on refrigerate, but it felt good when I walked inside. Between the wall of aquariums on the far end of the room and the varnished wood on the floors and the remaining walls, the inside of the local favorite bar and restaurant seemed a sanctuary from the oppressive heat. Jimmy Buffet sang "Cheeseburger in Paradise" over the speakers.

I climbed onto one of the high-backed barstools.

"Hey, Liz," Coy said. "What can I get for you?"

Tanned, muscled, with sun-drenched brown hair and an easy smile, he was a favorite with the local ladies of all ages. He was well aware of it.

"A Cheerwine please."

He set a bottle on the counter, opened it, and poured it over a glass of ice.

I took a sip. "I need to talk to you about Zeke."

He blanched. "What about him? I mean, I heard what happened."

"Tell me about the drone."

"Ah, man. I knew that was going to jam me up. Look. I did not do anything to Zeke. Whatever somebody did to him, it wasn't me that did it, okay?"

"Just tell me about the drone."

He clutched at his hair, shook his head. "I bought it from Sharper Image. It cost me three thousand dollars. It was a hobby. I took pictures with it. Nature pictures. Birds and shit. Yeah, I aggravated Zeke with it. But only because it riled him up so bad."

"And he destroyed it?"

"Blew it right out of the sky."

"I bet that made you mad," I said.

"Of course it did. I told you. It cost me three grand."

"And you threatened to kill him."

"Man, that was never meant as a real threat. I told you—I was mad. I said that in the heat of the moment. Come on now. Everybody has said that before, but they don't go around actually killing people."

He looked at me expectantly, waited for my agreement.

"The photographs you took. Your 'nature pictures'? Where

are they?"

"On my computer."

"I'll need to see those."

"No problem. I probably have a thousand. I'll put them in a cloud folder. Send you a link."

"Any of them have people in them? Maybe Zeke and Tammy Sue?" Or Zeke and Crystal.

"Nah. I might've looked at people on my live feed. But I didn't take pictures of them."

"You ever see anything unusual on your live feed that I need to know about? When you were harassing Zeke?"

"You mean like him arguing with somebody?" he asked.

"Yeah. Like that."

"Nah." He rolled his lips in and out, shook his head.

"Tell me about Crystal Chapman," I said.

"Crystal? What about her?"

"You and she date much?"

He shrugged. "Occasionally. It's not serious. We have fun. Why are you asking me about Crystal?"

"Did you take her to a party at Skip and Margie Robinson's back in March?" I asked.

"The bonfire. Yeah. What about it?"

"Bonfire?"

"The party was a bonfire on the beach."

"And you took Crystal as your date?"

"That's right."

"Did you leave with her?"

"Yeah. I took her home about three in the morning. Why? What's she saying?" He narrowed his eyes.

"Did the two of you have a good time at the party?"

"I guess. Yeah."

"Have you seen her since then?"

"No. She's been busy lately."

I waited to see if he'd elaborate on that. He didn't.

"Do you think she's seeing someone else?"

"Maybe. I don't know. I don't care much to tell you the truth. I told you. It's not serious."

"Are you seeing anyone else?" I asked.

"Not at the moment. I've been working a lot. Trying to make enough money to replace my drone."

"Where were you Monday late afternoon, early evening?"

"Monday's my day off. I was at the beach."

"Alone?"

"Yeah. Mostly."

"What does that mean?"

"There were other people at the beach. But I went there by myself."

"Did you talk to anyone you knew?"

"Sure."

"Who?"

He rattled off half a dozen names.

"What time did you see these folks?"

"Different times. I was there all afternoon."

"Exactly where were you on the beach?"

"Right at the north point, a hundred feet or so down from the inlet."

Not far from our house. It was a popular spot. "What time did you leave?"

"A little after five."

"Did you go straight home?"

"Yeah. I showered, then met some friends at Poe's on Sullivan's for drinks and dinner."

"What time did you meet them?"

"Seven o'clock."

He still would've had time to kill Zeke and leave his body in the trunk of the Mustang. It would've been tight. "I need their names and phone numbers." I slid my notebook and pencil towards him. "The names of everyone who saw you at the beach too."

"You think I killed Zeke?" His tone was accusing.

"Did you?"

"No way. Over a drone?"

"And then there's Crystal."

"I don't see the connection between Zeke and Crystal. You're going to have to explain that one to me."

"You didn't notice her flirting with him at Skip and Margie's?"

Coy blinked. "No. We don't keep tabs on each other at parties, okay? We were both having a good time."

"Who did you spend time with, aside from Crystal?"

"We were all sitting around the fire talking. I had a conversation with Connie Hicks, for one."

"Connie?"

"Yeah. She's nice. Intelligent. I like that in a woman."

"Are you planning to ask Connie out?"

He scratched behind his ear. "I don't know. Maybe."

"She's a nice girl. If you're just playing around, pass her on by."

"What are you now, the love police?"

That was a good question. I paid for my Cheerwine and left.

ELEVEN

Tammy Sue had undergone a miraculous transformation. In a pink linen sleeveless dress and matching sandals, she looked nothing like the woman I'd last seen under a pile of quilts. Oversized dark sunglasses hid her swollen eyes.

I parked behind the bank, which was right on the square in town, across Main Street from the police department and fire station. Tammy took a deep breath and we went inside.

Winter Simmons, the bank manager, spotted us seconds after we walked through the door. Her heels clicked on the marble floor as she approached. Winter was five nine flat-footed, six feet two in nude peep-toe pumps that I'd bet were Louboutins. The contrast between her cafe au lait complexion and cornflower blue eyes was startling. Her well-tailored black suit hugged her curves but no more than was ladylike.

"Tammy Sue." She clasped Tammy's hand with both of hers. "I'm so sorry for your loss. How are you holding up?"

Tammy drew a ragged breath. "As well as can be expected, I suppose."

Winter's gaze flicked my way. "Hello, Liz." Her voice wasn't cool, but it didn't ooze warmth either. She could've been holding a teensy grudge.

"Hey, Winter." I smiled sweetly.

"Tammy, how can we help you today?" She sounded compassionate—like she sincerely wanted to do something for Tammy.

"I need to get into my safe deposit box."

"I see," said Winter. "Let me check our records. Please have a seat." She gestured towards a seating area, then turned and clicked away. Yep. Those shoes were Louboutins all right. They had red soles.

"Tell me again how y'all are related?" said Tammy Sue as we settled into upholstered chairs.

"She married Spencer Simmons. He's my first cousin once removed." I didn't add that she'd married him fast, six months before their son was born. I'd only been fourteen at the time, but it was hard to keep these things quiet in a town our size.

"Isn't her sister Willa into voodoo and all such as that?" Tammy asked.

I sighed. "She is. She's also a gifted surgeon. But people tend to think of the voodoo first." Willa was our local Voodoo priestess. The story was that she put a spell on Spencer when she thought he wasn't going to marry Winter. Not everyone in my family was open-minded about spells and such, hence Winter's frosty disposition.

Winter walked back across the bank lobby. "We have a safe deposit box in Zeke's name. But I'm afraid you are not listed as co-owner. The box was sealed upon his death. The procedures for opening it are quite specific."

"Tammy Sue is Zeke's executor," I said.

"And as soon as the probate court has appointed her, I can let her in to inventory the box. The inventory will have to be notarized. Then we send it to the State for a tax waiver. Nothing other than a will, burial plot deed, or insurance policy can be removed until then."

"Hang on a second. Tammy, can I see that envelope please?"

"Sure." She handed me the large manila envelope Robert had given her. I slid out the papers, flipped through them, and handed Winter the order Hank Johnson had signed that morning.

Winter scanned the document. "Well that was fast. Come with me."

She led us into the vault and pulled out a large metal box. Tammy used her key, and Winter put in the bank's copy. Winter lifted the lid. Her eyes grew slightly, but she maintained her professional composure.

Inside was a stack of passports and two more straps, plus a partial strap of hundred dollar bills. I picked up the passport on top. It was British, in the name of William Grant, with Zeke's photo. All of the passports had photos of Zeke, some with glasses and different hair. Some with a beard and mustache. All the names were different. Two were U.S. passports. The others were from all over.

Winter logged each of the passports into her form and counted the cash twice. "I count twenty-five thousand dollars. Do you want me to count it again?"

"No," said Tammy Sue. "That's right."

Winter didn't ask any questions, and we didn't offer any explanations. After everything was logged, Winter called Connie Hicks away from the teller window to notarize the inventory.

We climbed into the Escape, and I rolled down the windows to blow out the hot air.

"Why on earth would Zeke have all those passports?" Tammy's eyes were round and anxious. "Is that legal? Am I in trouble?"

"No, of course not." I couldn't imagine she'd be in legal

trouble. Though there were all kinds of trouble, and I had a sinking suspicion it lurked close by. "Whatever Zeke was into, those were his passports, not yours."

"Why do you suppose he left those passports in a safe deposit box?" asked Tammy. "It looks to me like he'd have hidden them, not put them someplace where they'd be logged. What will Winter do with that log?"

I mulled that for a minute. I wondered if Winter had to report finding the passports, but didn't want to worry Tammy. "I imagine all Winter cares about is complying with probate laws. The State wants its cut of the cash. Maybe Zeke wanted an official record of those passports in case his past came hunting. If he had been killed in a way that made us suspect some foreign spy was responsible, maybe the passports would be a clue."

"But you don't think that's what happened?"

"No," I said. "But maybe after I talk to April I'll change my mind. She knows more about the spy game than I do."

"And the money? Why put that in the safe deposit box? Why not just deposit it in the bank?"

"It could be he did that because banks have to report deposits of more than ten thousand dollars. It's a transaction. But money in the safe deposit box hasn't crossed the counter, so there's no transaction to report."

"But why would he be hiding money like that?"

"My guess is in case he needed money to disappear for some reason. He may have more money stashed somewhere else. When you're up to it you should read through the will. Everything must be listed out there, except maybe cash stashed at the house. He gave you a heads up about that in the letter." I told her about the ten thousand dollars we'd found in the garage.

"I always knew there were things Zeke didn't tell me," she

said. "But I thought he was making things sound *more* exciting than they were, not the other way around. I thought he was happy running the shop. But that must've been such a different life than what he led for all those years."

"He chose to change careers, Tammy. He chose to run that auto shop. And with his education, he could've done most anything he wanted to do. It seems to me Zeke was one of the lucky ones who figured out what made him happy and changed his life to suit him."

"Then tell me this," she said. "Was he about to change it again, with Crystal? Would he have divorced me if he'd lived?"

I drew a deep breath, let it out slowly. "I don't know about that. Only Zeke knew what was in his heart. But everything I've seen indicates Zeke loved you very much."

"But was that old news? This is going to eat me up inside. Not knowing."

"There's no sense in torturing yourself this way. Hold on to what he told you in that letter. That's a solid, real love. This thing with Crystal was most likely a mid-life crisis type fling. Forgive him if you can."

She pressed her lips together, nodded, and sniffled.

"Did Zeke ever mention Harold Yates to you? He was a plumber in town."

Tammy nodded. "Zeke carried a lot of guilt about Mr. Yates. We used to take him casseroles, Christmas baskets, all like that."

"Why the guilt? What was their connection?" I asked.

"Zeke was a rascal as a teenager. That's what he told me anyway. Mr. Yates was always imagining the aliens were coming. Looking for flying saucers. Trying to communicate with them. The kids laughed at him, teased him, Zeke included. Then Zeke and a friend found his uncle's old AM radio transmitter in the attic. His uncle used to run a local radio station. It was real low power—would barely reach to Charleston, Zeke said. Anyway, Zeke had the idea to tell Mr. Yates that he read somewhere that aliens tried to contact folks on that channel when the moon was full. Next full moon, he and his friend used one of those voice modulators and broadcast that anyone who could hear them should come to the field off Marsh View Drive the next day and wait for the mother ship. Apparently, Mr. Yates stood out in that field all the next day. Didn't go in to work. He was a laughingstock."

"Oh, no. How old was Zeke?"

"He was only thirteen. But it weighed on him that Mr. Yates was still alone all those years later. He felt responsible, or at least like he made the situation worse. He said Mr. Yates was one of the invisible ones."

"Surely that one prank didn't change the course of that man's life," I said.

"I doubt it," said Tammy. "But I could never convince Zeke of that. We were the only people at his funeral. It nearly broke both our hearts."

"That is sad. It's hard to believe anyone in this town is that isolated."

"Small towns can be the loneliest places on earth if you feel like you're on the outside looking in at all that closeness."

She sounded like she understood that all too well.

TWELVE

When I'd started my day—it felt like a week ago—I'd planned to talk to Price Elliott again.

He left the shop on Monday inside the window of when Zeke was killed. He'd also failed to mention that he and Zeke had a fight regarding his work ethics and he'd come close to getting fired. That gave him a motive.

But after my unplanned visit with Winter, it seemed wise to interview my cousin Spencer before she had a chance to advise him not to even admit to socializing with Zeke Lyerly on account of the suspicious nature of the contents of his safe deposit box. I dropped Tammy off at Mamma and Daddy's house and zipped back downtown. Spencer was a dentist. His office was in the professional building on Main Street.

I found a parking spot half a block from Main on Palmetto Boulevard. To take advantage of the shade, I walked through the park that occupied our town square. It was quiet beneath the sprawling canopy the live oaks provided. The border beds burst with big blue hydrangeas and an assortment of day lilies. The garden club worked hard to make the park a welcoming centerpiece for the town.

I exited the park in front of the courthouse and walked a block to the professional building. I had to play the family emergency card to get Spencer's receptionist to tell him I was there. As she escorted me to Spencer's office, she gave me a look that put me on notice. Of what, it wasn't clear.

I waited for Spencer in a mid-century modern leather wing-back arm chair that called the Jetsons to mind.

Twenty minutes later, he opened the door. "Liz. This is a surprise." He closed the door behind him and crossed the room to take his seat at his desk. He was middle aged, with good bones, sandy, thinning hair, thick-framed glasses, and an extra twenty pounds. "What can I do for you?"

"I'm so sorry to interrupt your day. I know you have patients to see about. But Nate and I are investigating Zeke Lyerly's death."

"I see. How can I help?"

"Did you know Zeke well?" I asked.

"We were friends. We socialized occasionally."

"When was the last time you saw him socially?"

"I guess that would be at the Robinsons' bonfire."

"Did anything happen that night that sticks in your mind?"

He flushed. "Look, Liz, I don't know what someone told you, but there was nothing to it."

I smiled, gave him a quizzical look. "Nothing to what?"

He stared at me for a minute, then shrugged. "Winter had a little too much to drink."

"I hadn't heard that."

"Well, she did. She had one too many glasses of wine, and she may have been a bit inappropriate."

"Inappropriate? In what way?"

"She..." He looked flustered. "She flirted with Zeke, okay? But it was nothing. She did it to get a rise out of me. It worked."

"It made you angry?"

"Well, yes. But not angry enough to kill him, if that's what you're getting at."

"Tell me about this party."

He lifted a shoulder. "Skip and Margie invited folks over for a bonfire. They set up a grill on the beach, smoked some chicken. It was fun."

"Who all was there?" I now wanted to know everything there was to know about this party.

"Winter and me. Skip and Margie, of course. Zeke and Tammy. Coy Watson and his date...Crystal is her first name. I don't know her last name. Pete and Brenda Carter. Humphrey Pearson was there with Connie Hicks. That's it."

"Did anyone else have too much to drink?" I asked.

He raised an eyebrow, tilted his head, looked sheepish. "We all did, to tell you the truth."

"Aside from that night, did you ever have any reason to suspect anything was going on with Winter and Zeke?"

"No, of course not."

"Did anything else happen that night that seems remarkable to you in any way?" I asked.

He was quiet for a moment, then looked away, then back. "This probably didn't mean anything either. It was that kind of night. Things got a little out of hand."

"So noted."

"Zeke went for a walk on the beach. He asked if anyone else wanted to go. Tammy was cold. She stayed by the fire. That Crystal girl Coy brought...she'd been flirting with Zeke outrageously. I think that's why Winter backed off. The show Crystal put on was embarrassing. Regardless, she took off after Zeke. Tammy was upset. She tried to hide it, but it was plain as day."

"Did Zeke do anything to encourage Crystal?"

"Not that I saw."

"Anything else?"

He winced. "Yeah. Humphrey…"

"What about Humphrey?"

"He took it upon himself to cheer Tammy up. If you ask me, he was sitting way too close to a married woman. He's always liked Tammy a little too much. But if it were my wife, I'd be thinking he crossed a line. The way he tucked the quilt around her, talked to her real soft, brought her drinks…it just looked bad."

"What time did you and Winter leave?"

"Around two. We walked home. We both had too much to drink."

"Probably smart." I nodded. "Now don't go gettin' mad at me, but I need to ask you where you were Monday late afternoon, early evening."

He tilted his head at me and raised an eyebrow. "I left the office at five thirty. Went straight home. Had dinner with the family at seven."

I stood to leave. "Thanks, Spencer. I appreciate your time."

It was unlikely Spencer killed Zeke. I'd never known him to have that kind of temper—the kind a man would have to have to kill somebody because his wife got flirty. But just then I couldn't help but think that Spencer, who didn't work out and had likely never been in a situation where he had to defend himself, was perhaps the kind of guy who might use poison if he felt driven to murder. Coy and Price were both young and strong, and likely thought they were bulletproof. I didn't see either of them choosing poison as a weapon.

THIRTEEN

Carter's Exxon was on Main Street, a few doors down from The Cracked Pot. In addition to gas, oil, and whatnot, they sold the typical things you found in a convenience store. It was clean and cheerful, as mini-marts went. I decided to swing by on my way home. An electronic tone announced me.

Pete was behind the register. What with his neatly trimmed brown hair and plastic-framed glasses, Pete had always called to mind Clark Kent. He was preppy in a studious kind of way—not that there's anything wrong with it. Always somewhat reflective, that Wednesday afternoon he was downright subdued. I guess finding your friend in the trunk of a car would do that to a person.

"Hey, Liz."

"Hey, Pete," I said. "Is Brenda around?"

"Yeah, she's in back. How's it going? The investigation, I mean." He spoke as he walked towards the hall that lead to the back room.

"Good, good." I smiled.

"Brenda, could you come out here?" Pete called down the hall.

"How are you holding up?" I asked.

He drew a long breath, shook his head. "I'm okay. It was just such a shock, you know?"

"Yes, it was that."

"I'm sorry you had to see that. I should've…" He rubbed the back of his neck, at a loss.

"There was nothing you could do," I said. "My goodness, it wasn't your fault. It's a wonder that didn't give you a heart attack."

Brenda Carter stepped onto the sales floor. "Yes. It is a wonder." She gave me an expectant look. Slim, cool, and naturally pretty, Brenda had the grace of a ballet dancer.

"Hey, Brenda. I'm sorry to bother y'all, but I was hoping you could help me out with a few things."

"Of course." She moved closer to Pete, sidling up to him.

He put an arm around her. "We're still a bit shaken, I'm afraid. What can we help you with?"

"I know y'all are friends with Zeke and Tammy Sue. I wondered if either of you noticed anything off with Zeke lately. Did he seem like something was troubling him?" I asked.

Brenda looked at Pete.

He seemed to ponder that. "I've given that a lot of thought these last couple days. I didn't notice, to be honest, before Zeke's death. But I do think something was bothering him."

Brenda's forehead creased, but she didn't say anything.

"Why do you think that?" I asked.

Pete shrugged. "He just seemed distracted. Usually, Zeke was a happy-go-lucky guy. For the last month or so, he just wasn't himself."

"Did you see him often?" I asked.

"Sure," said Pete. "We had lunch together a couple times a week, at least. Sometimes, if he had a slow day, he'd stroll down here. Other days maybe I'd walk his way."

"When was the last time you saw him?" I asked.

"Hmm…I guess it was Saturday night. We went to The

Pirates' Den for dinner. Zeke and Tammy were there. We stopped by their table to say 'Hi.' They asked us to join them, but we needed some alone time. With two teenage boys, that's hard to come by in our house."

"Brenda, what about you? Is that the last time you saw Zeke?" I asked.

"Yes, it must've been," she said.

"And did either of you speak to him on the phone after that?" I asked.

"I did," Pete said. "I called him late Monday morning to see what time he was headed to the diner for lunch. We were going to meet there at noon, but then he drove by here a little after eleven and said he needed to run home instead."

That accounted for the call I'd seen on Zeke's cell. "Brenda?"

"No, I didn't speak to him by phone after Saturday," she said.

"Pete, did Zeke discuss his business with you much?" I asked.

"Sometimes." He shrugged. "Back when we did service and such, we would've been competitors. But we stopped all that years ago. We're mostly involved in the convenience side of things these days. The gas, well, you know. It's all self-service. But I still know some of the suppliers he uses. Used. Sometimes we talked shop."

"Did he discuss personnel with you?"

Pete winced. "You mean Price."

"Yes."

"Yeah, he told me he was having problems with Price. Said he showed up late all the time. Was always wanting to leave early for something," said Pete. "Said he spoke to him, and Price got a smart mouth. I think if he weren't Charlie Jacobs' grandson, Zeke would've fired him on the spot. When he gave him attitude."

"Did he ever mention if Price's habits improved?"

"He didn't, but he just told me that he'd given him a talking to last week. What day was that?" He squinted, looked towards the ceiling. "Thursday. The special at The Cracked Pot was meatloaf. I can't believe I'll never have lunch with him there again."

Brenda pulled him tighter and patted him on the chest.

"I know you miss him." I waited, gave them a moment. Finally, I said, "Pete, I don't know quite how to ask you this delicately, but I have to ask. You know how Zeke was always the one with big stories, right?"

Pete smiled a little. "Yeah, of course. That was just Zeke."

"Right." I returned the smile, but I was thinking about that safe deposit box. "Did you ever think any of that was true?"

He gave me a quizzical look. "The NASCAR stories? The bull riding thing? He told me once he was a fighter pilot. Another day, it was a helicopter pilot. I mean, I loved Zeke like a brother. But come on, Liz. All of that was a figment of his overactive imagination. He was like...Walter Mitty. He lived in a fantasy world. No. I never thought that stuff was real."

"No, I know it couldn't all be real, of course," I said. "But did he ever talk to you seriously about what he was doing for the twenty years he lived elsewhere? Did you ever think maybe *some* of it was real?"

Pete gave a look like maybe I'd suggested the Easter Bunny and the Tooth Fairy were coming over to my house for cocktails at six. "He talked plenty. Zeke loved to talk. Was he ever serious? I never thought so. I always figured he'd been in the Army the whole time, maybe traveled overseas a bit." He shrugged, shook his head. "The rest of it...no, he never said anything I took to be the truth."

I couldn't stop thinking about the hidden guns, the money, the passports. That stuff was real. Had anyone really known Zeke Lyerly? Or was he so delusional he imagined threats that didn't exist and concocted elaborate escape plans?

"I guess that's all I have for now," I said.

We said bye and all that.

On the way to the car, I was musing three things. Who was Zeke Lyerly? And Brenda Carter surely didn't have much to say. She seemed almost deferential to her husband. And Crystal Chapman was very likely what had zapped Zeke's joie de vivre, one way or another.

FOURTEEN

"Were you even going to tell me about the damn passports?" Blake was yelling when he climbed out of his car. Rhett barked hello and ran in a circle around the Tahoe.

"Of course," I said. "I just finished telling Nate." We'd pulled into the driveway at the same time and were walking up the steps. "Come inside. Our brains will melt out here." It was uncommonly hot for June. I hurried up the steps and into the house.

Nate, Blake, and Rhett followed me into the kitchen. I refilled Rhett's bowl in the mud room off the kitchen, then pulled a pitcher of water with lemon and mint out of the refrigerator, filled glasses with ice, and poured. "Here," I said. "We've got to stay hydrated." I climbed up onto one of the counter stools.

"You sound like your mamma." Nate grinned, drank deeply.

"Please. I'm an amateur." I turned to Blake. "Who told you about the passports?"

He set his glass on the counter. "Winter. She was all atwitter. Said she was going to fill out some damn report, but felt obligated to tell me as well. For some reason, she didn't seem to trust that you'd tell me."

I said, "She holds me responsible for Gram and Mamma not approving of Willa's hobbies. I've never said a word about it. I like Willa just fine. Winter has a chip on her shoulder."

"Winter said it usually took a lot longer to get an executor appointed by the probate court. What do you know about that?" Blake asked.

I explained about Robert's visit to Mamma and Daddy's house and the letter from Zeke. When the words CIA came out of my mouth, Blake tipped back his head and stared dramatically at the ceiling. "This is Zeke we're talking about. CIA my ass."

"Well, how else do you explain all those passports?" I asked.

Blake righted his head, seemed to ponder that. "Did they look real?"

"Real enough to get Winter all worked up," I said. "Yes. They looked real."

Nate looked at me. "You find this credible? Zeke as a CIA agent?"

"Given what we found at his house and in the safe deposit box, I do," I said. I told Blake about the hidden storage at the Lyerly home and all the guns. "Then there's Zeke's unnatural aversion to being photographed and all things to do with the internet."

Blake stared at me, practically vibrated with frustration. "You're telling me there's a damn arsenal in the Lyerly house. And you let it sit there all day and didn't call me."

I coated my voice in honey. "Well, I knew you'd been all through that house yesterday. I figured there was nothing there you hadn't already seen."

He cut me a look not filled with brotherly love, then blew out a breath. "I'll get Cooper to inventory everything and put it in evidence. Sounds like some high-dollar stuff of questionable legality."

"Remember I told you Daddy and the mayor had hired Zeke to thin the hog herd?" I asked.

Blake squinted. "Yeah. That's been a while back."

"Well, maybe he started hunting them at night. I hear that's when they're more active."

Blake snorted. "How did you come by that information?"

I shrugged. "After I caught Zeke in his secret operation, I guess I became more alert to feral pigs in the news. They're a growing problem in virtually every state, cause all kinds of damage to crops, parks, and forests."

"It's a moot point, what he was using that stuff for," said Blake. "Doesn't matter now. But I'll sleep better with it secured."

"Liz is going to talk to April tomorrow," said Nate, "see what she has to say. Unless she has something contradictory to offer, I think we have to assume Zeke was telling the truth. I mean, it's hard to believe a man would make up a lie and put it in his final letter to his wife."

Blake rubbed his left eyebrow. "Maybe. Then again, maybe he saw that as his last big tale. A whopper."

"Think, Blake. If this was some elaborate stunt, pulled by Zeke Lyerly, good ol' boy extraordinaire, where would he get the passports?"

He lifted his Red Sox cap, ran a hand through his hair, and resettled it. "Lab work came back on the samples from under Tammy Sue's fingernails. It was Zeke's skin cells all right. And he had fresh scratches on his face."

"She told us about that," I said. "The only reason we had her fingernails scraped is that she told us about the fight. Why would she do that if she killed him?"

"Maybe she's that smart," said Blake. "Figured it would make her look innocent."

"Wait. You can't see Zeke as a CIA agent, but you think Tammy Sue is a criminal mastermind?" I asked.

"Ah hell," said Blake. "None of this makes sense. All I know is she has the best motive. And that motive gets a lot stronger when you throw in life insurance."

"She didn't know about the life insurance," I said.

"Sis, are you really that gullible?" Blake said.

"I'm not gullible at all. You're just eager to make an arrest. And I'm telling you, Tammy is not the guilty party here," I said.

"Listen," said Nate. "It's only been a day. Tammy Sue is at your parents' house. It's almost like she's in custody, right? Tell your daddy to give you a heads up if she heads out. Meanwhile, give us another day to check out a few of these other leads."

"Who?" said Blake. "Who are your other leads?"

"Coy Watson, for one." I told Blake about the drone and about Crystal and Coy's relationship. "Or it could've been Price Elliott. Zeke threatened to fire him. Think about it. He failed out of college. His parents got him a job he thinks is beneath him, and he gets fired from that too? That could've been enough to send him over the edge. He's only twenty-four. His impulse control isn't fully developed yet. And he was the last one to see Zeke that we know of."

"But you said Zeke didn't fire him," said Blake.

"As far as anyone knows," I said. "But what if he wanted to leave early Monday, and Zeke lost it and fired him on the spot? Then Price gets mad and..."

Blake nodded. "Right. If he got mad, he might've hit him, stabbed him with a tool, or shot him even. But he wouldn't have had rat poison handy I don't think."

"That's true enough," Nate said. "I spent an hour at the hardware store today. Nothing they carry on the island has strychnine in it. You can't buy it here, and you can't have it shipped here. This definitely took some planning."

"Not a heat of the moment thing," said Blake.

"No," I said. "But Zeke and Price had argued before. He

could've set the whole thing up as a 'just in case' scenario."

"Do you have any other suspects?" Blake asked.

"Crystal. I think it's more likely she killed him from jealousy than Tammy Sue. Crystal is much tougher than Tammy. Or it could've been someone who cared for Tammy. Thus far the only name that's come up is Humphrey Pearson."

"Humphrey?" Blake gave me a pained look. "Humphrey is not the violent type. He's a poet for Pete's sake."

"Maybe the kind of person who would use poison?" I said.

"That's a stretch," said Blake.

"Maybe so," I said. "That's why he isn't at the top of our list."

"Is that your entire list?" Blake asked.

"Well...I did talk to Spencer today," I said.

"Spencer Simmons?" Blake's expression said *give me a break.*

"Yes. Winter was flirting with Zeke at this party at the Robinsons'. It's a long shot. Another long shot would be someone from Zeke's past—a spy. But I think we have to consider who would use poison and move his body to a car in his garage."

"I'll tell you who," said Blake. "Women use poison. Scorned wives. *That's* who uses poison. And the scorned wife we're talking about set the same car we're talking about on fire."

"I don't recall Zeke had his cap on," I said.

"What? When?" said Blake.

"When we discovered his body. His cap wasn't on his head. Did you find it in the trunk?"

"No," said Blake. "He probably ordered those by the dozen for the shop."

"And he normally wore them, right?"

"Right," Blake's tone begrudged me the point.

"He still had on his work shirt. Where was the cap?"

Blake shrugged. "Maybe he took it off."

"Whoever drove his truck home Monday evening was wearing one. Remember what Daddy said?" I said.

Blake nodded. "Yeah."

"So maybe the killer wore Zeke's cap as a disguise. Then he or she worried about leaving trace evidence on the cap, so they didn't leave it with the body. Can we please have one more day?" I asked.

"Fine," said Blake.

"Hey, have the sheriff's office techs gotten to Zeke's computer?" I asked.

Blake winced. "They had some trouble with it."

"What kind of trouble?" I asked.

Blake made a face, looked away.

"Blake?" I said. "What kind of trouble did they have with Zeke's computer?"

He made a chopping gesture with his right hand. "This does not mean Zeke was some kind of damned spy."

"Okay," I said.

"They were trying to break the password. Something went wrong. The disk was wiped clean. They're trying to recover it, but they're not optimistic."

Nate and I exchanged a glance. Blake could tell himself Zeke wasn't a CIA agent all he wanted to. I turned back to my brother and dipped my voice in honey. "Would you like to stay for dinner?"

"No, thanks," said Blake. "Heather is coming to my place for dinner."

Heather Wilder was an Environmental Studies grad student at College of Charleston. She was also the former resident of a house of questionable repute which Nate and I had recently investigated. Mamma was marginally less put out with me over introducing Blake to Heather than she was me being tangentially responsible for Daddy's pet pig.

"You're still seeing her?" Nate asked.

"Yeah." Blake grinned, his mood lifting.

"What does she think about your digs?" I asked. My brother lived on a houseboat. It was a very nice houseboat, but a lot of women didn't take to it. Heather's home in the historic house South of Broad that served as a boardinghouse of sorts had been quite luxurious.

"Ah...at first she loved it," said Blake. "Thought it was romantic. But I'm not so sure it's not wearing thin. She's used to nice big bathrooms, a walk-in closet. We'll see. But she's coming tonight."

"What are you cooking?" I grinned.

"Me cook? No. *She's* making me lasagna," he said.

"You know how to cook." I tilted my head at him, gave him a look that demanded an explanation.

"It's part of my system," said Blake. "If she doesn't mind cooking on the houseboat, maybe she's the right one. I'm not giving up the boat. If she gets tired of cooking in my galley, she's not the right girl for me."

"You're well defended." I shook my head.

After he left, Nate said. "She's not the right one, is she?"

"No," I said. "But not because she's getting tired of cooking in a galley. If she was the right one, he wouldn't be playing these games."

It stormed so bad that night the house shook with the thunder. Rain blew sideways against the windows so hard it came in around the seals. Rhett huddled with Nate and me in the sunroom until it passed. I fell asleep in bed with Nate spooned behind me, his hand clasped to my chest.

Later, I had the dream again. I'd had it half a dozen times now. It was always the same. There's a hurricane, a category 5. Nate and I have to evacuate in the middle of the night. Somehow, despite my hysterectomy several years ago, we have two children. We drive through a storm like I've never seen—trees falling all around us—to the marina because the ferry went down in the inlet. So many people are rushing onto boats at the marina—more people than have ever lived here. Too many people for the boats. Like every time before, a giant wave washes Nate off our boat.

Colleen was there when I woke up screaming at two thirty.

She hovered over the bed.

Nate held me close, rocked me back and forth. "Slugger, it's all right. Shh."

I clutched onto him for dear life.

After a few minutes he said, "Maybe tomorrow you'll tell me about this dream." He stared at Colleen hard, like maybe he thought she was responsible. Or maybe he just wanted her out of our bedroom.

"Talk to him," she whispered to me as she evanesced.

FIFTEEN

A massive brick building built in 1835 as a warehouse took up most of a block of Queen Street between State and East Bay. More than thirty years ago, a developer turned the building into apartments and named it Queens Gate. Some said Ann Margaret used to stay there when she slipped into town incognito back in the 1980s. A decade later the apartments were converted to condominiums. April Fox bought a one-bedroom after she and Zeke Lyerly divorced.

At nine a.m. that Thursday morning, I stood on the sidewalk in front of the arched entry. Queens Street was narrow, with another brick building on the opposite side.

It felt vaguely like being in a tunnel, the sensation abated by the bright blue Carolina sky above and on the horizon across East Bay, down Vendue Range, beyond Waterfront Park, and over the Cooper River. Palm trees and Crepe Myrtles grew in sidewalk cutouts.

I pressed the button to buzz April. She was expecting me. Robert had called ahead. I had the password Zeke had left. Briefly, I pondered the notion of leaving a password with your attorney so that after you were gone, folks would know whatever the attorney—or people he sent, like me—said was legitimate. Ten minutes and four tries later April still hadn't answered. Damnation.

Folks in Charleston were notoriously friendly and helpful. What the hell? I randomly pressed another button.

"Yes?" A male voice came over the speaker.

I employed my best helpless female voice. "This is April. I forgot my keys."

"April who?"

Well, there's one in every crowd.

I tried another button.

No answer.

One more. I bit my lip, looked around to see if anyone was watching me.

"Hello?" A woman's voice, older.

"Hey, this is April. I'm so sorry to bother you, but I forgot my keys. Could you buzz me in please?"

"Of course, dear. You should be more careful."

I heard a soft click.

"Thank you so much!" I lunged for the dark wood door, pulled it open, and stepped inside.

A small sitting area occupied the space near the bottom of the staircase. To my left was an elevator with a shiny gold door. I took the stairs to the second floor. Why didn't April answer? Had something happened to her? What if Zeke's death really did have something to do with his past?

I needed to make sure she was okay.

The heavy stained wood door to her condo showed no signs of tampering. I glanced over my shoulder. This would be risky. I knocked first.

No answer.

I knocked again.

If one of her neighbors caught me breaking into this high-dollar address in broad daylight, they would no doubt call the police.

I knocked three times.

No answer.

I took another look around. Everything was quiet. I hadn't seen another soul since I'd come in the door. I pulled my pick set and a pair of gloves out of my crossbody bag, slipped the gloves on, and unzipped the leather case.

The knob didn't have a lock, but the deadbolt above it looked serious. I went to work. Picking a lock is more art than science. It takes practice. I'd honed my craft. Five minutes later I opened the door and closed it softly behind me.

"Hello?" I called out. "April?"

A yellow tabby cat wandered out from the kitchen, which was immediately on my right.

"Hey kitty. Nice kitty." I reached down to pet her. "Where's Mamma?"

I surveyed the place. I could see most of it from where I stood. With twenty-foot ceilings, exposed brick, and heart of pine flooring, it had good bones. April's decorating taste was more modern than mine, and perhaps a bit masculine, with a brown leather sofa and abstract art in neutrals. She was also a bit of a slob. Dishes, beer bottles, and random articles of clothing were scattered about. A basket of laundry spilled into the sofa. Had her condo been ransacked?

I moved farther inside. The door to my left accessed a powder room. Above me, the ceiling had been lowered in part of the room to accommodate a loft above. Open stairs ran along the right side of the living room. Underneath the stairs was a black X-Base desk. Stacks of catalogues and unopened mail were strewn across it. I fanned the mail. It was all addressed to A.L. Fox. The senders were folks soliciting business. Nothing remotely personal.

April was clearly not downstairs. I scrutinized the loft from below, then climbed the steps. The loft was the bedroom, open to the downstairs. The clutter was more pronounced up there. Good grief. I stepped over a pile of laundry and pushed the closet open. Clothes were in seemingly random piles on the floor. Had someone gone through her closet? What were they looking for?

"Well, you're resourceful, I'll say that much for you."

My heart went to my throat.

I spun towards the voice. She'd come up the stairs without a sound.

She was roughly five foot three, with layered blonde hair, distressed denim jeans, and a fitted blue t-shirt. A butterfly tattoo peeked out from the neckline. She had a gun pointed at me, and she seemed comfortable with it.

"April?" I asked.

"I'll ask the questions, seeing as how you've broken into my home. I could shoot you right now where you stand and never spend a day in jail. You know that, right?"

I stared at the gun.

"Right?" Her i's were hard and stretched. *Riite?* She'd been raised in the South, no doubt. In the country.

"Right," I said. "I'm terribly sorry. I thought you'd been killed or possibly kidnapped."

"It don't look *that* bad in here."

"No," I said. "I didn't mean it that way. It's just with Zeke...Could you please put that gun down?"

"What's the password?"

"Mustang Sally."

She lowered the gun, but still held it in both hands. "He loved to sing that song on karaoke night."

I felt the corners of my mouth lift. "I've heard him do it. At The Pirates' Den."

"Who sent you?" April's eyes were still wary.

"Robert Pearson. He was Zeke's attorney."

"And you are?"

"I'm Liz Talbot. Zeke was a friend. He lived across the street from my parents."

She raised her chin. "Talbot you say. I met the couple across the street once. Nice people. Can't remember their names, but the lady brought me a pound cake when we moved into the house."

"That's my mamma, Carolyn Talbot."

"She makes a damn fine pound cake." She lowered the gun the rest of the way, took one hand off of it. Then she stepped away from the stairs. "I can't be too careful right now. You go on down. Have a seat in the leather chair in front of the window."

"All right." I complied. If she was this jumpy, it couldn't be too far-fetched that someone from her past with Zeke had killed him.

"What are you doing, poking around in people's laundry like that?" She followed me down the stairs.

"I was trying to figure out if someone had ransacked the place looking for something," I said.

"That's just cold." She slid the laundry basket over, tucked the errant pieces back in, and sat on the end of the sofa nearest me.

"I really am glad you're all right. Why didn't you just let me in when I pressed the buzzer?"

"Because how could I know for sure that really was Robert Pearson, the attorney, who called me, and not someone who tortured and killed Robert Pearson, the attorney?"

"I suppose that's a fair point." Something about her sassy attitude reminded me of Crystal. Did Zeke have a weakness for boisterous blondes?

"Do you have an envelope for me?"

"Yes," I said. "And some questions if you don't mind." I reached towards my purse.

"Careful there. Real slow like."

I pulled the envelope out and handed it to her.

"You can ask your questions," she said. "I'll let you know if I mind. Lemme read this first." She worked the letter out of the envelope and unfolded it with her left hand. She held onto the gun with her right.

I gave her time to read. When she looked up from the page, I said, "May I read it?"

She screwed up her face. "*No*, you can't read it. What's the matter with you, wantin' to read people's private mail?"

I sighed. "I'm just trying to figure out what happened to Zeke before my brother arrests Tammy Sue. I'm guessing some part of that letter asks you to take care of her, right?"

She shrugged, nodded. "Yeah, that's right. So lemme get this straight. You work with Zeke's attorney? And your brother—what? He's the sheriff or somethin'?"

"I'm actually a private investigator." I explained who was who, all the connections. "Do you think it's possible someone from your past killed Zeke?"

She narrowed her eyes. "What do you know about my past?"

"Hell's bells you sure are prickly," I said. "All I know is what was in Zeke's letter to Tammy Sue. That you were his partner. He told Tammy, in the letter, that the two of you were ex-CIA. Can that possibly be right?"

"What? You think I sound too redneck to be in the CIA?" she asked.

"No. I didn't say that. It's just that Zeke always seemed like a good ol' boy who told colorful stories. We never took him serious. Well, I kinda did, I guess. I wasn't sure what to make of him, to be honest. But—"

"You thought he was a yokel? A hick? White trash?" Her tone was defensive.

"*No*," I said. "Not at all. I liked Zeke."

"Let me tell you somethin'. Zeke and I had the best cover goin'. We were a real life Mr. and Mrs. Smith." A wide grin split her face. Mischief danced in her eyes. "You seen that movie? Brad Pitt and Angelina Jolie?"

"Then it's true?" Mr. Smith? The draft email in Zeke's phone flashed through my mind.

"For nearly twenty years," she said.

"Why'd you get out?"

She shrugged. "We were homesick. I grew up in the Lowcountry, near Goose Creek. Zeke was from Stella Maris. We both missed the smell of salt air. Being someplace where we had roots. And it got old. Pretending to be what you're not."

"Were you always just partners? Your marriage..."

"It was complicated between Zeke and me. The relationship started out as part of our cover. But we definitely had chemistry. The marriage was real. It takes more than chemistry to make a marriage work. In the end we just wanted different things. He wanted the white picket fence, Sunday chicken after church. That just wasn't my thing."

"Zeke really went to West Point?" I asked. "I haven't had a spare moment to try to verify that."

"He did." Her voice turned sad. "He was one of the smartest people I ever knew."

"Please," I said. "Tell me if you think there's any way his death has something to do with your job. Your former job."

"What happened to him? All that attorney told me was that he died," she said.

I outlined what we knew and what we suspected.

"Nah," she said. "If someone was out for revenge for something we did years ago—and I'm not sayin' what or where that was, you understand—they'd a put two bullets in his head. And they woulda hit me on the way out of town most likely."

I told her about the safety deposit box. "Why would Zeke leave the passports where they could be found like that? I'm thinking our bank manager is going to fill out some form—"

"An SAR."

"A what?"

"Suspicious Activity Report. She will. But it's fine. That's why he did it."

"He wanted the passports to be reported?" I asked.

"That much cash and that many passports are pretty dang suspicious, don't you think?"

"Well, yeah."

"That's the point. Those SARs are monitored by the CIA. That was Zeke's way of letting them know he was dead. If there was any chatter that makes them think someone was after us, they'd reach out to me."

"Fascinating," I said.

"Do you think Tammy Sue killed Zeke?" she asked.

"Hell's bells, no."

She screwed up her face again. "Is that some kinda ladylike cussin' or what? What is that? *Hell's bells*?" She rolled her eyes dramatically. "Do I need to teach you how to cuss?"

"Thank you so much, but no," I said.

"So who killed him?" she asked.

"I'm still working that out. Ah, if you don't mind me asking, where were you Monday between five and eight p.m.?"

She bristled. "You've got a helluva lot a nerve."

"I'm just eliminating folks that might've had a problem with

Zeke one by one. Not many people did. But the last time anyone saw you on Stella Maris, Zeke was arrested for assault with a deadly weapon."

"Those charges were dropped." She gave her head a dismissive shake.

"I understand. Where were you Monday?" I asked.

"At the spa at Charleston Place. I was there all day, didn't leave 'til close to seven. I had a massage, a yoga session, a seaweed wrap, a mani-pedi—the works. Call 'em up. Ask 'em. There's no way I coulda got to Stella Maris inside that window."

"Thank you." Just then I was mulling how everyone but me was getting in their spa treatments.

"But I would never have hurt Zeke in the first place. Just so you know. We were like family."

"Did you still see each other?" I asked.

"We had lunch once in a while," she said. "It was complicated. He was happy with Tammy. He really loved her. I'm glad he had that."

It crossed my mind to probe for insight as to why he was unfaithful to Tammy if he loved her so much. But that would've meant betraying my client's confidence. "I should go," I said. "Can I call you if I have more questions? Does Tammy know how to reach you if she needs to?"

She gave me a wary look, laid the gun on the coffee table, scribbled a number on a piece of paper, and handed it to me. "Don't wear it out. You can give it to Tammy. I woulda given it to her tomorrow night."

"Are you coming to the memorial?" I asked.

"Says in my letter it's a party. Zeke was real clear on that. Yeah. I'll be there."

"I'll see you there." I stood.

Her face got hard. "When you find out who killed Zeke, you

call me. You hear me?"

"Of course." I showed myself out.

SIXTEEN

I'd street parked half a block up on State. If April left by car, she'd exit the garage that occupied the first floor of her condo building on State Street. But if she left on foot, she'd most likely come through the Queen Street door I'd come in. Of course, she might not leave at all. But if she did, I wanted to see where she went. Something had her on high alert. As careful as she was being, she couldn't be as sure as she claimed that Zeke's death had nothing to do with their past. I didn't buy it.

There was no place I could park and monitor both doors. I went back to my car and opened the back. Keeping an eye on the garage door, I pulled a baseball cap from a plastic crate. I twisted my hair into a knot and tucked it underneath the cap. Then I swapped my Wayfarers for my largest pair of sunglasses and slipped a lightweight sweater on over my sleeveless top. My appearance altered as much as possible, I climbed into the passenger seat to wait.

I pulled out my iPad and propped it on the steering wheel so I could see it and still keep watch on the oversized metal garage door from the corner of my eye. This wasn't the best practice for stakeouts, and I typically didn't divide my attention like that. It was always better to stay fully focused on the subject of your surveillance. But I needed to know what April drove.

I did a quick search in one of our subscription databases

and found a silver 2014 Mazda MX-5 Miata registered to April Lynne Fox. Movement caught my attention. The garage door slid up. Moments later, a white Mercedes rolled out and turned left on State Street. I reached for a bottle of water in a small cooler on the front passenger seat.

Then I got antsy. What if she'd already come out the front door and taken off on foot? Maybe I'd just peek down Queen Street. I got out of the car and crossed State. I stayed close to the blue-grey house on the corner, peered down Queen Street, and checked pedestrian traffic as far as I could see. No sign of April.

I had taken one step towards the car, thinking how this could take a while, or it could be a dead-end, when the brown metal garage door rolled open. A silver MX-5 darted out and went left.

Sonavabitch.

I scooted for the car as quickly as I could without attracting undue attention. If she saw me tearing after her in the rearview mirror, she'd know she had a tail.

I climbed in, started the Escape, and eased into the traffic lane. The Miata was already sitting at the corner of State and Broad, but that was okay. I had to give April plenty of room. She was more experienced at spotting surveillance than most of the people I'd followed. She turned right on Broad. A red and white Chevrolet pickup rolled up behind her, too close for me to turn in front of it. Having a vehicle between us might be best in any case. I pulled in behind the truck.

Broad Street traffic was relatively light that morning. April passed through the intersection at Church, and I narrowly made the light. She pulled up at Meeting and Broad. The truck between us had to be twenty years old, and the back was filled to overflowing with lawn equipment. The truck's exhaust fumes were noxious.

The light changed and April hit the gas. The pickup in front of me rolled forward, inching up to five miles an hour. Breathe in. Breathe out. Good grief, was the truck burning? I coughed, tried to see around it.

April had already cleared King Street, and I was still in front of the court house.

Shit. Shit. *Shit.* I pulled on the steering wheel and willed the truck out of my way.

Gradually, we crept up to the light at Broad and King. It was yellow. The truck stopped. I stayed back as far as I could. It was easier to see around the truck and easier to breathe from a distance.

I leaned left and right, trying to see around the Chevrolet. I'd lost sight of April's Miata. After an eternity, the light changed, and the truck meandered forward. Nothing was coming in the opposite direction. I glanced around. No police cars in sight.

I swerved around the truck, waving to the driver as I passed. As soon as I cleared his bumper, I slid in front of it. Where was April?

I barreled past Legare and ran through a light that was turning red at Logan. No sign of the silver MX-5. Shit. Had she turned off?

When I made the right turn, where Broad becomes Lockwood, I sped up, zipped along the Ashley River. Still no April. Where had she been headed? I simply had no idea. I followed Lockwood past the Marina. Just as I was about to pass under the James Island Expressway, I caught a glint of silver from above. It was just a flash—could've been sunlight reflecting off any car. I took the ramp, accelerated.

Across the Ashley River, I caught sight of the Miata just as it moved out of sight off exit 1. She was headed out Highway 61.

I took the exit, but backed off the accelerator. We settled in for a scenic drive up Ashley River Road. Having lost her once, I kept April in front of me, giving her as much room as I could. Thirty minutes after we'd left downtown Charleston, she turned right and drove through the gate at Middleton Place Plantation. Surely she wasn't playing the tourist this morning.

I followed her underneath towering live oaks to the unpaved parking area. Middleton Place was popular that morning. April pulled in between a tree and a Taurus. I looped around and found a spot one row over. April climbed out of the Miata, scanned the area slowly as she rummaged in her purse, then set out towards the ticket booth.

I waited until she'd purchased her ticket and walked off towards the reflecting pond, then stood in line and bought a ticket for the self-guided garden and stableyards tour. I'd taken that tour several times, and it was gorgeous.

Middleton Place was a former rice plantation. Union troops had lit a fire to the original residential complex of a main house plus two flankers in early 1865, shortly before the end of the civil war. Williams Middleton had, after all, signed the Ordinance of Secession.

Only one of the flankers was rebuilt, and it served as the house museum on property. But the real charm of Middleton Place was the gardens—they were a national landmark, the oldest landscaped gardens in the country.

Designed by Henry Middleton in 1741 following the same principles used at Versailles, the gardens at Middleton Place reflected a grand classic style found in European gardens of the time. They were manicured, with walkways bordered by trees and shrubs that created outdoor rooms and secret passages. A riot of color when the azaleas bloomed, the gardens were designed so that something was always flowering. They had captivated my imagination as a child and held it still today as I pursued a former CIA agent. I took the path April had struck out on.

When I reached the reflecting pond, April turned off the path on the opposite side. She disappeared beyond a row of trees. As quickly as I could without causing a scene, I hustled down the walkway and followed.

When I stepped beyond the line of trees, I was in a verdant hall formed by a variety of trees and shrubs on both sides. April was nowhere to be seen. I hurried along the lane and made a right. Had I not been familiar with the garden layout, I might have wandered along its footpaths for days and not found April. As it was, I followed the path I was on to the next intersection and made a left.

The gardens were laid out geometrically, and the centermost section where I now stood was comprised of six large rectangles of grass, bordered by paths, trees, and shrubs. I stepped to my right. The four rectangles closest to the river had a large circle, cut into wedges like a pie made up of beds. Footpaths crisscrossed the circle. I had a clear view of this part of the garden. No April.

I moved to my left and scanned the gardens surrounding the remaining two rectangles of grass in that section. April was not among the pairs and groups strolling around the edges.

I moved back along the corridor between the trees and shrubs and proceeded towards the Middleton family tomb. Surrounded by trees, it was tucked away in an outdoor room in a corner near the Octagonal Sunken Garden. I turned off before I reached the tomb and circled behind it. I knew there was a bench near the tomb. If I were meeting someone for a private chat, I might meet them there. That is, if I were in need of inordinate secrecy.

I moved slowly along the path behind the tomb. No one in the area around the tomb could see me, nor I them. But I was hoping I could hear them.

I stood quietly admiring the octagonal garden and the view beyond to the river. Live oaks dripped with Spanish moss. The breeze smelled of magnolias. After a moment, through the stand of trees behind me, I heard a familiar voice.

"I 'preciate you coming on such short notice," said April.

"Of course. I hope everything is all right." A man's voice. European accent, one I couldn't place.

Damn. Damn. Damn. Europeans. CIA agents. This was getting out of hand fast.

"Zeke is dead." April's voice broke.

"What? When did this happen?"

"Don't pretend you're all sad about it. We both know that's a lie."

"I never wished him harm. Well, not in recent years in any event. Tell me what happened."

"He was poisoned."

"Cyanide?"

"Strychnine they think," said April. "But that's not official."

"Strychnine. That is very odd."

"What I thought too. I wanted to be sure you had nothing to do with this."

"My dear, I assure you. I had no reason to harm him anymore. You know this."

"Don't touch me, dammit."

"I apologize. I only meant to offer comfort."

"Is there anyone new in the office?"

"Not recently. I cannot believe Zeke's unfortunate death has anything to do with our work here."

"Well, keep your ear to the ground. Send me a message if

you hear anything that might be connected, okay?"

"Of course. And if you change your mind about dinner, likewise, you must send me a message."

"Dammit, Sergei. Stop that shit right now."

"Of course, my dear. Again, I apologize."

The voices fell silent. Sergei? I moved towards the tomb. I wanted to get a look at Sergei.

When I reached the bench, a tall man was on the path moving towards the reflection pond. I followed him. He was slim with broad shoulders and dark hair. He wore khaki pants and a long-sleeved button-down shirt with the sleeves rolled up. He was alone. That had to be Sergei. I trailed him back to the parking area.

April's Miata rolled out of the lot and turned down the dirt lane. Sergei climbed inside a black BMW. I followed him all the way back down Ashley River Road. He took Sam Rittenberg, then hopped on I-26 and got off on Meeting Street. A few blocks down, he turned left onto Cool Blow by Meeting Street Academy. He pulled to the curb and went inside a modern three-story concrete and glass office building. I drove almost to the end of the block and walked back to the door he'd gone inside.

The sign on the building listed the occupants. My breath caught.

The Georgian Honorary Consulate was in Suite 322.

SEVENTEEN

On the way back to Stella Maris, I focused on my breathing. In. Out. I needed to think about something normal for a while. I'd talked Mamma out of her last ripe June Pink, so I went home for a late lunch. There's just nothing better than a homegrown heirloom tomato sandwich. I sliced the tomato thick, salt and peppered it, and let it sit while I made a fresh pitcher of tea.

Nate was spending the day surreptitiously scouting the island for anything with strychnine in it. He'd left early, in old clothes, and I was grateful I wasn't the one who'd be poking through sheds and garages. What could I make him for dinner?

Most of the year, I eat only whole grain bread. But you need the cheap white stuff that's bad for you to make a decent tomato sandwich. I coated two slices thick with Duke's mayonnaise and layered on the June Pinks. Then I took my concoction and a glass of tea to the deck and ate it standing over the rail while I sucked in great lungfuls of salt air and thought about what April had said. And about Sergei.

I believed that Zeke and April had been CIA agents. On the one hand, her hunch that Zeke's murder didn't look like some sort of spy thing matched my own. But on the other hand, it was hard to ignore something as significant as your murder victim being an ex-spy. How could it not be connected?

I sincerely wanted this to be a normal case—something we had experience dealing with, your everyday lunacy. I was too far out of my element with Georgians named Sergei. Who knew there was a Georgian consulate in Charleston? What on earth did they do there? I needed to mull the next steps to take down that investigative path.

And in truth, I did have several other possibilities in mind. I decided to focus on those for the moment. It felt like the sane choice. I washed my hands and went to my office to spend some quality time with the case board.

Thus far, my possibilities and suspects list was slim. Tammy Sue, Crystal, Coy, Price, "Someone From Zeke's Past," and "Someone Smitten With Tammy Sue." Under the heading of "Someone From Zeke's Past," I wrote Sergei.

Then I pondered my conversation with Spencer from the day before and what Tammy had told me. I erased "Someone Smitten With Tammy Sue" and replaced it with Humphrey Pearson. Unenthusiastically, but to be thorough, I added Spencer Simmons to the persons of interest row.

The bonfire at Skip and Margie Robinson's tickled my brain. It kept coming up. The trouble between Zeke and Tammy had started then, with Crystal. How would things be different for them if they'd never gone to that party? With the exception of Price Elliott and now Sergei, everyone on my case board had been at that bonfire. Should I add Skip and Margie to the case board? What about Pete and Brenda Carter? They'd been there too. Who else? Connie Hicks. Winter. I was reaching. But I did need to talk to all of them.

Surely someone had taken pictures. I moved to the desk, opened a browser window, and logged on to Facebook. Folks would be squeamish if they knew how often private investigators and even law enforcement employed social media. It came in handy.

I'd already scanned Tammy Sue's photos. I pulled up Margie Robinson's page and clicked on the photos tab. Margie clearly wasn't one of those who posted every day. I didn't have to scroll back far to find shots with a bonfire, Adirondack chairs, and tiki torches.

A shot of Tammy Sue with a plate full of chicken, shrimp, corn, beans, and slaw caught my eye. She was smiling, toasting the camera with a wineglass. Candid shots of everyone at the party except Zeke with piled high plates and either wine or a beer followed. It looked like a fun time.

As the light grew dimmer, the shots with food gave way to pictures of people relaxing in the chairs by the fire. Coy and Skip tossed a football back and forth. Pete and Brenda threw corn hole bags with Zeke and Tammy Sue.

Photos taken still later in the evening showed everyone around the fire. Even Zeke. Had he known someone took this photo? He wasn't tagged, no one was. He grinned wide. My heart ached for the happy soul whose life had been stolen from him.

Margie's photos jumped to a series taken around the marina. I searched for Brenda's page. Her first name was unusual. Tyne, like the actress, Tyne Daly. I'd never heard Brenda use the name.

Brenda hadn't posted photos from the bonfire. Most of her Facebook posts were of her and Pete's two sons. They both looked like her: tall, slim, and fair. In the few photos she'd posted of herself, she looked as if she wore no makeup. Some women would envy Brenda Carter. I moved on to Winter's photos.

Here were more shots of everyone with food, then playing games, then later around the fire. They were all smiling, laughing. There was a picture of Coy leaning down to pick something up in the sand near the fire. What was that? A green wine bottle. A few photos later, there was Zeke, in another untagged photo, bending down apparently to pick up the same bottle. That was odd.

When I got to the picture of Humphrey bending over the same bottle, I realized no one was picking it up. What in this world? Most of these folks were married. They couldn't be playing spin the bottle, could they? Surely not. It had to be Truth or Dare. Still unexpected for this group, but better than spin the bottle. That must've been some party.

Winter had photos of everyone except herself spinning that wine bottle. I was now more curious than ever about the Robinsons' bonfire. I closed Facebook and remembered something from my conversation with April. She'd made a joke about her and Zeke being like the movie, "Mr. and Mrs. Smith," where Brad Pitt and Angelina Jolie had starred as married spies. That had reminded me of the email on Zeke's phone. With the information that Zeke had been a CIA agent, I saw that draft in a new light. Had he been using the draft folder of an email account to communicate with someone without having to send the email? I'd heard of people doing that. Two or more people logged into the same account.

Thankfully, I hadn't dropped the phone off at the police station yet. I unlocked my desk drawer, pulled out the evidence bag, and slipped out the phone. I typed in the passcode and opened the email application, then tapped on the drafts folder.

There were now two drafts, the one I'd seen the day before from "Mr. Jones" to "Mr. Smith," and another, dated today.

Mr. Jones,
The governor requests the honor of your presence at his

home this morning at eleven.

Ms. Smith

Of course. This was how April had set up a meeting with Sergei. He must be Mr. Jones. The governor was a reference to Henry Middleton, one of the people buried in the Middleton tomb in the gardens. He'd been the governor of South Carolina for a while back in the early 1800s. Henry Middleton was also a minister to Russia—for far longer than he was the governor of South Carolina. I pondered for a moment how Russia was right next door to Georgia, and Georgia was a former Soviet republic.

The original email from Mr. Jones...Had that been Sergei letting Zeke and April know he was moving to Charleston? Why had he addressed it only to Zeke? He'd said he harbored no ill will. Had there been bad blood between Zeke and Sergei? Clearly there must have been if April had needed to verify that Sergei's hands were clean in the matter of Zeke's death. But why would she trust what he said? I needed to talk to April again.

But...why would Sergei have poisoned Zeke and moved his body to the trunk of his classic car? Why would anyone? That felt especially wrong for a professional spy. I shook my head to clear out the Russians and returned Zeke's phone to my desk drawer.

My thoughts skipped back to my conversation in the car at the bank parking lot with Tammy Sue. Harold Yates bugged me too. Not because I saw a connection to Zeke's death. Harold had been dead for three years and he had no family. But because he was a lonely soul who lived in the shadows of our happy town, and only Zeke had thought to care for him. Who else was invisible?

I spoke to myself sternly and refocused on the case board.

Profiles. I needed profiles for Humphrey and Spencer, people I'd known my entire life. I suffered a profound lack of enthusiasm for either as a suspect, but I needed to make sure all the bases were covered. Often the person I least suspected surprised me.

For the next hour, I dutifully documented what I knew about Humphrey and Spencer and came up with no red flags. Then I checked my email, retrieved the link Coy had sent me, and sifted through more pictures of birds and alligators than I'd seen in a while. If Coy had in fact taken pictures of people, he'd left those out of the cloud folder. If more evidence later pointed to him, Blake would have to get a warrant to explore Coy's computer further.

Nate's ringtone, a rift of blues, sang from my phone.

"Hey, handsome," I answered.

"I found the strychnine."

I came halfway out of my chair. "Where?"

"In the Elliotts' garage. Gopher bait. I called in an anonymous tip to Blake. He's getting a search warrant."

I bit my lip. "Oh, no. This is going to kill Charlie Jacobs." Somewhere, in a corner of my mind, I acknowledged relief that this pointed away from the Sergei angle.

"The former police chief? Blake's predecessor? What's he got to do with this?"

"Price Elliott is his grandson. Glenda Elliott is his daughter. Are you still at the Elliotts' house?"

"No. I'm at The Cracked Pot grabbing lunch."

"Price is out of work for the moment. Wasn't he at home?"

"His Subaru was there, as was Glenda's car."

"How did you manage to get in and out of their garage in broad daylight without them seeing you?"

"They left the walk-through door unlocked."

"Most people here do—it's a small town. We're fairly

isolated." My voice sounded defensive to my own ears.

"I know, I know. I had a pretext ready in case I got caught. They have a pet door, just like the one we have for Rhett. I figured if they came downstairs, I'd say I saw a raccoon run in through it and gave chase to be neighborly. It being broad daylight and all, that critter would very likely be rabid. Fortunately, they never knew I was there."

"I'm going to talk to Price again before Blake gets there with a warrant. Before Price knows we know."

"Be careful, Slugger. He's young and clearly hot-headed. Probably impulsive."

I scrunched up my face. "It just doesn't fit very well, does it? He may be impulsive, but whoever killed Zeke took the time to plan it out. He or she waited. They used gopher bait."

"Hmm. Maybe ask Grant and Glenda how they came by that gopher bait. Price likely found it in the garage and used it because it was there. That's my guess, anyhow. It was an instrument of opportunity."

"Price would've had his own cap."

"Come again?"

"The cap. Price wouldn't've needed to wear Zeke's. If he was the one Daddy saw in Zeke's truck Monday afternoon, he could've worn his own cap. But come to think of it, he wasn't wearing one Tuesday morning at the shop."

"Zeke's cap could be anywhere. Could've come off while his body was being moved, or he might've taken it off earlier."

"True. I'm headed out."

"Should I meet you there?"

"No, I've got this. If we both show up he'll know something's up right off."

"As you wish. Hey, I made reservations for us tonight at 82 Queen."

"Tonight?"

"Tomorrow night is Zeke's memorial. That leaves tonight for date night."

"Sounds wonderful." And it did. I loved 82 Queen, and date night was one of the rituals we kept for us. But I hadn't slept well the night before, and it had been a long day already. I still hadn't told Nate about Sergei.

EIGHTEEN

Grant and Glenda Elliott lived in Sea Farm, a golf course neighborhood that occupied most of what used to be Pearson family land. The Elliott home was a green stucco affair. It sat, like many homes on our island, on top of oversized double garages. The wide driveway and parking area took up a swath of the front yard. A double staircase led from either side to a wider set of steps that ascended to the front porch. I started a voice memo, climbed the steps, and rang the bell.

Glenda answered the door. In her early forties, she sported a short brown bob and a black Under Armour warmup suit. Immediately, I felt bad for her. Things were about to go sideways for her family.

"Hey, Glenda. How're you? I'm sorry to intrude on your afternoon, but could I have a word with Price?"

She seemed startled. "Price? Why do you want to speak with Price?" She held onto the door, keeping it open no more than civility absolutely required.

"You heard about Zeke, I guess."

"Of course. That's the reason Price is home today." Her look held me accountable for Zeke's shop being closed.

"Nate and I are investigating. I just need to ask Price a few questions. He could really help our case. He was the last person to see Zeke before someone killed him." I felt so guilty for playing her it made me sick to my stomach.

Apprehension was writ large across her face. She hesitated, then stepped back and opened the door wide enough to let me in. "I'll get him. Have a seat in the family room." She closed the door and headed upstairs.

The foyer and the great room were vaulted. I watched as Glenda walked across the second floor balcony that must've connected the two upstairs bedrooms. The Elliotts also had a daughter. I settled into an overstuffed tropical print sofa.

Moments later, Glenda came back downstairs, followed by Price. He had the look about him of one who'd only recently woken up, or perhaps had been closeted in the dark with a video game. Barefoot with baggy athletic shorts, a tank, and an open hoodie, he looked like a kid. And something white was taped to the side of his face.

"I'll just check on the laundry." Glenda moved towards the kitchen. The openness of the floor plan meant she would no doubt be able to hear everything we said.

"You wanted to see me?" Price remained standing. The James Dean snarl seemed at home on his face. But whatever it was he had taped to his jaw took some of the edge off. What in the name of common sense was that? It wasn't a Band-Aid. He shoved his hands into the pockets of the hoodie.

"Would you sit with me?" I asked.

"Whatever." He rolled his eyes elaborately and sat on the sofa across from me.

"The logoed caps for Lyerly Automotive...do you typically wear those to work? I noticed you weren't wearing one the other morning when I came by the shop."

He blew out a short breath. "Yes, I wore the stupid caps. When Zeke was there. It was a thing with him. Damn things messed up my hair."

"Did he have a lot of those made up?"

"Hundreds. He gave them out to anyone who would take them. I have four or five myself."

"How nice." That was unfortunate. "Back to Tuesday morning... you made coffee, right?"

He gave me a look that suggested I was an idiot. "Yeah. I made coffee. Is that a crime now?"

"No, of course not." I smiled. "Did you happen to spill any?"

"What?" The sneer deepened. He had a chip on his shoulder the size of Mt. Everest.

"In Zeke's office. Did you spill anything on the floor?"

"How is that German?"

"How is it what?" I squinted at him.

"German. What's it got to do with anything?" His face flushed.

Oh my stars. Germane. He meant germane. I moistened my lips. "Price, I know it doesn't seem important to you, but it might actually be key to what happened to Zeke. Did you spill anything in Zeke's office?"

Again with the eyeroll. "No. I did not spill anything on the floor. I got some coffee on the counter, but I wiped it up."

"Was it typical for you to make the coffee, or did you only do it on Tuesday because Zeke wasn't there?"

"He usually made the first pot of the day. After that, sometimes it was me, sometimes him."

"When Zeke was there did you use the bathroom in his office?"

"Well, yeah. It's the only one."

"Okay. So you went into Zeke's office every day then."

"Yeah."

"Did you notice anything different than usual on Tuesday,

anything missing or out of place?"

"No." He slouched, exhaled loudly.

The thing on his face looked like a big lump held in place by clear shipping tape.

"It's fatback."

I might've been staring at the bandage. "I'm sorry. What did you say?"

"It's fatback. It'll draw a cyst to a head. It's a natural cure." He shrugged. "I have a cyst."

Sweet reason. "I've never heard that." Laughter welled up, threatened to escape. Surely this could not be our killer.

He nodded. "Zeke's the one who told me about it. It's an old-timey cure. His grandmother knew all kinds of stuff like that. She was like, a medicine woman."

Zeke...the ex-CIA agent, class valedictorian, shotgun enthusiast, dispenser of home remedies. I swallowed my giggles.

"I also wanted to ask you about a coffee mug Zeke liked to use."

"That ugly brown thing with the face?"

"That sounds right." Tammy had described it as pottery. Perhaps Price didn't care for pottery.

"What about it?"

"Do you recall if Zeke was drinking out of it on Monday?"

He winced. "Man, I don't pay attention to that kinda thing. He used it every day. Probably." His face changed. "Wait. He had it in bay one when he got back from lunch. He made a fresh pot of coffee. I remember thinking he'd made a whole pot and it wouldn't get drank. I can't stand it the way he drinks it—way too strong. That time of day, didn't seem like he'd drink a whole pot by himself."

"Do you remember an accident—maybe he dropped something? Did anything happen where the mug might've ended up broken?"

"Nah. I'd remember that too. Tammy gave it to him. He was real particular about it. Did it get broken? I didn't have nothing to do with that."

"It looks like it did." I waited a minute, gave him time to keep talking if he was of a mind. He wasn't. "Tell me about the argument you and Zeke had."

"Who says we had an argument?" He lifted his chin.

I caught myself staring at the fatback again, raised my hand to cover my smile.

"It doesn't matter who told me about it. You had an argument. What was it about?"

He examined the ceiling. "He said I was late too much. Lectured me about my work habits. My future. What did he know? He was a mechanic in a rinky-dink town."

I felt my eyebrow creep up, gave him a long look. Like most people in town, he'd had no idea who Zeke Lyerly was. Just like Zeke wanted.

"No disrespect." He waved a hand dismissively.

"To Zeke, or our hometown?" I didn't care for his attitude about either. Who was he to criticize, sitting there with fatback taped to his face?

He flashed me a look filled with disdain, then looked away.

"Why were you late?" I asked.

"I wasn't late much. Maybe five, ten minutes, that's all. I worked hard for him when I got there. What's the big deal, whether I'm there at seven thirty or 7:35?"

"How did you react to this...lecture?"

"It pissed me off, okay?"

"You and he fought?"

"No, we didn't fight. He lectured me. I got pissed off. I told him he didn't pay me enough for how hard I worked. He said if I was more contentious I might get a raise. We went back and forth a while."

I rolled my lips in and out, nodded. Zeke must've told him to be more conscientious. Good grief. "Sounds like a fight to me."

"It was a disagreement."

"When exactly did you have this disagreement?" I asked.

"A week ago this past Wednesday, I think."

"Was that the end of it?"

He shrugged. "Yeah. I've been there fifteen minutes early every day since. Until you closed the place down, anyways."

I studied him, looking for any sign he wasn't being truthful. It was hard to tell, what with his sullen act and all. And it was hard to take him seriously when he had raw pork on his head. My phone vibrated with an incoming text. I pulled my phone out of the side pocket of my purse.

It was from Nate: *Warrant delayed. Judge gone fishing.*

Hell's bells. I didn't think Price was a flight risk. But I was worried he'd think to ditch the rest of the strychnine before Blake could execute a search warrant. I couldn't ask Glenda and Grant about the gopher killer until after it was officially found.

"That's good," I said to Price. "Tammy Sue is going to need your help as soon as she reopens."

Behind me, Glenda's voice floated into the room. "When do you suppose that will be?"

"Maybe tomorrow." I really had no idea, but that came right out of my mouth, nonetheless. "Tammy will call Price to let him know, I'm sure."

Glenda stepped into the room, looked pointedly at me. "Is there anything else?"

It crossed my mind that maybe she should make her son see a dermatologist, but I didn't offer my opinion on the matter.

Price stood. He apparently sensed his mamma was sending me packing.

I offered them my sunniest smile. "No, but thank you so much, Price, for your help. I think that coffee mug may be important. It's real helpful to know Zeke had it Monday afternoon. I'm grateful to you."

Don't laugh. Don't laugh. Don't laugh. I said my goodbyes and headed out.

From the Escape I called Blake. "You might want to get Clay Cooper to sit on the Elliott house until you can get a search warrant. Just in case Price gets antsy and decides to get rid of the gopher killer."

"Why can't my outside investigators take care of that?"

"Because Zeke's memorial is Friday night, so date night got moved to tonight. We're going into Charleston."

"Fine. I'll talk to Clay. But that'll cost me overtime."

"His rates are better than ours. I'd charge you overtime too."

He grumbled under his breath.

"You kept the strychnine quiet, right?" I asked.

"Yeah. No one knows that's likely what killed him except you, Nate, and me. And Warren Harper, of course." He sighed. "And Mom and Dad. But they know better than to talk about that."

"And April. I told her. And the killer," I said. "The killer knows."

"I'll send Cooper over to watch him," he said.

But I still wasn't sure Price was our guy.

NINETEEN

The storm the night before had brought the temperature down. It was comfortable enough to sit in the brick courtyard, which was my favorite spot at 82 Queen. Our table was tucked beside the pink garden wall, next to an old wrought iron gate. The lush green plantings made it feel private. White lights strung in the trees added to the romance. Nate held my chair, then took his seat.

The waiter handed him the wine list, and each of us dinner and specialty drink menus. "Would you care for a cocktail?"

"I'd like a Charleston Sparkler." I was particularly fond of that concoction, which was made of Acai vodka, fresh lime juice, pomegranate simple syrup, and sparkling wine.

"Woodford Reserve, two rocks," said Nate.

"Very good." Our waiter disappeared.

"Shall we decide on dinner before we continue our conversation?" asked Nate.

"Sounds good. I adore the She Crab Soup. I'll start with that."

"Hmm..." Nate studied his menu. "I'll have the Brown Sugar Pork Belly with grilled polenta."

"That's not a healthy choice." I gave him a disapproving look.

He grinned. "Perhaps we should tally the nutritional

content of She Crab Soup."

"Okay, you have a point." I returned to my menu. "I think I'll have the Queen Street Chicken Bog for my entree."

"Excellent choice. I'll have the ribeye. Do you want a salad?"

"I'll never be able to eat all that. I should have something green, but no. We need to have salads tomorrow."

"I doubt they'll serve that at the memorial service. We'd better get our greens at lunch."

The waiter brought our cocktails and took our dinner order.

"And we'd like a bottle of the Lyric Pinot Noir," said Nate.

All efficiency and unobtrusiveness, the waiter murmured in the affirmative and disappeared.

"Price Elliott is a kid," I said.

"And kids much younger than he, unfortunately, have committed murder," said Nate.

I sighed. "I know. It's just...honestly, I don't think he cares enough about that job to kill over it. He'd likely've been quite happy to lose it. Nate. He had *fatback* taped to his head." I started to giggle.

"Come again?"

"He'd taken packing tape and taped a chunk of fatback to the side of his face. He thinks it will bring a cyst to a head. Surely someone that unsophisticated didn't kill a former CIA agent. Oh, wait. It was Zeke who taught him that fatback trick."

We both laughed.

Nate seemed to mull that. "But there's close to a hundred pounds of gopher bait under the Elliotts' house. Strychnine is the active ingredient. As hard as that stuff is to get ahold of, that's pretty damning evidence someone in that house poisoned Zeke. You don't suspect Grant or Glenda, do you?"

"No," I said. "The only possible motive there would be that

Zeke might've hurt Price's feelings or some such thing, but neither Grant nor Glenda are that irrational."

"Then I think this case is solved," said Nate.

"Well...I haven't told you about the guy from Georgia."

"Near where Tammy Sue is from?" Nate sipped his bourbon.

"Not that Georgia." I started with April's condo and finished with figuring out the email trick.

"Why is there a Georgian consulate in Charleston?" asked Nate.

"I have no idea. But since you've found strychnine on the island, surely this case has a solution that doesn't involve spies."

"I don't understand why you're so set against it being Price," said Nate.

I shrugged. "It's just a feeling. You went through Skip and Margie's garage with a fine-tooth comb?"

"I did."

"Is there a shed...some other place Coy would have access to?" I asked.

"Coy?"

"Yes, Coy. If you'd found strychnine at Skip and Margie's, I'd say we needed to take a harder look at Coy. He lives above their garage. He had two motives, and his alibi is a poor excuse."

"You know how much I hate to disappoint you. There's storage next door at the marina, all right. But I went through that as well. No trace of strychnine."

"Well, damn."

"And I checked your cousin Spencer's garage for good measure. And Humphrey Pearson's place. He doesn't have a garage, but there's a shed out back. No gopher killer, but he has some healthy marijuana plants behind the shed."

"Maybe forget to mention that to Blake. There's no sense

getting Humphrey into trouble when we were trespassing to begin with."

"Agreed. It's one thing to use the fruits of an illegal search to bring a murderer to justice. Quite another to hassle a grown man about his recreational habits."

The waiter brought our wine and made quick work of the presentation. As soon as he'd poured, someone brought our first course. I turned my attention to my soup. The first silky, creamy, savory sip was heavenly. I closed my eyes and nearly moaned with pleasure.

I opened my eyes and ladled a second spoonful.

Nate grinned at me. "That must be really good soup."

"You want a taste?" I asked.

"No, thank you. Would you like to try mine?"

"No, thanks. Maybe we should search a few more garages," I said.

"What, randomly?" His forehead creased.

I winced. "No, of course not. Maybe. I don't know. I just get a certain feeling when we're on the right path. I don't have that feeling yet."

"Have you seen Colleen today?" asked Nate.

I shook my head. "Not since she popped in to harass us at Zeke's house."

"I think she was more harassing your ex than us."

"He's not my ex."

Nate raised his eyebrows.

"Okay, he is my ex, of course. But in the context of this case, he's a contractor we had to call. Him being my ex is incidental."

"Fair enough. Nonetheless, we have seen her since then."

Right. The dream. I took a sip of wine. "I wonder if Colleen has been reprimanded," I said. "I worry about her."

"I'm sure she's fine. She's quite industrious. And it is nice to have dinner alone." He lifted his wine glass.

"Indeed it is." I smiled and touched my glass to his.

Worry clouded his smoky blue eyes. "You had another nightmare last night."

I sipped my wine, then set down my glass. "I did."

"They're becoming quite frequent. And they seem to frighten you profoundly."

I studied the label on the wine bottle. "They do."

"You mentioned they had to do with Colleen keeping the island population from growing. But you haven't told me yet what happens that scares you so much you wake up trembling and screaming."

I drew a deep breath. "Colleen told me they are an impressionist version of things that might possibly happen, depending on the choices people—including you and me—make. I shouldn't take them literally, she said."

"All right." He waited.

"In the dream, you and I have two children. The girl is named Emma Rae, after my Gram." My eyes glistened. "We're evacuating. There's a super hurricane bearing down on the island. The ferry's gone down, so we have to go to the marina. In the dream, we have a boat. A cabin cruiser. There are so many people trying to escape the storm. Too many people. It's clear some are not going to make it. They're swarming the boats—our boat too. Then a giant wave washes you away. The children and I are standing there screaming. There's nothing we can do."

He sipped his wine. "Do you think this dream is a warning?"

"Yes. I do."

He nodded. "Then perhaps we should heed it. If there's a storm in the Atlantic, we leave town with days to spare. Problem solved."

"I don't think it's that simple," I said. "Colleen said the forecast models aren't always that accurate." I wasn't even going to mention the earthquake/tsunami scenario Colleen had brought up the last time we'd talked about this. Nate might start to wonder if he'd married a nutcase.

"So, what do we need to do?" asked Nate.

I shrugged. "According to Colleen, all we can do is be prepared and be alert."

"Then why are you still worried?"

A tear escaped. "Because I can't imagine life without you."

TWENTY

The next morning, Nate went by the police station to check in with Blake and to log Zeke's phone and Price's keys to the shop into evidence. Because I couldn't warm up to the idea of either Price Elliott or Sergei the Georgian as a murder suspect, I took my second cup of coffee and a bag of Dove Dark Chocolate Promises into the office and stared at the case board. When it wouldn't confess, I opened the file on my laptop and scanned my notes. Then I went back to the beginning.

I pulled up the video I'd shot Tuesday morning, right after Pete Carter had taken a crowbar to the trunk of Zeke's Mustang. Had the killer been among the crowd watching from neighboring yards? Who all was there but didn't live in the immediate neighborhood? The people front and center were neighbors, folks whose names hadn't otherwise come up in the course of the investigation so far. The clip was only twenty seconds long. I reached for a piece of chocolate and started it over.

After I'd watched it a few times, I zoomed in. Frame by frame, I scanned the video. I froze the screen on a familiar bearded face among the crowd. Why would Humphrey Pearson be there? He didn't live close enough that he would've heard Tammy Sue's commotion and come to see what was going on. Word of Zeke's death had not yet had a chance to spread at that point. I needed to talk to Humphrey.

For good measure, I resolved to speak to everyone at the Robinsons' bonfire who I hadn't already spoken to. It's not that I suspected any of them really. I was turning over rocks, hoping to find a snake under one of them.

Where would I find Humphrey on a Friday morning? When he worked, he did carpentry and odd jobs for Michael Devlin, who I sincerely did not want to call again. Where was Michael working? Since he hadn't been able to sell his spec house, he hadn't started another new home on Stella Maris.

I hopped in the Escape and started my search for Humphrey at his place. His grandfather had built the beachfront cottage in the early 1900s, way before the island had restrictions about building so close to the beach. It was specifically held back when a large chunk of Pearson land was sold to build Sea Farm, which bordered Humphrey's property.

The cottage was at the end of Pitt Street, where it dead-ended in the sand. Humphrey had meticulously maintained it over the years. Its white picket fence and white painted wood siding had a fresh coat of paint. It wasn't in the same neighborhood as Mamma and Daddy's house and the Lyerly home. But it wasn't but a few blocks away either.

I pulled into the dirt driveway and parked beside the well-loved Jeep Wrangler Humphrey had driven for as long as I could remember. I knocked on the door and waited, praying he would answer fully clothed. Humphrey's wardrobe preference was none, but he generally didn't force that proclivity on the rest of us. Dropping in on him was risky.

Without warning, the door opened. Humphrey had clearly walked to the door in bare feet, which explained why I didn't hear him coming.

"Liz." His warm smile was guileless. Untamed blond hair hung to his shoulders in waves. In contrast, his beard and mustache were closely trimmed. A vibrant blue print sarong hung around his waist.

"Hey, Humphrey. Sorry to come by unannounced. Do you have a few minutes to chat?"

"Sure. Come on out by the pool." He opened the door wide.

As I stepped inside, my gaze fell to a set of pegs by the door. Along with several jackets and a spare sarong, there hung a Lyerly Automotive cap. Too bad it wasn't a limited edition.

A large living area with a kitchen at the left end formed the heart of the house. I followed Humphrey across the room and out the french doors to the brick patio.

A wooden trellis to the left labored under mounds of bougainvillea. Mimosa trees and bright pink hibiscus shrubs ran along the right side of the patio. The pool in the center was crystal clear and inviting. While I admired it, Humphrey dropped his sarong and dove in.

Instinctively, I covered my eyes.

Humphrey surfaced, slicked his hair from his eyes and laughed. "It's okay. You can't see me under the water."

"Are you sure?"

"Yes. I'm sure. You should jump in. The water's nice." His eyes twinkled. "You swim naked. In the ocean."

I took my hands off my eyes. "How do you know that?" He was right. All I could see was a flesh-colored blur below the waterline. Not that I was looking.

"Everyone knows that. Except your mother. She prefers not to know."

"Yeah. That sounds about right."

"To what do I owe this pleasure?" he asked.

"I need to talk to you about Zeke."

"Zeke." His expression fell, saddened. "What about him?"

"You and he were friends, right?"

"We were. From kindergarten. It hasn't sunk in yet, you know?"

"I understand. I'm sorry for your loss. We weren't close, but I always liked Zeke. Nate and I are helping Blake with the investigation. Do you know of anyone Zeke had trouble with?" I perched on the end of a lounge chair. Before I talked to April and tailed her to her meeting with Sergei, I would've maybe asked Humphrey if he thought his friend was a spy or some such thing. I was reasonably sure I knew the answer to that.

"Throw me a towel, would you?" He pointed to a stack of thick blue beach towels.

I grabbed the one on top and handed it to him, then averted my eyes as he climbed the steps.

"You're safe now." He wore the towel the same way he'd worn the sarong.

I returned to the lounge chair and sat on the end. He took the chair beside me, sat facing me, with his legs between the two chairs. It was unnerving, knowing he had nothing on beneath that towel. I tried not to think about it.

"I can't think of anyone who would've killed Zeke," he said. "I'd like to think I don't know anyone capable of that."

"I hear you. But unfortunately, it's likely we both do. When was the last time you saw him?'

"Saturday night. It's been less than a week. It's hard to believe I'll never see him again."

"What did y'all do Saturday?" I asked.

"I went to The Pirates' Den. He and Tammy were there for dinner. They asked me to join them. Later Connie came over to the table. It was an ordinary Saturday night. Like a hundred others."

"Are you and Connie seeing each other?"

"Nah. We've been friends for years. She's like a little sister to me. I look out for her, I guess."

"Did you take her to a party at Skip and Margie's a while back?"

"You mean the bonfire?"

"Yeah. The bonfire."

"Sure. But it wasn't like a date."

"What do you remember about that night?" I asked. "Did anything happen out of the ordinary?"

A shade seemed to lower over his eyes. He shrugged. "Not really. Friends, food, too much alcohol maybe."

"Tell me about that."

"What do you mean?'

"Did anyone have too much to drink, act out?" I asked.

He shook his head. "No more than usual. We were cutting up, sure."

"Did you play any games?" I was fishing, of course.

"Sure. Corn hole, football, we tossed a frisbee around. Typical stuff."

"Nothing else? Anything involving a wine bottle?"

"A wine bottle?" He rolled his lips in, shook his head. "Not while I was around. Not that I remember."

I switched directions. "You went to school with Zeke, right?"

"Stella Maris High class of 1987. Go Dolphins." He grinned.

"I heard that Mustang was his first car."

"It was. Sweet ride. Zeke's daddy bought it for him on his fifteenth birthday."

"It was sentimental for Zeke to hang onto it," I mused.

"I guess. It was a collectible. Zeke was always into cars. His daddy was too."

"Did he ever wreck that car?" I continued my fishing expedition. Humphrey was more cooperative than many of the folks I'd talked to in the last few days.

"Wreck it? No. He nearly drove the wheels off it. But he never wrecked it. Not that I know of. Hard to imagine I wouldn't've."

"I'm just trying to figure out why someone would've put him in the trunk of the car. Seems like a statement to me."

"I can't help you there."

"Zeke hung onto a lot of things from high school. His yearbooks are on his office shelves. Trophies, all like that."

Humphrey shrugged. "I guess he was sentimental."

"Who did Zeke date in high school?" I'd run out of things to ask him about, but wanted to keep him talking. And I was curious, I confess.

Humphrey chuckled. "That would be Brenda. Dated her all through school."

"Brenda Carter?"

"She was Brenda Williams then. Barely knew Pete Carter. He went to private school. One of the church schools I think." Humphrey seemed lost in the memories. "Brenda was a firecracker. Tom Boy."

"I'm sorry?"

"That was Brenda's nickname. Her first name is Tyne. Some fancy notion her mamma had. Brenda hates it. Always went by Brenda. But her initials were TB. And she was a tomboy from the word go. That's what everyone called her. Tom Boy. Always thought she could outrun us, out whatever us. And she was three years younger. But she tagged along from the time she could walk."

"With you and Zeke?"

"That's right."

"You and he were close back then?" It was one thing to be friends since kindergarten. It was quite another to have a close friendship that endured through the years.

"Most of our lives, I guess."

I smiled. "Did you play baseball too?"

"Third base," he said. "I never had the bat Zeke had. I wasn't as serious about it. Zeke coulda played in the big leagues."

"That's interesting," I said. "I always think of you as the artistic type, not the jock."

He shrugged. "I guess I was a bit of both when I was a teenager."

"Would you say you and Zeke were best friends?"

"Not really. If Zeke had a best friend in school, it was Brenda. Zeke was friends with everyone. But he spent every spare moment with her."

"It must've been hard on both of them when he joined the army," I said.

"It was," he said. "At first they planned to marry after boot camp. But life happens, you know? Zeke went to school. They drifted apart. Brenda married Pete. I guess the rest is history."

I nodded. "Have you seen Zeke talking to anyone you don't know? Anyone who isn't from here?" Had Sergei been to Stella Maris?

He shook his head slowly. "Not that I can recall."

"So, how did you end up in the crowd at Zeke's house Tuesday morning?" I kept my voice nonchalant.

He looked at me sideways. "Like everyone else. I went to see what was going on."

"Could you hear it from here?" I squinted at him.

"I went for a walk after breakfast. I do that most mornings. When I walked down Sweetgrass, Tammy Sue already had the fire lit and a crowd was gathering."

"Are you and Tammy close?"

He hesitated. "I'd say so."

"Why didn't you come over and try to talk to her? Calm her down? Especially after we found Zeke..."

"I wanted to." He looked away. "But it seemed like a bad idea."

"Why?"

He didn't say anything, looked away.

"Was there more than friendship between you and Tammy Sue?"

"You see?" Frustration crept into his voice. "That. That right there is why I did not go over there."

"What do you mean?"

"I'm very fond of Tammy. But there has never been anything inappropriate between us. Clearly, she and Zeke were having trouble. I didn't want to add fuel to the gossip fires. You know how this town is."

"I see what you mean," I said. "You said the last time you saw Zeke was Saturday night. Did you talk to him after that?"

"No."

Had he forgotten that Zeke called him Sunday afternoon, or was he hiding something?

"He didn't call you?"

"Not that I remember."

Interesting. "I just have one more question, and please don't take this the wrong way."

"What?"

"Where were you Monday between five and eight p.m.?"

He drew back like I'd slapped him. "I can't believe you'd ask me that. Surely you can't think—"

"No, of course not. It's just what we do. We ask everyone that. Even Tammy Sue. It's like a check list thing."

He regarded me from under lowered brows. "I was walking

on the beach."

"Nice day for it." I nodded, gestured with an open palm as if to say, *well, there you go*. "You run into anyone?"

"No. No, I didn't."

I would have been way less concerned about that if he hadn't been surreptitiously watching Tammy burn Zeke's belongings from across the street. And if he'd told me about Zeke calling him Sunday afternoon. And the game involving the wine bottle in the sand. Then there was the cap, which proved absolutely nothing but could still mean something.

Humphrey had moved up on my suspects list. But he wasn't the only friend of Zeke's I needed to take a closer look at. I mulled Brenda's relationship with Zeke as I drove home. It sounded like they'd had an uncommon bond. She and Pete had built a good life for themselves. But what if she'd never gotten over Zeke leaving her here when he joined the army? Was she holding onto feelings for her first love? The Carters had been at the Robinson's bonfire. And they had been inside the Elliott garage.

Nate called to let me know he was going to have lunch with Blake at The Cracked Pot. I made myself a tomato sandwich and took it with a glass of Cheerwine to my office. I ate while I updated my case notes. Then I created profiles for Brenda and Pete Carter, starting with basic background data.

Tyne Brenda Williams was born on Stella Maris, April 4, 1970. She was nearly a year and a half older than Peter Nash Carter, who'd also been born here, on August 23, 1971. Neither of them had gone to college. They'd gotten married the June after Pete graduated from high school. He was only eighteen and she was barely twenty. That was awfully young. I wondered what the story was there. Was she getting back at Zeke?

Pete's parents, Ingram Carter and the former Robin Smith,

had no other children. Robin Carter died June 22, 1982, when Pete was only ten. Brenda's parents had moved to The Villages in central Florida five years ago. Like Pete, Brenda was an only child.

Pete and Brenda had two sons. Aside from Brenda and the boys, his only remaining family was his mother's sister, Rita, who married Boone Newberry. Rita and Boone Newberry still lived in Stella Maris.

The Carters jointly owned the Exxon station. They had a mortgage on their house, but it had never been late. Neither of them had ever been charged with a crime, nor been a defendant in a civil complaint. Their digital footprints held little of interest. Certainly I'd found nothing that would suggest a long-buried motive for murder.

After digging for a couple of hours, I stared once more at the case board. Tammy Sue, Crystal, Coy, Price, Sergei, Humphrey, Spencer, Pete, or Brenda? Humphrey was definitely at the top of my list, with Crystal and Coy tied for the second spot. But there was enough circumstantial evidence against Price Elliott that I knew I wouldn't be able to persuade Blake to hold off. At least it wasn't Tammy Sue he'd be arresting.

TWENTY-ONE

The Pirates' Den was packed to capacity for Zeke's memorial party. Under strict orders from our host, there was no eulogy.

To kick things off, Humphrey read a simple note from Zeke: "Y'all this is the last party I'll get to throw. Have fun, and if anybody tries to give a speech about me, toss 'em out for me, would you?" Humphrey wore a sad smile. Something about him seemed broken. Could he possibly have killed his friend?

When Humphrey climbed off the stage, Blake and his band, the Back Porch Prophets, started playing. They alternated sets with a DJ so they could enjoy the party too. John and Alma Glendawn had put together a buffet to Zeke's specifications, and it had all his favorites: Caribbean shredded pork, black beans, saffron rice, fried plantains, shrimp and grits, cold peel-and-eat shrimp, Lowcountry Boil, and fried oysters. For dessert there was pineapple pudding or homemade ice cream. And there was an open bar. As Zeke had wanted, there was food, revelry, dancing, and liquor. Mamma didn't quite know what to make of it.

Tammy's one contribution to the event, which Zeke had perhaps not thought to forbid, was a photo montage of Zeke projected on the wall above the stage. Because he'd been so camera shy for the last thirty years, most of the pictures were from the first eighteen years of his life.

Zeke at about eight or nine with a group of kids in front of a massive sandcastle. Early teen Zeke, tall and lanky, with a proud grin and a big fish. Zeke in a baseball uniform, jumping and stretching to make a catch. Zeke in the same uniform sliding in to home plate. The images changed every ten seconds. From the distance of time, Zeke's childhood and teenage years looked idyllic. Were they?

Nate and I sat at a table overlooking the ocean with Mamma and Daddy, Blake, Tammy Sue, and my friend Calista, who was the most recent in a long line of Blake's former girlfriends. The DJ was playing, so Blake had a break, and we were feasting off plates piled high. Tammy's family hadn't made it to town after all, according to Tammy, because she wasn't having a "real funeral."

About the only person in town not at the party was Clay Cooper, who was still tailing the Elliotts, who were at the party. Clay was across the street in a rental car. Judge Johnson had told Blake he'd take his request for a search warrant under advisement. He wasn't a fan of anonymous tips, and Charlie Jacobs was an old friend. We were in a holding pattern, which made me antsy. Whether Price or Humphrey had killed Zeke or someone else had, it was almost a certainty the killer was in the room.

I took a sip of my margarita.

Mamma eyed me from across the table, her porcelain features drawn with consternation. "I declare, I've never heard of such. Serving liquor at a memorial service? This is sacred. But I don't want to be rude." Her strawberry daiquiri remained untouched.

"We have to honor Zeke's wishes, Mamma," I said. "But you surely don't have to drink if you don't want to. Zeke wouldn't want you to be uncomfortable."

"Wouldn't make any sense to be the only sober people

here," said Daddy, always the pragmatist.

Mamma looked at him sideways, shook her head. "Zeke was a character, sure enough. But he was a good-hearted soul. I declare I'll miss him."

"Carolyn, you'd best be careful not to make a speech," Daddy said. "I'd hate to have to escort you out."

"I'd like to see you try," she said mildly.

Calista's eyes twinkled mischievously. "Let's get the DJ to play that Don Henley song Liz likes so much...'All She Wants to do is Dance.'"

"No," Blake and Nate said together.

I might've gotten a teensy bit tipsy and danced on a table to that song a time or two. But never when Mamma was around. I was in no danger of getting that relaxed with Mamma here. I rolled my eyes at Nate and Blake.

"Is Heather not coming?" I asked Blake.

"Nah. She didn't know Zeke," he said.

I caught Calista's eye as I stood. Was she going to take advantage of an opportunity to reconnect with Blake? "I'm going to get another margarita. Anyone else want one?"

"I'll get it," said Nate.

"Thank you, sweetheart. But I need to stretch, walk around." I rubbed his arm.

The DJ was taking requests but had been filling in with Zeke's favorites, which were heavy on Genesis and Fleetwood Mac. At that moment, he was playing "The Chain." It was a great song, but nobody could dance to that. Everyone was clustered around chatting over the music.

Heads turned when April walked in the door. She wore a skin tight black dress that Mamma would no doubt tsk over and red cowboy boots. She looked fabulous. And she had Sergei the Georgian on her arm—or she was on his.

I made my way through the crowd to say hey and get an introduction. April caught my eye and grinned. She said something to Sergei and they headed towards me.

"Hey, April," I said. "Good to see you." I offered Sergei my sunniest smile.

Sergei was tall, dark, handsome, and smooth. "Sergei Ivanov. Delighted to make your acquaintance."

"Nice to meet you, Sergei." I offered him my hand. "I'm Liz Talbot."

"Sergei knows Zeke from way back," said April.

"Really? How far back? Sergei, did you meet Zeke when he was in the army?"

"Yes." He smiled and nodded.

"And you came all the way from—where are you from, exactly?—for Zeke's service?" I kept smiling. Butter wouldn't've melted in my mouth. But I wasn't going to miss this opportunity.

"Originally from Georgia," said Sergei. "But I live in Charleston at present."

"Do tell?" I tilted my head, looked up at him. "What brings you to the South Carolina Lowcountry?"

"Job relocation. April, dear, would you like a drink?"

"Yeah, thanks, Sergei. That's a good idea. I'd like a shot of Patron—or the best Tequila they have. Zeke and I used to drink shots of Patron. Seems fitting."

"Of course. I'll be right back." Sergei smiled and moved towards the bar.

"He was a friend of Zeke's?" I asked.

"They had a complicated relationship," said April.

"Is that why you went to meet with him yesterday after I left your apartment?"

"Well." She gave me an appraising look. "Perhaps I

underestimated you. Yes, that's why I went to meet him. I needed to make sure he had nothing to do with Zeke's death."

"Why would you think he might?" I asked.

"Listen up," she said. "There's a bunch I can't tell you, okay? But what you need to know is this: Sergei's interest here is me. Period. He's had the hots for me for years, and most of the drama between him and Zeke was related to that. But he would've had no reason to want Zeke dead. We'd been divorced for years, and Zeke was a happily married man."

Well, mostly happy. "You're absolutely convinced he had nothing to do with Zeke's death?"

"Absolutely," she said.

"How can you be sure of that?" I asked.

"Because I'm highly trained to read people," she said. "And because he was at a Chris Botti concert at the Charleston Music Hall Monday evening."

"How do you know that?"

"I have ways of finding out, okay? And you need to remember, I was a helluva lot closer to Zeke than you, so if you think I'd cover for anybody, you're crazy as hell."

"And he's here as your date?"

"Hell no," she said. "He'd like that, yeah. He's here to pay his respects, like everyone else."

I mulled all of that for a minute. It would've been easier if Zeke had been killed by a foreign agent of some sort. That would've meant someone we all knew hadn't killed one of our own. But my instincts told me that was exactly what had happened. "We're at that table in the corner." I pointed, wondered briefly what the etiquette rules were for wives and ex-wives at funerals, and decided all that went out the window when Zeke hired the DJ.

"We'll stop by and pay our respects to Tammy." Her eyes

were glued to the stage. No, the picture of Zeke above it. "I've never seen these." Her voice was softer than I'd heard it, seemed almost wistful. "Who is that?"

The photo was of Zeke at maybe thirteen with another blonde. Both kids were barefoot, all tanned legs and arms and sun-streaked hair. His arm was wrapped around her shoulder and she looked up at him, her expression averted. He grinned at the camera. Was that Brenda? It was hard to tell, but I'd bet it was Brenda, the original sassy blonde in Zeke's life, the root of the attraction. The picture changed.

"I didn't recognize her," I said.

"Some things never change." She seemed to snap out of her reverie. "What the hell is that DJ playin'? That Zeke." April shook her head. "He loved Fleetwood Mac. Only the Stevie Nicks years, though. We got to get this guy to play some dancin' music. Ima go talk to him soon as I get my drink. Then I'll see you over there."

"I need another margarita myself." I moved towards the bar.

As I made my way through the crowd, I caught sight of Crystal Chapman. In a black dress, she hovered near the edge of the dance floor across the room from our table where Tammy Sue sat. Crystal seemed to be keeping her distance, which was a good idea. Who was she talking to? The person to her right leaned in as if to hear her better. Price Elliott. Good grief, what were the two of them talking about?

John Glendawn was behind the bar with Coy. He also had two extra bartenders that night. They all stayed plenty busy. I ordered my margarita and continued scanning the crowd.

Margie Robinson stood beside me, waiting for her drink. She smiled. "Hey, Liz."

"Hey, Margie. How are you?"

"Like everyone else, I guess. A little sad, but I want to celebrate the way Zeke wanted. Honor his wishes."

The bartender set down both our drinks at the same time.

"Want to get some air?" she asked.

"Sure." I'd been trying to talk to her for days, but hadn't been able to get to it. This might be better. She'd be less guarded since she'd asked me to walk outside with her. I wasn't interviewing her, exactly.

We walked through the crowd, out the french doors to the deck.

"That's better," Margie said as the doors closed behind us.

The night was clear and warm. The sky looked like diamonds on black velvet.

She picked a spot against the rail overlooking the ocean. It was too dark for much of a view, but moonlight reflected off the waves, and their cadence worked a soothing magic.

"I'll miss Zeke," Margie said.

"Me too."

"I'm in a melancholy mood, I guess," she said. "To be expected under the circumstances. But..."

Clearly, Margie wanted to talk, which worked out well for me.

"What's wrong?"

"I just feel somehow responsible," she said.

"How could you be responsible for Zeke's death?" I asked.

She laughed softly. "I didn't kill him, I promise. It's just...everything changed after this party we had back in March."

"The bonfire?" I asked.

"You heard about that?"

"Just that Crystal snared Zeke there," I said.

Margie nodded. "She did. I thought maybe I should talk to Tammy about it. But I figured she knew. And how do you talk to a friend about that kind of thing, especially if you feel liable."

"Crystal and Zeke were both adults," I said. "I hear that was quite a party."

"It was."

"I heard you played some interesting games," I said.

She closed her eyes. "Who told you about that?"

"I can't reveal my sources."

"We were all having fun. But things went sideways after the Truth or Dare."

I was right. "I haven't played that since high school."

"Yeah, none of us had either. It was stupid. It was my idea. I thought it would be a bonding thing. It seemed to have the opposite effect."

"What do you mean? What happened?"

"We all trotted out stuff better left unsaid. Humphrey's in love with a married woman—like no one knew that. Winter has some wild fantasies I'm betting Spencer wishes she'd kept quiet about. And poor Zeke..."

"What did he tell?"

"Do you remember Harold Yates, the plumber who died a few years ago?"

For simplicity's sake, I said I did.

"Zeke told us a story about tricking him into standing in a field all day. Zeke was only thirteen. Harold believed in UFOs. It's a long story. He missed a whole day of work. Zeke still felt guilty after all those years. He thought he was the reason Harold died a lonely man. I personally don't think it was that simple. But after he told that story, the group just broke up. He went for a walk on the beach. Crystal went after him. The mood of the party changed. Honestly, I don't think any of us have been the same since."

"I'm sure you're reading too much into it," I said. "It just seems that way because something happened to Zeke."

"Maybe you're right," she said.

"Margie, how long did you know Zeke?"

She shrugged. "Most of my life. He was four years ahead of me in school."

"How about Brenda Carter?" I asked.

"Brenda? She's one of my closest friends."

"I understand she and Zeke dated all through school."

"They were inseparable as far back as I can remember. It started way before dating. They always had a special bond. Zeke's first wife, April. I saw her earlier. She reminds me of Brenda."

"Did Zeke have a thing for blondes?"

"No, I wouldn't say that exactly. It's more the fire inside. They are both blonde, of course."

"So is Crystal," I said. "And that just confuses the hell out of me."

"What do you mean?"

"Everything points to Zeke adored his wife," I said.

"I think he did," said Margie. "But Zeke had a restless spirit. He was happy coming home, building a life here. And he was happy with Tammy Sue. But once in a while, I think he just got a little crazy. And yeah, Crystal was his type."

"It's just hard for me to understand a man who loves his wife being unfaithful."

"People often do things that make no sense to the rest of us," she said. "The challenge is to love them anyway. I like to think Tammy Sue would've forgiven Zeke."

"I think she has," I said.

We enjoyed the air and the stars for a few more minutes.

"I'm going to head back in," I said.

"I'll be in shortly."

I rubbed her arm and went inside.

The DJ was playing "Watch Me" by Silento, and the dance floor was full of folks doing the whip and nae nae.

I didn't see April at the table as I made my way back. Were things awkward between her and Tammy Sue? Where was Crystal, and what was she up to? I scanned the room, then took my seat.

"Where'd Blake run off to?" I asked.

Nate said, "He went to dance with April."

Mamma looked profoundly unhappy.

Daddy grinned from ear to ear. "Red Bird, you'd better have a sip of that strawberry daiquiri."

"What about Calista?" I asked.

"She's dancing with Sergei, that foreign fella with April," said Daddy.

TWENTY-TWO

Our morning runs are therapeutic. More than that, sucking in all that oxygen helps me process things. The next morning, it was still pitch black as we sprinted past Sullivan's Bed & Breakfast, around the north point of the island, and then south along the Intracoastal Waterway towards the marina.

"We're not racing here," said Nate.

I ran faster, not to be contrary, but to work out my tension. Nate matched my pace. Rhett raced on ahead, as was his custom.

It was only a little after five. We hadn't been running long. I was still pent up.

"What's eating at you?" asked Nate.

"I'm missing something," I said. "It's not Sergei. It's not Price. And it's surely not Tammy Sue. And I really don't think it's Coy. Or Crystal, for that matter."

"This is a hunch?" said Nate.

"Yeah." My feet pounded the sand, then the asphalt as we cut across the marina parking lot. I suppressed a shudder as the dream flitted across my mind. I shoved it aside.

"I'm normally a fan of your hunches," said Nate. "But in this particular case, we have several good suspects, and one of them had access to our murder weapon."

"I know," I said. "But I won't rest until I kick over a few more rocks."

"What can I do to help?" asked Nate.

"I'm pondering it," I said.

We crossed back into the sand beyond the marina. It was far enough behind us that the lights from the parking lot no longer broke the pre-dawn dark. The blackness was thicker here on the west side of the island, but our path was well-worn, familiar. Nothing stirred but us in the soft morning air.

Before long we approached Heron Creek. Weeping willows, live oaks, and mimosa trees crowded its banks, their mass turning the horizon in front of us a deeper shade of black. The sand gave way to grass. This was where we turned around every day. I pulled up to take a sip of water.

Nate stopped too, but Rhett ran past us and darted through the tree line to the creek.

"He's going to get all nasty," I said.

"Rhett," Nate called.

Rhett went to barking like a hound of hell.

"What in the world?" I turned back to face the creek.

Crack. The noise pierced the morning quiet.

Something whizzed by my head.

A bullet.

Another crack.

Rhett barked relentlessly.

"Get down," yelled Nate.

There was nowhere to take cover. I flattened myself to the ground. "Nate?"

"Are you all right?" He was to my left.

Crack.

"Yeah. You good?"

"For the moment. Hard to tell where it's coming from," he said.

"The creek. Rhett! *Come!*" I couldn't see him for the trees. I only knew he was okay because he was still barking.

Crack.

"We're pinned," said Nate. "Keep your head down."

Crack.

A bullet hit the grass next to my ear.

"Shit," I said. "*Rhett*! Here boy."

"We can't stay here," said Nate. "We've got to move."

"All right," I said.

"Roll towards the water. Fast. Go."

I rolled hard. I rolled as fast as I could. Scrubby grass, stones, and sticks littered the ground. I plowed over everything.

Crack.

"When you hit the water...dive and swim towards the marina," said Nate. He was still to my left. I would go into the Intracoastal Waterway first.

Crack.

It seemed like I rolled for an hour. I was disoriented. Was I even moving in the right direction anymore? Finally, the ground tapered off and I spun down a bank and into the water. Thank God it was high tide. If we'd landed in mud and swamp grass, it would've been over right then. I wriggled around and pushed myself farther into the waterway, then pushed off the bottom and scooped big circles of brine with my arms. I dove and swam north.

Seconds later I felt movement in the water beside me. Nate.

I broke the surface and gasped for air.

"Stay down," he said.

I ducked back under and kept swimming. The current was with us, but the water was black. I felt claustrophobic in a way I never do in the water. I tamped down panic. Panic could get you killed in the water.

The next time I surfaced, I flipped onto my back and looked

towards Heron Creek. We'd put two piers with Boston Whalers tied off between us and whoever was shooting at us. There was no sign of anyone. Rhett was still barking. I flipped and swam in an adrenaline-fueled fast crawl towards the marina.

When the boat slips at Robinson's came into view, my tension eased.

"Second pier," Nate called.

I swam past the first row of boat slips, towards a ladder at the end of the second dock.

I grabbed the ladder and pulled myself to it, gasping.

Nate pulled up beside me, sucking in air. "Are you okay?"

"Yes. Are you?"

"I'm fine. Let's move to the houseboat. Stay low."

We climbed the ladder and crouched as we moved quickly onto Blake's floating home. I sat on the teak rail and swung my legs over. Nate climbed over behind me. I banged three times on the wood and glass door, then tried the knob.

It was locked.

I rattled the knob and banged harder. Had our assailant pursued us?

"Coming." The door swung open. Blake gaped at me. He was dressed, but his hair was still wet from the shower. "The hell? Liz?"

We pushed past him.

"Close the door," I said.

We collapsed on the built-in sofa.

"Are you guys all right?" Blake asked.

"I think so." I was still panting. "Rhett." I looked at Nate.

"What happened? You're soaking wet, scraped all over..." Blake stepped into the bathroom and returned seconds later with a stack of towels. "You've got..." he leaned in, looked closer "...sand spurs in your hair."

I wrapped a towel around me. "Thanks." My teeth chattered, more from shock than cold.

Nate held his side. "Our morning run was rudely interrupted by a shooter beyond the tree line at Heron Creek."

Blake looked me up and down. "Are you sure you're all right?"

"I'm fine. Whoever that was, the gunshots were muffled. I mean, they were loud, but not as loud as they should've been."

"Definitely a sound suppressor," said Nate.

Guns weren't always silenced as much as it seemed on TV. It depended on the equipment. But the sound could be deadened significantly. "The shots came from above," I said. "He was in a tree."

Nate said, "And he must've had night vision goggles or a scope. It's too black over by Heron Creek this time of morning to hope to shoot somebody otherwise."

"You rattled somebody's cage," said Blake. "Whose?"

"I don't know," I said. "Price Elliott is likely the most perturbed. But this doesn't feel like something Price would do. The last person I interviewed was Humphrey Pearson, but it's hard to imagine him with a gun."

Blake turned to Nate. Alarm washed over Blake's face. "You've been hit."

I spun to Nate. His towel was turning red, his hand bloody where he'd been holding his side. A stain spread across his shirt.

White hot pain hit me in a wave. I tasted metal. We were at the marina. Nate was in trouble. Dizzy. I was so dizzy. Get a grip. Get a grip. *Get a grip.*

"Oh my God," I said. "We've got to get you to the hospital." I stood.

Shock bleached Nate's tanned face. He stared at his hand unbelieving.

Blake grabbed his keys with one hand and his phone with the other. "Doc Harper's closer. Nate, you okay to get to the car?"

"Yeah." He shook his head, seemed dazed. "I didn't realize I'd been shot."

Blake spoke into the phone. "Coop, get over to Heron Creek. Take Rodney and Sam with you. We had a shooter this morning. Up in a tree. Find him. And be on the lookout for my sister's golden retriever."

Blake took Nate's arm and ducked under it. "Let's move."

Nate staggered to a stand.

I moved in on his other side. He kept his right arm close to his body, his hand pressing the towel against his abdomen. The blood. Oh dear God. The blood. I slipped an arm around his waist.

"I'm the first one through that door," said Blake.

The three of us moved sideways out the door, looking for movement. The sky was lightening. A boat engine started. I craned my neck to see. Just a fisherman heading out. The lights inside the marina store were on now. Clay Cooper's siren howled, still blocks away.

We moved as quickly as we could to Blake's Tahoe. Nate was getting weaker, slowing down. My heart pounded so loud I could barely hear Blake's voice.

"Nate, let's get you in the back." Blake swung open the back passenger door.

"Roger that." Nate's voice slurred. He winced as he lifted a leg to climb inside the SUV.

Blake helped him in, then he was on the phone. "Doc, I'll be there in five with my brother-in-law. He's got a gunshot wound to his right side."

I ran around the car, crawled in the other door, and

slammed it shut. Nate leaned over in the seat, towards the center. His face was ashen, grim. He was out of breath. I slid my arm around him. "Drive, Blake. *Drive.*"

I was terrified, shaking.

"Slugger, I'll be fine. This isn't anything but a scratch."

"Shh. Hush now. Rest."

The Tahoe shot out of the parking lot. I prayed quietly, but fervently. *Father God, save my husband, your servant, Nate. Heal his body.*

How long had we been in the water? How long had he been bleeding?

A silver aura filled the backseat, bathing us in light.

Colleen.

I felt a surge of hope mixed with anger. *How could you let this happen?*

She faded in, but remained transparent. Her eyes were moist. "Keep praying. We'll talk later."

"What the hell is—?" Blake drifted right, then jerked the steering wheel back center.

"It's fine," I said. "Please just drive."

Nate mumbled something I couldn't make out. At least he was still conscious.

Colleen put one hand on Nate and one on me. Shimmers of soft gold and white swirled around us. And we prayed.

Blake's phone rang. He answered it hands free.

"Drive to the parking lot at the high school," said Doc Harper. "A Medicare helicopter will meet us there. We're going to MUSC. Can't take any chances with a gunshot to the torso."

"Roger that." Blake made a hard left. Then a right. Minutes later we turned into the school parking lot.

Doc Harper was waiting for us. He ran to the car as Blake pulled to a stop.

Colleen turned off the special effects but stayed in the back of the car with us, perched on the console.

Blake popped the door lock. Doc opened the door to check on Nate.

He looked at the wound, took his pulse. "Looks like the bullet passed through. We need to do some imaging, see what's hit."

"Scratch," said Nate.

"Maybe so," said Doc Harper. "But we can't bank on that. We're going to take good care of you. How much pain are you in on a scale of one to ten?"

Nate's eyes fluttered shut.

"*Nate.* No. No. No. Stay awake with me, sweetheart."

"He's passed out," said Doc Harper. "Might be for the best."

And then I heard the rhythmic thrum of the helicopter approaching. It hovered over us, then descended to the parking lot. The rails had barely touched the asphalt when the door slid open and a medical crew sprung out.

Everything that happened next was a blur.

Nate on a stretcher, unconscious.

The medics examining him—taking his vitals, calling things to each other in a language I couldn't decipher.

Them lifting him into the helicopter.

Blake and me climbing in after him.

Colleen crying and telling me to keep praying.

And the helicopter rising above the island, then shooting through the dawn sky towards Charleston, leaving Colleen in Stella Maris.

TWENTY-THREE

That morning aged me by ten years. It seemed surreal. Blake and I moved from one waiting room to another as they ran tests to see if Nate needed surgery. Blake called Mamma and Daddy and Merry—neither Nate nor I had so much as our cell phones with us.

Because I asked him to, somehow, Blake convinced them to stay put until we knew more. It was my family's protocol that everyone gathered at the hospital if any one of us was having more than a routine test. I wanted them there, needed the comfort of family around me. But some part of me felt like as long as we weren't all in the waiting room, it couldn't be life-threatening. I kept praying.

By some miracle of an answered prayer, the bullet missed Nate's organs. It wasn't a scratch. But it wasn't a mortal injury either. They cleaned the wound and stitched him up. The doctor wanted to keep him overnight, but Nate was adamant.

"If they keep me here," he said, "nothing will drag you away. That's the way you operate."

He was right. As long as he was in that hospital, I would be by his side. No matter how good the medical center, I held a conviction that patients with an advocate on hand got better care. Finding Zeke's killer—and who shot Nate—was important to me. But if I had to choose between Nate's welfare and any case, he would win every time. "I won't apologize for that."

"No need. I'd do the same if the situation were reversed. But I can't be lying about while Zeke's killer absconds to parts unknown. And even if I could talk you into going back to work, they'd have to knock me out to keep me here while you chased a killer. The only solution here is I'm going home."

The doctor wasn't happy. But after Nate signed and initialed a forty-seven-page release, we left with antibiotics, painkillers, and discharge instructions.

Blake was exasperated. He agreed with the doctor and thought Nate and I were being foolhardy. Nate was loopy on painkillers, and I was crazy with relief. The three of us laughed at the absurdity of Ubering from the hospital to the ferry dock on Isle of Palms, where Clay Cooper picked us up in his patrol car.

"I dropped Rhett off at your house an hour ago," Clay said. "Found him wandering around Sea Farm. He's fine."

"Oh, thank goodness," I said. "Thank you so much, Clay."

"Happy to help," said Clay. "I wondered if he'd tailed your shooter home, but Rhett, he wasn't talking."

"About the shooter..." said Blake.

Coop shook his head. "He'd cleared out by the time we got over to Heron Creek. We found a piece of navy fabric snagged on a live oak and two shell casings in the brush. Looks like he climbed up in the tree all right."

When Blake finally dropped us off at the house, Rhett ran out to greet us. I looked him over from head to tail.

"Are you all right, boy?" I hugged him tight. "Good boy. You're such a good boy."

"*E-liz-a-beth Su-zanne Tal-bot.*" Mamma stood at the top of our porch steps looking down, her expression heavy with worry. "Are you all right?"

"I'm fine, Mamma." I'd called her from the hospital. Daddy and Tammy Sue hovered behind her.

"Then bring your husband inside," Mamma said. "Rhett is perfectly fine. I've given him some chicken. You and Nate need food."

"Carolyn, I'm so happy to see you." Nate climbed out of Blake's Tahoe. "I haven't eaten all day." He shot me a playful grin.

Mamma's look accused me of being an unfit wife.

"The doctors wouldn't let him eat until they'd thoroughly checked him out, Mamma."

Her gaze didn't let me off the hook that easily. "What exactly did the doctors say?"

I'd already told her this on the phone, the second time I called. Blake, Nate, and I climbed the steps.

Nate said, "The bullet went straight through. Just a flesh wound. A scratch, really. Didn't hit anything important. They patched me up. I've got a couple prescriptions. I'll be good as new in no time. Unless I starve." Again with the grin. He was playing to Mamma.

"I've got a late lunch inside," Mamma checked him out good, hugged him hard, then led us all indoors.

"Mamma, I've got to get a shower," I said. "I'm too nasty to be in the house."

She scrutinized me, must've seen the truth of what I said. "Hurry up," she said. "The food will be cold."

I watched Nate like a hawk all the way up the steps, afraid he was going to faint from blood loss or infection or some damn thing. When we made it to our bathroom, I breathed a sigh of relief.

I turned on the shower, got the water warm. "I'm not sure

about that waterproof bandage."

"It's tight as a drum," he said. "I need a shower." He had that mulish look on his face again.

"Fine," I said, "you go first."

He raised an eyebrow. "What, you're not going to wash me?"

I gave him a quelling look. "Mamma and Daddy are downstairs." Then I hugged him tight, held onto him. "Are you really okay?"

"I really am."

"I'm worried Colleen must've been reassigned. I can't believe she wasn't there," I said.

"But she was there in the car," said Nate. "Or did I dream that?"

"No. She was there. But why wasn't she there to keep you from getting shot?"

"The way she tackled you in Charleston a while back?"

"Exactly," I said.

"I guess it was a wake-up call. We can't depend on her to always run interference. Maybe we've gotten sloppy."

We were both famished. We showered and changed and were back downstairs in record time. Nate moved gingerly, slowly, but he wouldn't hear a word about being waited on.

We ate in the dining room. It had been four years since Gram left me the beach house. This was the first time we'd eaten a family meal at the dining room table that had seen so many happy family memories. It was time. Daddy sat in Gram's place at the head of the table and Mamma spent extra time thanking God before we ate. Tears of gratitude slipped down my face as she prayed.

"Liz, are you going to fix Nate a plate?" asked Mamma.

"Of course." I averted my face and wiped my cheeks as I

rose.

Nate put a hand on my arm. "Please sit down. You're exhausted and haven't eaten yourself. Carolyn, if you don't mind, I'd like to pick my own chicken. Liz doesn't put near enough on my plate. Unfortunately, she's prejudiced against fried foods."

"Certainly," said Mamma. "Frank, pass Nate the chicken."

Daddy handed the turkey platter, piled high with fried chicken, to me. "When you children get some food in you, I'd like to hear exactly what happened." His tone notified me that this was not an idle request.

"Of course, Daddy." I set the platter between Nate and me. "Have all you want."

He grinned at me.

We were all quiet for a few minutes as we heaped chicken, mashed potatoes, biscuits and gravy, green beans, sliced tomatoes, butter peas, and fried squash on our plates. I cheerfully poured gravy all over my potatoes and my biscuit.

Tammy Sue sat across from me, next to Blake. "I just hate that Nate was hurt. Somehow I feel responsible for all of this."

"Nonsense," said Mamma. "How on earth are you responsible for what some reprehensible scoundrel did? It's hard to believe such things going on here in Stella Maris." She shook her head.

"Y'all were out for your morning run?" Daddy prompted.

"That's right," said Nate. "We were closing in on Heron Creek when someone in a tree along the bank opened fire. We're reasonably sure they were using a sound suppressor and night vision equipment."

I told Daddy about the fabric in the tree and the shell casings Clay Cooper had found.

"Up in a tree," mused Daddy. "Not everybody can climb a

tree."

I mulled that. "Did you take custody of Zeke's guns? The...accessories?"

"Yeah. Everything's locked up," said Blake.

"His shotguns? Why would you lock up his shotguns?" asked Daddy.

Blake, Nate, and I shared a look. We hadn't told Mamma and Daddy about the number and variety of weapons in Zeke's gun collection.

"Well, it's not like I need to shoot something," said Tammy Sue. "I've never fired a gun in my life."

Blake looked at her. "How is that even possible? Being married to Zeke?"

"I just don't care for guns." Tammy broke off a bite of biscuit and smeared it with butter.

"Who can blame you?" said Mamma.

"Whoever was shooting at us had to have night vision goggles or a scope," I said. "There's no way he could've seen us otherwise. And the shots sounded loud, but not nearly loud enough."

"Agreed," said Nate. "The shooter used a sound suppressor. Who else on the island owns that kind of equipment?"

Blake grimaced. "I wouldn't've thought anyone had it. Island's too small for that kind of hunting."

"Unless you're part of the hog reduction team." I'd lost all patience with Daddy's secret impeding me getting a straight answer. "Daddy, who else was working with Zeke?"

"Working with Zeke to do what?" Daddy worked hard to look innocent, but came up short.

"Frank." Mamma eyed him. "What is she talking about?"

Daddy gave me a look that promised we'd talk about this later. "Now, I did hear that Zeke was working on thinning the feral hog population, if that's what you're talking about."

Mamma shuddered. "Oh my goodness. Surely not."

"I'm afraid so, Carolyn," said Tammy Sue. "He was convinced they were a threat to agriculture, our parks, our yards. He was working for the mayor."

"Tammy," I said. "Was he doing that at night?"

"Well, yes," she said. "He said that's when they were active."

Blake said, "He use night vision scopes? Goggles?"

"That's right." Tammy Sue might've saved Daddy's skin by mentioning the mayor but no one else involved in the hog project.

"Do you know if anyone else was working with him at night?" I asked.

"He never mentioned it to me if they were," said Tammy.

"Dad?" asked Blake.

"How would I know?" He studied the bite of food on his fork.

"Frank," said Mamma. "Don't think for a minute I believe your hands are clean in this."

Irritation flooded Daddy's face. "As far as I know he was working alone. He liked hunting alone."

"Well," Nate said. "Looks like we're closer than we thought. Someone is spooked."

Blake nodded. "Price Elliott. I called Judge Johnson and told him what happened this morning. We've got our warrant."

"No," I said. "I'm telling you, it wasn't Price. Do you really see him at five in the morning, climbing a tree with an automatic rifle? Blake, he plays video games."

"All the more reason," Blake said. "Those things desensitize you to violence."

I shook my head. "We need to look for someone who had access to the strychnine and a gun with a night scope or goggles—and who knew how to use the gun. We can figure out the motive. There can't be more than one person on this island who could've put their hands on both those weapons."

Blake stood, wrapped a biscuit in a napkin. "Until you have a better idea, I'm locking Price Elliott up right now."

"Fine, hard head," I said. "I'm coming with you."

"We'll be right behind you." Nate winced as he negotiated himself out of his chair.

He needed to be in bed. "Sweetheart—"

"Nate Andrews," Mamma said. "I am not having this. Uh-uh. No. You need your rest. Elizabeth, if you have more important things to take care of, your father and I can stay here."

Nate's eyes grew, sought mine. His look said, *Help.*

"She's right," I said. "I'll stay here."

He closed his eyes, gave his head a little shake. "No. Go on now. Kick over some rocks. Let me know what you find. And Liz?"

"Yes?"

"You've got your weapon, right?"

"It's in the car," I said. "It's been too hot for a jacket to cover a holster. I'll swap out my purse so I can carry it with me."

TWENTY-FOUR

Blake and Clay Cooper searched the Elliott home for gopher bait. I waited in the family room with Glenda, Grant, and Price.

"I don't understand this," said Glenda for the third time.

"Is Kelsey out of town?" I asked. Kelsey was their daughter. I didn't suspect her of anything, but I was methodically compiling a list of anyone who had access to the strychnine.

"She's studying abroad this summer," said Grant.

Blake didn't waste much time. He knew where the gopher bait was. Nate had told him. We heard footsteps on the steps leading from the garage below the house into the kitchen. Blake stepped into the room.

"I'm removing two bags of Gopher 50 from the premises," he said. "One of them has been opened and is half empty. Grant, could I get you to sign this form?"

Grant's face creased. "Come on, Blake. Is that what this is all about? The gopher bait? Good grief. Half empty?"

"Sign here, please," said Blake.

"This is ridiculous." Grant shook his head, but signed the form.

"Grant," I said. "Where did you purchase the gopher bait?"

He ran a hand through his hair. I'd seen Price use the same mannerism. "I had my brother get it for me. He lives in Florida. You can't have it shipped to South Carolina. I've tried everything they have at Island Hardware, and everything they have at Lowes. I can't get rid of the damn gophers. I asked my brother to help me out. I was desperate. Surely you've got bigger things to worry about." He looked at Blake hard.

"I don't think I do," said Blake. "Do you have any firearms in the house?"

Grant said, "Yeah, I have a shotgun and two hunting rifles in the bedroom closet. Why?"

Blake said, "Master on this floor?"

"Yeah," said Grant. "Right through there."

Blake nodded at Cooper, who went to retrieve the guns. "Is that it?"

"Yeah," said Grant.

"Any accessories?"

Grant screwed up his face. "Accessories?"

"Do you own any night vision goggles or scopes or any sound suppressors, anything like that?" asked Blake.

Glenda paled, looked at Grant.

"No, of course not," said Grant.

"I'm going to finish looking around downstairs," said Blake. "Clay Cooper will be up here. This may take a while. I need the keys to your cars, please."

"I don't understand," said Grant. "I thought this was about the gopher killer." He handed Blake his keys.

"We'll finish as quick as we can," said Blake.

Clay walked back through the room with the family shotgun and hunting rifles. He logged them, had Grant sign a receipt, and carried them outside.

"Grant, Glenda," I said. "Price...were y'all all home early this morning, between five and six?"

"Glenda and I didn't get up until seven thirty," said Grant. "It's Saturday. Price slept 'til lunchtime."

"Do you have an alarm system?" I asked.

"No," said Grant.

"Was anyone else here?" I asked.

"Just the three of us," said Grant.

"Did anyone else know you bought the gopher bait?" I asked.

"No," Grant shook his head. "I haven't mentioned it to anyone. Have you, Glen?"

"No," said Glenda.

"Has anyone had the occasion to be in your garage, where they might have seen it?" I asked.

They were quiet for a moment. Finally, Glenda said, "It's been a while...back towards the first of April, maybe. Brenda and Pete were over for dinner. They left through the garage because it was raining so hard. The door was just a few feet from where they parked. But they'd never..." She looked away.

"Was the gopher bait in the garage that long ago?" Brenda's name kept popping up. But it seemed unlikely that Zeke's high school girlfriend had decided to take revenge for some long ago crime or a recent slight when they'd lived as friends and neighbors for nearly ten years. What motive would she have had?

"Yeah," said Grant. "I picked it up middle of March. Three bags. I used one of 'em. Figured I should get plenty while I was getting it."

"Anyone else in your garage since then?" I asked. "Price, have any of your friends been down there?"

He looked sullen, but not worried. If he'd had any inkling someone thought he'd used that poison—if he even knew the gopher killer was poison—to kill someone, surely he'd be nervous. "Nope," he said.

Grant said, "Humphrey helped me carry in my new grill

table a few weeks back."

"Humphrey Pearson?" There was only one Humphrey I knew of on the island. Still.

Grant nodded. "Yeah, but he...I mean Humphrey wouldn't...I have no idea what you think we've done beyond surreptitiously ordering gopher killer."

Damnation. Humphrey. Humphrey with a gun? That was a hard notion to subscribe to. But people had surprised me a time or two. Aside from Price, Humphrey had the closest thing approaching a motive of those who had access to the poison. And he'd lied to me. He had something to hide.

For the next couple hours, I tried to engage the Elliotts in conversation, which was difficult given the circumstances. Finally, at a few minutes past six, Blake and Clay came back into the family room.

"Grant, Glenda." Blake nodded, took a deep breath. "We removed the items you've signed for, nothing more. We'll get them back to you as soon as we can." He turned to Price. "Keaton Price Elliott, you have the right to remain silent..."

Glenda gasped. "Blake. What in this world?"

Grant said, "Now hold on a damn minute."

Blake proceeded to read Price his rights.

For his part, Price finally looked alert, but also confused.

Blake said, "You're under arrest for the murder of Zeke Lyerly."

Grant and Glenda both jumped to their feet.

Price went to stuttering—all the cool evaporated right off of him.

"Price, shut up," said Grant. "That's just damned crazy."

"I'm calling Daddy," said Glenda.

This was going to kill Charlie Jacobs.

Blake cuffed Price and led him out.

"Price," said Grant. "Don't answer any questions, you hear me, son? Don't say a word. Not. One. Word. I'm calling Robert Pearson."

"Maybe call a different attorney," I said.

"What?" Glenda said. "Why?"

"Robert represents Zeke's estate, and also Tammy Sue Lyerly. There may be a conflict of interest," I said.

"Liz..." Glenda was sobbing now. "You need to keep investigating. Keep looking. I'm telling you, Price could not possibly have killed anyone."

Grant said, "Call your Daddy, Glenda. Let's see what he says about an attorney."

I said my goodbyes and showed myself out.

TWENTY-FIVE

Seven p.m. is magic hour on our island in June. The sun wouldn't set for another hour and a half, but softening light bathed the foam-topped waves in shades of pink and gold. Humphrey Pearson had a front-row seat to the show every night.

His wide front porch, rustic shutters, metal roof, and blue front door welcomed me inside. Humphrey wasn't home, but I accepted the invitation anyway.

I made quick work of picking the lock, stepped through the door, and closed it behind me. I had no idea where Humphrey was, or when he would be back. As unlikely as it seemed, I had to entertain the notion that he'd shot at me just that morning. I was on edge.

Humphrey had a crush on Tammy Sue. It seemed common knowledge in their circle of friends. I wouldn't put it past Zeke to've kept Humphrey close so he could keep an eye on his old friend. But had Humphrey decided he was tired of waiting on Tammy? He had access to the poison—Nate had walked right inside the Elliott's garage. Humphrey knew their schedule. He could've helped himself at any time.

Nate had already searched the shed out back. I focused on the house, looking for any sign of leftover gopher bait, automatic rifles, night vision goggles, or scopes and whatnot.

The cottage was maybe twelve hundred square feet with an open floor plan. Places to stash things were limited. I started with the master bedroom.

Like the rest of the house, the ceiling and walls were made of stained wood boards. There was no sheetrock to hide cubbies between studs. I moved to the closet, which was not a walk-in affair, but modest. Humphrey's aversion to clothes perhaps kept the neat row of Hawaiian shirts and linen pants and shorts sparse. There was no rifle hidden in the back.

I made short work of the dresser, chest, and nightstand, mindful of being cornered in the back of the house should Humphrey return home. He lived simply. There wasn't any clutter to conceal contraband. The second bedroom had even fewer opportunities to hide things.

In the bathroom, Humphrey's medicine cabinet had aspirin and the usual toiletries. I made my way back to the living area, searching for attic access. There didn't seem to be any.

I scanned the great room. It was modest, but homey. Creamy painted trim set off the wood panel walls. A sofa, two chairs, and a coffee table were the only furniture in the living area. Two sets of french doors led to a brick patio with a pool and a variety of lush palms. There were even fewer places to hide things in here.

I tried the stove, the refrigerator, and two sets of hung cabinets with no luck. But when I opened the cabinet under the kitchen sink, a pint-sized Mason jar caught my eye. I pulled out my iPhone and snapped a photo. The contents looked like large grains. I held it up.

A key slid into the lock.

I put the jar back in place, closed the cabinet, and bolted for the french doors.

When Humphrey opened his front door, I stood on the

outside of the french doors on the pool deck. I smiled my sunniest smile and waved real big. "Hey, Humphrey! I thought maybe you were out back. You got a minute?"

He wore a quizzical look. "Liz. Sure. I thought that was your car." He crossed to the patio doors in a few long strides. His Hawaiian shirt was a muted green. In linen pants and sandals, he looked like a large Golden Retriever. He seemed harmless. Had he used that image to his advantage?

Humphrey looked crossways at the door handle. "Thought I locked that." He swung it open. "What can I do for you this evening?"

What indeed. "Well, I...ah...I wondered if you could tell me more about Zeke."

His expression looked genuinely sad. "What about him?"

"I wondered, since y'all were friends since—well, all your lives—if you might could help me out with some more background."

"Have a seat." He gestured towards the sofa and sat in a wicker chair. "What did you want to know?"

What topic would be safest? Get me out the quickest and cleanest? Not set him off? "Do you know if he was really in the Army?"

Humphrey chuckled. "He was. I don't know if he was ever a Ranger or not."

I gave him my best clueless blonde look. "I'm just trying to figure what he was doing for twenty years, you know, while he lived somewhere else? I'm thinking maybe someone from off came looking for him. Maybe someone who had a grudge from his Army days, you know what I mean?"

Humphrey nodded, sad-faced. "I wish I could help you there. But whatever he was doing, he never shared that with me."

I popped up. "Well, thank you anyway. I'd better be going. I told Blake I was going to pop by here on my way to dinner, but I'm running late."

"Oh. Okay." He stood and followed me to the door. "I hope you figure this whole thing out soon."

He seemed truly sincere. But what was that in the Mason jar?

TWENTY-SIX

Nate had dinner ready when I got home. Chicken with Champagne Mustard sauce with wild rice and broccoli.

"This is delicious," I said. "But how did you get Mamma to clear out, and why are you out of bed?"

"Slugger, I have a scratch. I'm fine. I thanked your mamma profusely, had a big ol' piece of her lemon pound cake, and told her it was hard for me to sleep with everyone in the house. She got Tammy and your Daddy out of here PDQ. I took a nap. And then I was bored out of my mind and needed something to do."

"Scratches don't soak shirts and towels with blood," I said. "It's more than a scratch."

"I'll be good as new in a few days. Did you tell Blake about the Mason jar under Humphrey's sink?"

"I sent him a photo." I pulled out my phone and showed it to Nate.

"That looks like the stuff in the Elliott's garage all right."

"Hell fire. I didn't want it to be Humphrey."

"I hope he doesn't ditch the poison. Is Blake going over there?"

"He's asked for a search warrant. Judge Johnson is not going to like this, since he just signed one for Blake to search the Elliott's place. But surely he'll do it with such a limited scope."

"Surely," said Nate. "I just hope he does it quickly enough. If he's smart, Humphrey got rid of that as soon as you were a block away."

"Let's hope he doesn't suspect I was inside."

Nate gave me a look that said how slim he thought that chance was.

I stood and picked up our plates. "I'll clean this up. You go get comfortable on the sofa. You want to look into Humphrey's background? You're not as familiar with it as I am—not as prone to overlooking things, maybe."

"Sure, I can do that." He picked up his water glass and headed down the hall.

I loaded the dishwasher and wiped everything down, then headed into the office. On one end of the green velvet sofa that had been Gram's favorite piece, Nate stared intently at his laptop. I tucked myself into the other end and put my legs up between us.

Once more we were in a holding pattern, waiting for a warrant. Since Nate was doing background on Humphrey, I went back over the other profiles, scanning for anything I might've missed. Humphrey was a Pearson. His family had been on Stella Maris since before there was a town. Humphrey was a part of the fabric of our community. Before I let Blake arrest him, I wanted to be damn sure I hadn't overlooked something. I started with Crystal and worked my way through.

When I got to the Carters, I mulled why they'd married so young. What had caused Zeke and Brenda to break up after so many years of being inseparable? Was it simply that they'd grown up and apart? Had a long-distance romance proven too difficult to maintain?

"I'd like to have a glass of ice tea and a nice long chat on Rita Newberry's front porch," I said.

"Rita Newberry?"

"Pete Carter's aunt."

"Why is that?"

"Because she had a front row seat to whatever happened way back between Zeke and Brenda Carter."

"You think that's relevant?"

I shrugged. "I'd like to be sure it's not before Blake arrests Humphrey Pearson. Maybe Brenda was looking to rekindle the old flame. She wouldn't be the only woman on this island to flirt with Zeke. In fact, based just on the Robinsons' bonfire, she'd be in the minority if she didn't."

"You're thinking Pete maybe didn't care for that, I'm guessing."

"It's a possibility I think we have to consider. Zeke's parents aren't here for me to talk to. Brenda's moved to Florida years ago. This case has a lot of layers. I'd like some perspective on some of the history. Rita Newberry could at least help me understand the nuances better."

"Ciao." Colleen appeared, roosted atop a wing back chair across from the sofa.

"Where have you been?" I asked. "I was worried sick you'd been reassigned. And then you were in the car, on the way to the hospital. I don't understand what's going on."

Her expression was solemn. "I'm so sorry you were hurt, Nate," she said. "I would never've let that happen if I'd had a choice."

"It was my fault," said Nate. "I didn't realize we'd gotten close enough to rattle our killer. Clearly we need to be more careful, even on friendly turf, when we're working a case."

"But I thought protecting us was part of your mission," I said.

"It is," she said. "But it isn't my only mission. Sometimes I have to make difficult choices. Weigh the alternative scenarios."

"What could possibly have been more important than keeping Nate from getting shot?" I asked.

"I had business in Milan," she said.

"I'm sorry," I said. "Did you say *Milan*? Like in Italy?"

"Si."

"That's why you've been speaking Italian," said Nate.

"Si," said Colleen.

"What on God's green earth do folks in Milan have to do with Stella Maris?" I asked.

"There's a young woman there who came here on vacation with her family last year. She fell in love with the island."

"Lots of folks do," I said.

"Well, this particular young woman is the object of a billionaire's affection. He wants to marry her. And he'd like to give her a chunk of this island as a wedding present. If he does that, down the road, she'll get it in a divorce, and her second husband will talk her into developing it."

"But who would sell it to this billionaire to begin with?" I asked.

"Michael Devlin," said Colleen.

I caught my breath. "Seriously?"

Colleen bit her lip. "He might be feeling a little desperate. That's my fault. I have to control the situation, so the unintended consequences aren't worse than Michael building more new houses here."

"But surely you knew we were getting shot at," I said.

She nodded. "I always know when you're in danger. If you'd been in mortal danger, I would've dropped what I was doing, of course. But..."

"But what?" I asked.

She swallowed, looked away, then back. "When I protect

you, and you're sure that I will...It makes you overconfident, I'm told, perhaps reckless even. Or it could, if I continue doing it. You're going to have to be more careful."

"It's not that I expect it," I said. "It's just that you said—"

"It is part of my mission. But maybe I wasn't supposed to tell you that. I think I screwed up. You're taking more risks. I'm so sorry Nate got hurt." Her eyes glistened.

"Nate's right," I said. "It's not your fault. We'll be more careful."

She shimmered. "Promise me."

"I promise," I said.

Colleen disappeared.

"I've always wanted to go to Italy," said Nate.

"You know I have a fondness for Italian wine," I said. "I hadn't realized we'd come to count on her as our 911."

"I don't think we have," said Nate. "But we do need to be more cautious."

After a few minutes, we settled back in to work. I returned my attention to the Carters and Nate dove back into Humphrey Pearson's background.

I dug for an hour, dotting i's, crossing t's, and basically feeling bored with what seemed like irrelevant data. I sat back, closed my eyes for a minute—they were tired. It had been a ridiculously long day. When I opened my eyes, I stared at the report I'd just read.

"Sweet reason." Every muscle in my body tensed.

"What's wrong?" asked Nate.

"Pete Carter's mother died June 22, 1982."

"June 22, that's—"

"The same day someone killed Zeke," I said.

"I don't care for coincidence."

"Me neither." I started digging into Robin Smith Carter.

The first thing I came across was a newspaper article. "Car accident," I said, reading ahead. "Dear Heaven, a drunk driver hit her at three in the afternoon."

"That's a horrible tragedy. Was the driver related to Zeke?"

"No," I said. "It was Bridgette Glendawn."

"Is she—"

I nodded. "John Glendawn's sister. Oh my stars. She's a recluse. This must be why. She never married. But what does this have to do with Zeke?"

"That's the Final Jeopardy question," said Nate.

"Is this just a rabbit hole?" I asked. "What did you find on Humphrey?"

Nate grimaced. "Humphrey has a long arrest record, but it falls into only two categories: civil disobedience and marijuana-related. Some of them are both. But there's nothing that would make you think he was a killer."

"I need to walk around," I said. "I'm going to start the dishwasher. Do you need anything from the kitchen?"

"I need to stretch too."

We wandered back into the kitchen. Rhett came bounding in from the mudroom to join us. I ruffled his fur and baby-talked him as I opened the cabinet under the sink to get the dishwasher detergent.

"Sonavabitch." I recoiled.

"Slugger, what's wrong?" asked Nate.

"Where did that come from? That wasn't here this morning."

"What?"

"The Mason jar. Whatever's in it, it's the exact same thing I found under Humphrey's sink."

TWENTY-SEVEN

At ten o'clock the next morning, Nate and I walked into Blake's office. He stood, an eager look on his face.

"What did you find?" asked Blake.

We slid into the visitors' chairs in front of his desk.

"The same exact kind of Mason jar with identical-looking contents is under Tammy Sue's sink," I said. "It definitely was not there when we searched the house on Wednesday. And there's not one under Mamma's sink."

Blake reached into his bottom desk drawer and pulled out his baseball glove and an old ball. He tossed the ball towards the ceiling and caught it. Up. Down. "I've got Price Elliott and Humphrey Pearson both in holding cells. And I don't have much more on either of them than I do on you."

"Did you check under your sink?" asked Nate.

Up. Down. "Yeah. Nothing there."

"The question is," I said, "is either Humphrey or Price smart enough to put the bait under my sink and Tammy's to confuse things? Or is someone else doing that?"

Nate said, "Whoever it is must've decided when he couldn't kill us that he had to neutralize us another way. The best evidence we have on anyone is the gopher bait. If a lot of people have it..."

"We need to know who all has Mason jars under their

kitchen sinks," said Blake. "And there's no way I'm going to be able to convince Hank Johnson I need that many search warrants."

"It's not practical in any case," I said. "And most people would let us look if we asked."

Nate shrugged. "Then let's ask."

I grimaced. "Well, the innocent folks would let us look. But then we'd likely tip off the person who planted it in the process. What if we just check the people with known connections to the case?"

"But what if there's someone with a connection you don't know about?" said Blake.

"Maybe you could put a notice in the *Citizen*," I said. "Ask people to check under their sinks. Let them know that if they have a Mason jar of something that's unfamiliar, it may be a dangerous poison, and they should call you right away."

Blake nodded. "I'll do that. Meantime, you and Nate go check everyone with a known connection."

TWENTY-EIGHT

The Carters lived in Sea Farm, two blocks over from the Elliotts. The Carter home had the look of a much older home—traditional double porches, white lap siding, mature landscaping. Nate and I climbed the steps to the front porch.

"Nice place," said Nate.

"Someone has a green thumb." I admired the container gardens by the front door as I rang the bell.

When no one answered, I rang again. The house seemed quiet, no sounds of anyone coming to the door. We waited five minutes.

"It's a Monday morning in June," I said. "They could all four be at the Exxon station." I figured Pete and Brenda would be at work, but I had anticipated their two teenage boys being home.

"Or," said Nate, "the teenagers could still be in bed."

"In which case we might get in and out without them even knowing we've been here." I bit my lip, mulled the situation. "There's a fifty-fifty chance they have a security system. I don't see one of those signs that's supposed to scare off burglars."

Nate peered in the wide sidelight. "No control panel in the foyer. Let's walk around back."

We wended our way between beds mounded high with pine

needles. Out back, a large screened porch ran the length of the house. The screen door was unlocked. We stepped inside and peered in the kitchen windows. No sign of life. And no sign of an alarm panel.

"I say we go in," I said. "If we trip an alarm, the alarm company is going to call Blake. I'll text him and let him know we're here." I pulled out my phone.

"I'm more concerned about the teenagers," said Nate. "Or what if Brenda isn't at the Exxon station? She could be at the grocery store, come home any minute."

"Good point," I said. "What if you park the car down the block and watch for anyone pulling in the driveway? I'll go have a look around."

Nate said, "Or you could be the lookout and I'll go have a look around."

"You're injured. Not in top form for a quick getaway."

"I have a scratch. But it'll be quicker if I just give you your way and get on with it."

I slipped on gloves and went to picking the lock, and Nate headed out front.

The kitchen was more modern than I would've expected in this house—all angles, sleek white cabinets, and minimalist decor. I closed the door to the screened porch behind me and scanned again for an alarm panel. If the home had an alarm system, the panel was hidden.

I moved quickly to the kitchen sink. Another Mason jar exactly like all the others. I snapped a picture. Since I was already inside, it would be a waste not to snoop around a little further. Now where would this family keep the guns? I did a quick tour of the downstairs. It was all white on white, with the occasional pop of turquoise, not a gun cabinet in sight.

I returned to the kitchen and checked the broom closet and

the pantry. No luck. I headed upstairs. On the second step, I heard a door open upstairs.

Footsteps.

Someone was home and headed towards the stairs.

I tiptoed back down the steps and hightailed it out of there. We had what we came for.

I climbed into the passenger seat of the Escape. "That was close."

"Teenagers?" asked Nate.

"I didn't stick around to find out. Spencer and Winter's house next?"

"What's a little breaking and entering between family?"

We found identical Mason jars of gopher bait under Spencer and Winter's kitchen sink and at Connie Hicks's cottage on Magnolia. I hadn't picked that many locks in one morning since I'd been learning how.

The last house on our list was the Robinsons' waterfront home near the marina. Nate rang the bell and we waited on the wide front porch. The house had an elevated first floor to protect it from flooding. White, with Charleston green shutters and a shiny metal roof, it screamed South Carolina Lowcountry. It was a relief when Margie Robinson answered the door.

"Liz. Nate." She smiled a welcome. "I heard you'd been shot. I'm happy to see it's not as serious as the gossip mill reported."

"Just a scratch," said Nate.

I punched his arm. "Will you stop saying that?" I turned to Margie. "It scared me to death. We're very grateful it wasn't as serious as it looked at first."

"Please, come in." She stepped back to let us inside. "What brings you by?"

"This is going to sound strange, but could I look under your kitchen sink, please?"

She startled a bit. "If you like. The kitchen is through here." She led us to the large living area in the center of the house and through a pass-through door to the left. The kitchen called to mind a farmhouse, but the appliances were modern. Margie gestured to the porcelain farmhouse sink. "Help yourself."

I pulled open the white painted doors. Margie and Nate hovered behind me.

The Mason jar was front and center. I snapped a picture.

"What is that?" Margie asked.

"Poison," I said. "Leave it where it is for now. When did you last look under your sink?"

Margie thought for a moment. "Saturday morning. That's the last time I ran the dishwasher. With just me and Skip, I don't run it every day. That jar wasn't there then. I have no idea where that came from."

"Has anyone come over since Saturday morning?" Nate asked.

"Supper club," said Margie. "We had a progressive picnic. Ordinarily I'd have run the dishwasher three times after that group. But we had one course at each house, and we used paper products. Dessert was here. I made trifle." Her voice trailed off. She stared at the Mason jar.

"Who all is in your supper club?" I asked.

"Glenda and Grant Elliott. Winter and Spencer Simmons. Brenda and Pete Carter. Rita and Boone Newberry. And Lauren and Warren Harper."

I looked at Nate. "No one else has come by?"

"Not that I can think of, no," said Margie.

"Humphrey didn't come by for any reason?" I asked.

"Humphrey?" Margie shook her head. "No."

"Does Coy have access to your house?" Nate asked.

"He has a key for emergencies," said Margie. "Sometimes if we're out of town, he'll let a repairman in or something."

I closed the doors to the cabinet. "We should check Coy's kitchen as well."

She let us outside, and up the steps to Coy's apartment over the garage. There was a Mason jar under his sink too.

"What's going on?" Margie asked.

"We're trying to figure that out," I said. "Just don't touch those jars or what's inside. Even a small amount is deadly poison."

We followed her back to her kitchen.

"I'm going to make a pot of coffee, y'all want some?" she asked.

"Sounds good, thanks," I said.

"Y'all sit down." She gestured to the painted yellow kitchen table.

Nate and I slid into chairs.

"This is crazy," said Margie. "Who would sneak something under my kitchen sink? And Coy's too?"

Just then I was thinking how everyone who had been at the bonfire had poison under their sink. The party guests, plus Nate and me. Price Elliott had the original supply in his garage, but no Mason jar under the sink. How sure was I that Margie and Skip were innocent? Should we drink the coffee Margie was brewing?

"You know what?" I said. "I slap lost track of time. Nate, we need to get back and brief Blake. He's expecting us."

TWENTY-NINE

We climbed into the Explorer.

"What was that all about?" asked Nate.

"I'm just rattled," I said. "Let's go home and kick this around."

"As you wish." Nate started the car.

"Wait."

Nate looked at me expectantly.

"Let's see if the Newberrys are at home." Margie mentioning Pete Carter's aunt and uncle reminded me that I had questions for Rita.

"You want to drop by and ask if she'll sit on the porch and sip tea with you? Have you ever met this woman?"

"Well, no, actually. But Pete and Brenda had access to the poison. One of them could've planted it at the Robinsons' and Spencer and Winter's house during the progressive dinner."

"But when did they—or anyone—plant it at our house? Whoever put those decoy jars under people's sinks had to have access to our house too. And Tammy Sue's and Humphrey's and the Carters' if it wasn't one of them. But several of those folks had reasonable access to all the houses. The key is, who had access to ours?"

"Anyone." I sighed. "I didn't set the alarm when we went

running Saturday morning. I just forgot. I was distracted. And then we went straight to the hospital, and we were gone until dinnertime."

Nate's forehead creased. "What time did your parents arrive with Tammy?"

"Around three."

"So our culprit probably put the Mason jar under our sink first, before three o'clock. He could've gone by Tammy Sue's anytime. Humphrey's house...he'd just have to catch him on the beach. All the other houses were part of the progressive picnic thing."

"Right. Back to the Newberrys..."

"You're going to have your way here, aren't you, Slugger?"

"I'm afraid so. The thing with the date of Pete Carter's mamma's death is a huge red flag to me."

"But what does that have to do with Zeke and Brenda's history, and a possible jealousy motive?"

"Maybe nothing. I just feel like we need to know more about Pete than I can find in databases."

"Where do they live?" Nate asked.

I pulled up the town directory. "On Magnolia. Three doors down from Merry's house."

"Do you want to call ahead?" Nate asked.

Ordinarily, I wouldn't dream of dropping in on folks that weren't family unannounced. But this was far from an ordinary situation. "No," I said. "Let's act like we're checking under their sink. They'll see that in the paper tomorrow. Let's talk our way in and see where it goes."

Nate closed his eyes for a moment, gave his head a little shake, then started the car.

"Thank you for humoring me," I said.

"At least we have a pretext handy," he said. "It's not like we have to pull out Tommy and Suzanne."

"I miss them," I said. "We haven't played them in a while." Tommy and Suzanne were personalities we sometimes used when it was necessary to con our way into places.

The Newberrys lived in a red brick ranch that was probably built in the 1960s. The yard was well kept, the beds full of dahlias, gladiolus, and canna lilies.

"Hey, Mr. and Mrs. Newberry," I said when they opened the door. "Y'all may not remember me. I'm Liz Talbot. This is my husband, Nate." I offered them a bright smile. In truth, as I'd told Nate, we'd never met. But Stella Maris was a small town. They knew my people.

"Of course, dear." Rita Newberry wore a warmup suit and tennis shoes. "Boone, you remember Liz. She's Frank and Carolyn Talbot's middle child. Merry's older sister."

"Hmm." Boone Newberry didn't look too sure about that.

"What can we do for you?" asked Rita.

Nate said, "We're helping Blake out by checking homes on the island for a toxic substance that's been discovered in several houses."

That was true, and just vague enough. I nodded sincerely.

"Oh my," said Rita. "It isn't mold, is it? We've heard horror stories."

"Is it the mold?" Boone squinted.

"No," I said. "Not mold. And there's probably nothing at all to worry about. Could we check under your kitchen sink?"

"Sounds like mold to me," said Boone.

"No, sir," said Nate. "This was sold as a pesticide, but some of it has been found not properly labeled."

I shot Nate a glance. He was so good at this. Again, truth, but no troublesome details.

"Oh, all right then." Boone stepped back, opened the door

so we could come in.

"Right this way." Rita turned and headed through the family room. She led us into a homey kitchen that had last been updated perhaps twenty years ago. The cabinet doors were painted white, the wallpaper a cheery pink floral. She stopped to one side of the sink.

Rita and Boone hovered as I opened the doors under the sink. No Mason jar.

"All clear." And good to know that our pattern was still holding. No one aside from the people who'd attended the bonfire—except for Nate and me—had surreptitious poison under the sink. "That's a relief. My goodness, this has been a long day." I leaned against the counter, closed my eyes, my hand to my temple.

"Come sit a spell," said Rita.

I felt bad for conning her. She was a sweet lady. "You're so kind. Perhaps just for a moment."

"I'll get us some iced tea. You go on in the den."

"Oh, no thank—"

"Go on now." Rita's tone was a lot like the one Mamma used to get us to mind.

Nate raised an eyebrow at me. We moved to the den and took seats on the sofa.

"What were you looking for again?" Boone sat in the recliner and put out the foot rest.

"A pesticide," I said. "You have a lovely home. Merry is always talking about your beautiful magnolia out front. How old is that tree?"

"It was planted when the house was built in 1965," said Boone. "We bought the place in 1974, the year before our Rachel was born."

"Does Rachel still live in town?" I asked.

"My, no." Rita set a tray on the coffee table and served us each a glass of iced tea. "She's been in Atlanta since she graduated high school. She loves the city. Me, I can't abide it. It's too loud."

Nate said, "Is she your only child?"

"Yes," said Rita. "But our nephew lived with us from the time he was ten. You know Pete Carter? Owns the Exxon station."

"Right," I said. "We know Pete."

"That's right." A cloud crossed Rita's face. "Pete was my sister Robin's boy. Robin died in a car accident."

"I'm terribly sorry," I said. "Was Pete's father in the accident as well?" Of course I knew he hadn't been.

"No." Rita sighed. "But he might just as well have been. It killed him too. He just couldn't cope with losing Robin. Drank. We thought at first if we took Pete for a little while, maybe Ingram would pull himself together."

Boone shook his head. "Never did. He lived 'til 2002, but it wasn't much of a life, to tell you the truth. Pete was better off with us. We raised him like ours."

"He's very fortunate to have had you," I said.

"It helped." Rita looked at her hands. "It was hard for me, losing my sister. Having Pete here...it was like holding on to part of her."

"It was hard on all of us," said Boone.

"I imagine so," said Nate.

"The guilt..." Boone shook his head.

I felt my face creasing. Why did Boone Newberry feel guilty? Bridgette Glendawn had been driving the car that killed Robin Carter. "I'm sorry?"

Rita looked at Boone. "It was my fault."

"How could that be, Mrs. Newberry?" I asked.

"No," said Boone. "It was my fault. I should've picked Rachel up at school, let someone else worry about the damn busted pipe."

Nate said, "Busted pipe?"

"You see," said Rita, "Robin was killed on the way to pick up Rachel at school. I had a migraine. I never got over that. Knowing that if I had just gone to pick up Rachel, my sister would be alive."

"No," said Boone. "I should've picked her up. How could you drive with a migraine? I shouldn'ta ever gone to see about that burst pipe at the diner. I shoulda just said, I have to go pick up my daughter."

They both looked utterly miserable. I felt horrible for bringing up such painful memories. "I'm so terribly sorry. We should go."

Then it hit me. "You're a plumber, then, Mr. Newberry?"

"Well, I wasn't then. I was a handyman. But the plumber, Harold Yates, no one could get ahold of him. I guess he was sick, that's what I heard. After I fixed that pipe, I figured maybe plumbing was a good field. The island only had one. Seemed like something we needed."

THIRTY

"Yes?" Brenda Carter opened the front door. She wore a pale blue tank top and white shorts. I didn't know Brenda well, had never spent much time in her company.

"Hey, Brenda, how're you this evening?" I smiled real friendly.

"Good, and you?" Her expression inquired as to my business on her front porch at nearly nine p.m. on a Monday night.

I studied her. She was tall, lanky, her blonde hair styled in a careless layered bob.

I knew in that moment there was a fifty percent chance I had this figured wrong. Too late to turn back now.

"I'm good. Is Pete home?" I asked.

"Yes. I'll get him. Come in." She opened the door, stepped back. "Have a seat in the living room."

She moved towards the kitchen. I sat in a white wing back facing the fireplace. When she came back, Pete was with her. We said hey and all that. They perched on the sofa. Brenda reminded me of an exotic cat that might pounce on me if she took a notion.

"What can we do for you?" Pete seemed stiffer today than he had in the Exxon station last Wednesday, less open.

"Look, I know Zeke's death is still fresh, and it's difficult to talk about him, but I'm asking all his close friends if they can help me figure out something in Zeke's past...something we can't explain, and we think could be related to his death."

He shrugged. "I'll help if I can, of course."

"Good, good," I said. "Do you know what Zeke's connection to Harold Yates could possibly have been?"

Pete turned white, looked stricken. Brenda straightened. Neither of them said a word.

"Zeke kept Harold's obituary. Did you know he and Tammy Sue were the only people in town at Harold's funeral?"

"I didn't know that, no." Pete cleared his voice, adjusted his glasses.

"He was such a lonely man," I said. "It's hard to think someone could live in our small town and be that isolated."

"Maybe he would've had more friends if he would've shut up about the damn flying saucers," said Pete.

Brenda put a hand on his knee.

"Did you know Harold?" I asked.

"Not really," said Pete. "I knew about him."

"You hated him, didn't you?" I kept my voice soft.

"What?" Pete tried to look shocked, but failed. "No. Why would I hate him?"

"Because he went out into a field looking for UFOs one day and didn't come to work all day. No one could find him. When the pipe burst at the diner, they called your uncle, Boone Newberry. The only other man in town to call for a broken pipe."

"I don't know what you're talking about." Pete's high color testified otherwise.

"Your Aunt Rita had a migraine. Boone couldn't pick up your cousin at school, because he had to fix the pipe in the diner. So they called your mom. And on her way to pick up Rachel, she was broadsided by a drunk driver. All because Harold Yates was out standing in a field."

Pete stared at me. Brenda seemed to be gripping his knee.

"I'm very sorry for what happened to your mother," I said.

"You don't understand anything about it." Pete was shaking.

"I think I do," I said. "You hated Harold Yates. The only person you hated more was Zeke Lyerly."

Pete drew back as if I'd slapped him. "I didn't hate Zeke. I told you. We were friends."

I nodded. "I believe you were, all these years. It must have killed you to find out at Margie and Skip's bonfire that Zeke was the one who caused Harold to go out into that field with his prank. Truth or Dare. All those years, you were his friend. And then you find out he was responsible for your mother's death."

"I don't know what you're talking about," said Pete.

Brenda stared at me hard. "Pete needs a glass of water. And something to calm his nerves. His blood pressure must be going through the roof. I'll be right back." She stood and moved towards the kitchen.

I looked at Pete.

He shook his head. "You've got this all wrong."

"I wish I did, Pete," I said. "And I really wish you hadn't shot my husband—tried to kill us both."

"I did no such thing. Liz. Come on, now." He reached for a look of disbelief, but it fell flat.

"You know what the only thing I haven't figured out is?"

Brenda walked back into the room with a glass of water, handed Pete a pill. They both stared at me with something like dread. Pete swallowed the medication, took a sip of water.

"Zeke told everyone at the bonfire that he and a friend played that prank on Harold Yates. He didn't name the friend. I wondered why, thought at first he didn't want to lay blame at someone else's feet. He felt remorse for that stunt but didn't want to make anyone else look bad."

Something flickered in Brenda's eyes.

"But that wasn't the only reason why, was it, Brenda?" I asked.

"How would I know?" she asked.

"Because you were Zeke's best friend from the time you were what, nine? You were the tomboy running with Zeke until you were Zeke's girlfriend in high school."

"That was a long time ago," she said.

"It was," I said. "Does Pete know it was you with Zeke and that old a.m. radio? It was you who helped play the prank that led to his mother's death?"

Pete dropped the water glass. It shattered on the hardwood floor, sending glass and water in every direction. His head swiveled, a crazed look in his eye. "Brenda?"

And there it was. Well, it could've gone either way.

"Pete, be quiet." Brenda's voice was nearly a whisper.

"*Noooo,*" he howled through clenched teeth.

Tears slipped down Brenda's cheeks.

"All these years," he said. "You never told me. You made a vow before God to honor me and you kept *that* from me?"

"I just—"

He jumped to his feet, lunged toward her. "Not one word."

He had a gun. Must've had it in his waistband. Sonavabitch. I reached for my Sig 9.

"Freeze." Pete pointed the gun at me.

"Pete, you're scaring me," said Brenda.

"Pull your gun out slowly, by the barrel," said Pete. "And give it to me."

"Pete, you don't want to do this," I said.

"Do it now. Seriously? I have *nothing* to lose. You do not

want to fuck with me."

"Okay." I nodded fast. "All right." I pulled out the Sig and handed it to him.

"I'm curious about one other thing," I said.

"Really?" Pete raised both brows dramatically. "Too bad. You're all done asking questions."

I pressed on. "I can't figure out why you would've put Zeke's body in his car trunk. I bet you never expected you'd be the one to open that trunk, right? That must've been quite the quandary. You're the only one who knew what you'd find there. But you couldn't've anticipated Tammy Sue would set fire to the car."

Brenda said, "Pete, don't say anything. Let's call a lawyer."

He seethed. "It's too late for lawyers. It's too late for...anything. Our whole marriage has been a lie."

"Don't say that," said Brenda. "It's not true. We're a family. The boys..." Her face twisted in grief, perhaps for the life they'd all shared which was clearly a memory.

He looked like he'd been sucker punched. "Where are the boys?"

"They're at the beach with friends," she said. "They'll be home soon."

"Well, we'll just have to take this party somewhere else." He gestured with the gun. "Both of you, in the garage."

"What?" I said. "You haven't answered my question yet."

He looked at the ceiling. "Fine. Putting Zeke in his car was a poetic gesture of sorts. He prowled the town in that car when we were teenagers. It was his pride and joy. Stuffing him inside it just felt right."

"Oh my God," said Brenda.

"Shut up," said Pete. "The garage. Now."

Brenda gave her husband a look that said he'd clearly lost his mind. "Pete? You're going to shoot me? What the hell is going on here? I'm not going anywhere with you and a gun."

"I'd hate to kill you here, where our sons will see the blood, but I will if you make me." Pete's tone was ice. "Move. Into the garage." He gestured towards the pass-through door in the kitchen.

"Where are we going?" I asked.

"To the lighthouse," said Pete. "Move."

"Lighthouse?" Brenda had the look of someone watching aliens land.

Pete jammed the barrel of the gun into his wife's kidney.

"Better do as he says, Brenda," I said. "It'll be okay." No sense getting her shot. Pete was becoming increasingly unstable.

"Get in your car," said Pete. "In the driver's seat. Liz, you get in the backseat with me."

Like she was in a trance, Brenda walked through the kitchen, opened the door to the garage, and passed through. She climbed into the driver's seat of a BMW crossover. I got into the backseat, and Pete slid in behind Brenda.

"Head to the lighthouse," Pete said.

Brenda's shoulders rose and fell.

"Go ahead, Brenda," I said.

She looked at me in the rearview mirror. I nodded as slightly as I could manage, trying to reassure her. I hoped she received the message I was sending.

She started the car and backed out of the garage.

I said, "Pete, that was smart what you did with all the gopher bait, divvying it up between everyone's house to neutralize it as evidence. Shame you didn't think of that before you shot Nate."

"It's a shame I didn't kill both of you," said Pete. "But I'll enjoy killing you today that much more."

"Like you enjoyed killing Zeke?" I asked.

"Not that much," he said. "He died slow and painful. Like he damn well deserved."

"How'd you get him to swallow that strychnine?" I asked. "That stuff's got an awful bitter taste."

"You wouldn't believe how easy that was. I showed up at closing time with a thermos of coffee," he said. "Zeke liked it strong. I had my cup in my hand. Of course I didn't pour mine from that thermos. Told him it was the best coffee I'd ever tasted. Poured him a cup in that ugly mug of his."

"I figured," I said. "The thing that gave you away was the car. You should never have put his body in the back of that Mustang. You might've gotten away with it."

"It doesn't matter anymore," he said. "Nothing matters anymore."

"Now Pete, that can't be true. What about your sons? Don't you want to see them grow up?"

"Huh," he said. "Like you're going to allow that to happen."

Brenda parked the car in the parking lot at the base of the lighthouse.

"Give me the keys," said Pete.

Brenda handed him the key fob.

"Get out of the car, slowly," said Pete.

We both climbed out and shut the doors.

"Now climb." He gestured towards the lighthouse.

"There's just one other thing I don't get," I said.

"I don't give a damn," said Pete. "Climb, or I'll shoot you both right here."

"Here works for me," I said. "No sense in doing all that work and then getting shot. Besides, you—what? Want to make it look like Brenda killed me, then jumped or something?"

He seethed.

"Tell me what I want to know and I'll climb up those steps,"

I said.

"What the hell else do you want to know?" he snapped. "What else is there?"

"Why did you try to shoot Nate and me? Up until then, you were barely on our radar as a suspect—certainly not at the top of the list."

He looked at me with pure hatred. "Is that a fact? I overheard you and Margie Robinson talking at the Pirates' Den Friday night. She told you that sob story of Zeke's—he felt so bad about poor Harold. It would only've been a matter of time before you figured it out."

"Ah," I said. "Maybe so. Bonus question."

"Climb," he said through gritted teeth.

"I think he's finished talking, Brenda. I don't want to climb those steps, do you?" I said.

She looked at me like I'd lost my mind.

"Rumpelstiltskin," I said.

And four sets of car lights came on, lighting the parking area.

"Pete Carter, drop the gun," said Blake. "You're under arrest."

THIRTY-ONE

That Wednesday night, we had dinner at Mamma and Daddy's house. As was her custom, Mamma put on a spread of fried foods not often seen outside country buffet restaurants. We fixed plates in the kitchen and gathered around her mahogany Duncan Phyfe dining room table.

Daddy said, "You're telling me Pete Carter is the one who was shooting at y'all from up in a tree?"

"He was," I said. "I think maybe he was hunting hogs with Zeke. They really were good friends right up until that moment at the Robinsons' bonfire when Zeke told that story. And it's sad how random all that was. Zeke was not one to open up like that. And he couldn't have known what that stunt he pulled on Harold Yates cost Pete Carter."

Mamma looked at me wide-eyed. "Poor Brenda. She'll have to finish raising those boys by herself."

Blake said, "The thing I don't get is why someone good with guns would choose to kill someone with poison. Pete's lawyered up. Not telling me anything."

"The only way he could've killed Zeke with a gun and not risk Zeke taking the gun away from him was to do it from a distance—the way he tried to shoot us," I said. "I think he wanted Zeke to know he was the one killing him and why. He wanted him to suffer. Pete was eaten up with rage. It had been stewing in him for thirty some odd years."

Nate said, "He'd likely been planning since the bonfire to kill Zeke on the anniversary of his mother's death. Then in April, when he saw the gopher bait in the Elliotts' garage, he decided it would make the perfect murder weapon. He went back later and helped himself. Grant didn't notice half a bag was missing because he'd already used what he needed. I guess Saturday, after he didn't kill Liz and me, he decided to get rid of the remaining poison in a manner that would muddy our investigation."

"Liz, I wish you wouldn't go into these situations by yourself," Mamma said.

"I was never by myself, Mamma," I said. "I had a microphone on and a camera in my sunglasses, which were propped on top of my head. Blake, Nate, and the rest of the cavalry were never far away."

"That's how they knew to wait for you at the lighthouse?" she asked.

"That's right," I said. "I had to get Pete to talk while he still thought he was in control of the situation. So we let things play out a bit."

"That's the dangerous part." She gave me a worried look. "When people are desperate, you don't know what they'll do."

"I'm fine, Mamma," I said. "How is Tammy Sue? Have you talked to her this week?"

"I have." Mamma cut a slice of tomato. "I took her a casserole. I invited her over here any night she wants to come. But she's grieving, said she needs to be alone. It's going to take time. I'll keep an eye on her."

"Did she say whether she'd talked to April at all?" I wondered if the two would bond in the aftermath of Zeke's death.

"She didn't mention it," said Mamma. "Those two are cut

from very different cloth."

"How's poor little Crystal?" Daddy forked a bite of country fried steak and gravy.

Mamma gave him a quelling look. "She's not one of the sympathetic characters in this story, Frank."

I rolled my eyes. "She's fine as far as I know."

"Why in the world would Zeke run around on a sweet wife like Tammy Sue?" Mamma asked. "I feel like he really did love her."

"I think he did too, Mamma," I said. "But from what we learned, it seems Zeke had a type. It started with Brenda—blonde and a bit rowdy, unconventional. But when Zeke went off to the army and then wherever else he went, Brenda wasn't willing to wait to see if he came home. Or maybe he told her not to—who knows. In any case, she married Pete."

Blake said, "And Zeke replaced her with April, who's cut from the same mold."

"But that blew up because they were too much alike," I said. "Then Zeke met Tammy Sue, fell in love, and might've lived happily ever after, but then Crystal started pursuing him, and he just couldn't turn down that type. She had too much of Brenda in her."

Colleen faded in, perched on top of Mamma's buffet. "Crystal was familiar."

He didn't know her all that well. I threw the thought at her.

"Sassy blondes were Zeke's downfall—not what was good for him, but what was familiar. Too often that's what you mortals chase. He found true contentment with Tammy Sue, but it was unfamiliar, so he destroyed it. Not intentionally, but nevertheless."

What's wrong with sassy blondes?

"I didn't say anything was," said Colleen. "That's just not

what Zeke needed. He needed stability. He had enough of a wild streak himself. He needed someone steady to balance that out."

Well thank you for your analysis after the fact. I might have been a teensy bit sarcastic.

"Liz?" Mamma looked at me expectantly. "Sugar, what's wrong? You look like you've seen a ghost."

Nate and I both burst out laughing. Colleen bray-snorted exuberantly.

"What in this world?" Mamma looked at Nate and me like we'd lost our minds.

Blake looked up from his plate. "Hey, did y'all hear Michael Devlin is selling the family home?"

"What?" Please not to the Italians.

"Yep," said Blake. "He discounted that spec house way low. Put the Devlin place on the market, says he's moving to Savannah."

"Does he have an offer?" I asked.

"Not yet," said Blake. "He just listed it."

"The Italians have lost interest," said Colleen. "Hopefully someone local will buy it." She stared at Blake.

Blake didn't have that kind of money. *What are you thinking?*

"Savannah," said Daddy. "What's in Savannah?"

Blake looked at me mischievously. "I think it's more who's *not* in Savannah."

"Oh, please," I said. "This has nothing to do with me." I cut my eyes to Colleen.

Daddy was clearly tired already of Michael Devlin as a topic of conversation. "Red Bird, did you tell Liz about that woman in the grocery store that tried to take me home with her?" He grinned.

Mamma covered her face. "Frank."

"Tell her," said Daddy.

"What happened?" I asked.

"We were in Edwards Grocery. I gave your Daddy my list, and he was helping me shop. I turned around to look at the meat, and he disappeared. Fifteen minutes later, I saw him putting groceries in another woman's cart. I said, 'Frank, what are you doing?' He looked up, came hurrying down the canned goods aisle. He said, 'You see that woman right there with clothes on the same color as yours? I've been following her around the store.'"

We all laughed. We needed to laugh. The week had brought violence to our small island town that wasn't as unheard of as it used to be. Things were changing. The idyllic life we enjoyed had been once again marred by violence committed by one of our own, against one of our own. The anxious feeling in my stomach was diminished by the laughter, but it was becoming harder and harder to tamp down my anxiety with a lighter mood.

I couldn't shake the feeling that something ominous was headed our way.

The worried look on Colleen's face did nothing to assuage my fear.

Susan M. Boyer

Susan M. Boyer is the author of the *USA Today* bestselling Liz Talbot mystery series. Her debut novel, *Lowcountry Boil*, won the Agatha Award for Best First Novel, the Daphne du Maurier Award for Excellence in Mystery/Suspense, and garnered several other award nominations, including the Macavity. The third in the series, *Lowcountry Boneyard*, was a Southern Independent Booksellers Alliance (SIBA) Okra Pick, a Daphne du Maurier Award finalist, and short-listed for the Pat Conroy Beach Music Mystery Prize. Susan loves beaches, Southern food, and small towns where everyone knows everyone, and everyone has crazy relatives. You'll find all of the above in her novels. She lives in Greenville, SC, with her husband and an inordinate number of houseplants.

The Liz Talbot Mystery Series
By Susan M. Boyer

LOWCOUNTRY BOIL (#1)

LOWCOUNTRY BOMBSHELL (#2)

LOWCOUNTRY BONEYARD (#3)

LOWCOUNTRY BORDELLO (#4)

LOWCOUNTRY BOOK CLUB (#5)

LOWCOUNTRY BONFIRE (#6)

Available at booksellers nationwide and online

Visit www.henerypress.com for details

Henery Press Mystery Books

And finally, before you go...
Here are a few other mysteries
you might enjoy:

FIXIN' TO DIE

Tonya Kappes

A Kenni Lowry Mystery (#1)

Kenni Lowry likes to think the zero crime rate in Cottonwood, Kentucky is due to her being sheriff, but she quickly discovers the ghost of her grandfather, the town's previous sheriff, has been scaring off any would-be criminals since she was elected. When the town's most beloved doctor is found murdered on the very same day as a jewelry store robbery, and a mysterious symbol ties the crime scenes together, Kenni must satisfy her hankerin' for justice by nabbing the culprits.

With the help of her Poppa, a lone deputy, and an annoyingly cute, too-big-for-his-britches State Reserve officer, Kenni must solve both cases and prove to the whole town, and herself, that she's worth her salt before time runs out.

Available at booksellers nationwide and online

Visit www.henerypress.com for details

ARTIFACT
Gigi Pandian

A Jaya Jones Treasure Hunt Mystery (#1)

Historian Jaya Jones discovers the secrets of a lost Indian treasure may be hidden in a Scottish legend from the days of the British Raj. But she's not the only one on the trail...

From San Francisco to London to the Highlands of Scotland, Jaya must evade a shadowy stalker as she follows hints from the hastily scrawled note of her dead lover to a remote archaeological dig. Helping her decipher the cryptic clues are her magician best friend, a devastatingly handsome art historian with something to hide, and a charming archaeologist running for his life.

Available at booksellers nationwide and online

Visit www.henerypress.com for details

MURDER ON A SILVER PLATTER

Shawn Reilly Simmons

A Red Carpet Catering Mystery (#1)

Penelope Sutherland and her Red Carpet Catering company just got their big break as the on-set caterer for an upcoming blockbuster. But when she discovers a dead body outside her house, Penelope finds herself in hot water. Things start to boil over when serious accidents threaten the lives of the cast and crew. And when the film's star, who happens to be Penelope's best friend, is poisoned, the entire production is nearly shut down.

Threats and accusations send Penelope out of the frying pan and into the fire as she struggles to keep her company afloat. Before Penelope can dish up dessert, she must find the killer or she'll be the one served up on a silver platter.

Available at booksellers nationwide and online

Visit www.henerypress.com for details